ANNIE

Not His Vampire

Not His Vampire

Annie Nicholas

Published 2017
Copyright by Annie Nicholas

This is a work of fiction. The characters, incidents and dialogues in this book are of the author's imagination and are not to be construed as real. Any resemblance to actual events or persons, living or dead, is completely coincidental and not intended by the author.

Manufactured in the United States of America

I love hearing feedback.   Email: annienicholas@ymail.com
To be kept up to date on Annie's releases sign-up for her newsletter.

Books by Annie Nicholas

Not this Series
Not his Dragon
Not his Werewolf
Not his Vampire

Vanguard Elite
Bootcamp of Misfit Wolves
A Taste of Shifter Geekdom
Blind Wolf Bluff
Penny of the Paranormal
Pallas

The Vanguards series
The Omegas
The Alpha
The Beta
Omegas in Love
Sigma
Prima

The Angler series
Bait (Free)
Catch
Hunting Colby
Release

Chronicles of Eorthe
Scent of Salvation
Scent of Valor
Scent of a Scandal

Lake City Series
Ravenous (Free)
Starved for Love
Sinful Cravings

Stand Alone Books
Irresistible
Koishi
No Refuge
Boarded

For more information on coming releases go to
http://www.annienicholas.com

CHAPTER ONE

The dragon's castle loomed ahead. Rumor was people who trespassed on his land went missing. No one ever found proof so it could all be urban legend, or so Trixie Russell told herself over and over as she coaxed her animal control truck up the steep incline.

Apparently, the castle had a rodent problem. Brave rats to want to live with dragons. Trixie wiped her sweaty palms on her work jumpsuit so the steering wheel would stop slipping in her grip. Her cell phone went off and she jumped. It was her sister, Ruby.

"Hello," she answered via Bluetooth.

"Where are you? You were supposed to be home thirty minutes ago. I was worried." Ruby treated her as if she still wore diapers. They lived together in a part of town where women shouldn't walk around alone. Even at the crack ass of dawn, like now.

"I have to run one more errand." She hoped the dragon was a morning person.

"Where?" Ruby yawned. "I want to know how much longer I have to stay awake."

"Go to bed. I'll be fine." Her sister worked the night shift too, waiting at an all-night diner. Ruby was always exhausted.

"Patricia Bella Russell, where are you?"

Trixie could lie. She *should* lie. There would be less yelling and Ruby wouldn't worry. "I'm just retrieving some kennels a customer borrowed." But she sucked at lying. Ruby would know immediately and there would be more than just yelling. So, she stretched the truth. Win-win, Ruby could relax, maybe fall asleep while she waited on Trixie, and she *would* wait—well, shit. Trixie got nothing out of the deal because she'd feel guilty either way. "It shouldn't be more than an hour."

Ruby grumbled something under her breath about Trixie's boss. She silently agreed. "Fine. I'll put on a pot of coffee. Call me if you'll be longer."

"Sure thing, sissy." Trixie hung up and counted her blessings. If Ruby knew where she was headed, she'd be so pissed off *neither* of them would get any sleep today. Ruby wasn't the most responsible person, except when it came to Trixie. She wished Ruby could adjust her priorities. Make them a little less about Trixie and a little more toward herself.

When Trixie's boss had threatened to fire her over some missing cat kennels, she had promised to have them back in city hands by tonight. She knew where they were, but if she told boss-man then she'd definitely lose her job.

The dragon had them.

Trixie had an invitation to the castle…of sorts. The black dragon of New Port, harbinger of smoke and darkness, had adopted all of her best friend's cats, so her friend had lent him all the kennels to transport the animals to the castle without Trixie's consent or knowledge.

Yeah, that's what friends were for, right?

The transmission of her truck ground as she shifted into a lower gear and crept the last half mile to the top of the mountain. Stone gargoyles watched her progress with focused interest. They decorated the castle wall and tied her stomach in knots. A forest filled with shadows surrounded the area and was so dense she couldn't distinguish the tree trunks from each other. Her gaze kept drifting to New Port, her home, which sat at the base of the mountain. She wanted to be below with all the other humans.

She liked that New Port had dragons and was proud of the honor, but she'd never desired meeting one.

She parked her animal control vehicle in front of the castle's massive wooden doors and stepped outside. The cool air played with her hair, whipping the pink strands around her face.

Hands buried in her one-piece overalls, she stared at the old building. Its age made her bones ache and her whole neighborhood could have fit inside. The gargoyles' gazes followed her even when she strolled a few feet to the left then back again.

That wasn't creepy. Nope, not at all.

A wooden chest sat on the ground by the door. Curiosity got the better of her and she peeked inside. Clothes. Men's and women's. Not very nice ones, either. She didn't understand, but then again, she wasn't a dragon.

She drew closer to the entrance and one of the gargoyles turned, watching a bird fly overhead.

She screamed. The sound left her breathless as she scrambled away from the castle, tripping over every conceivable rock between her and her vehicle. Fuck this. Her boss could have her job and come here himself.

The bird's shadow circled her, blocking out the sun. Every muscle in her body turned to stone as she stared above.

The dragon circled slowly until it landed next to her. White scales covered her sleek body and long white feathers grew from her wings and tail. She swung her long, graceful neck in her direction. "Aren't you Betty's friend? The human one at her soulmating. I can't forget the hair."

Trixie tried to answer but even her jaw was frozen.

The dragon sniffed the air. "You don't have to be afraid. I'm Angie. The nice dragon." She winked. "I don't eat people, only pop tarts."

Trixie didn't know dragons came in the nice variety. Or that they made pop tarts that big.

Angie changed shape until a petite naked woman with a dark, pixie haircut stood in the dragon's place. Trixie couldn't pull off short hair properly. Her face was too narrow and her eyes too big. Angie moved toward the trunk by the door and pulled out some clothes.

The gargoyle gave a high-pitched whistle of appreciation.

Angie's face turned shades of pink to rival Trixie's hair. The dragon scowled at the castle wall where the gargoyle had returned to stone. "Which one was it?"

Trixie kept her gaze pinned to the castle, trying not to stare at the naked dragon-woman. Shifters. Until a few weeks ago, she hadn't known any. Now they paraded through her life. Most of the time without clothes on. She should be used to it by now, but Trixie wasn't as liberated as her sister.

Scanning the wall, she pointed to a trio on the right corner of the tower. "I thought it was that one." She shrugged. "But they all kind of look alike from this distance."

"Eoin says their turning to stone is a defense mechanism. They infest a castle, mimicking the existing stone work so we can't tell which ones are the troublemakers." Angie yanked the wooden doors open and stomped inside. "They're as bad as the rats."

The gargoyle in question waggled his fingers at Trixie in a friendly wave.

"I think there's only one of them." Was this conversation real or was she having an acid flashback?

"That's how it starts. One moves in then the rest of his family follows." Angie's voice echoed from deep inside the building.

Not wanting to lose her, Trixie hurried into the foyer, pushing thoughts of gargoyles to the back of her mind. She was here for the kennels, then she could return to her normal human life. Work her job, collect her paycheck, and hang out with her sister and their friends. Life was good. Normal was better. She was happy being human.

Especially after witnessing what poor Betty had gone through finding her soulmate. Trixie would hate for some stranger to march into her life and turn everything inside out.

Wings, changing shape, raging hormones? It sounded like puberty on steroids. No thanks. She liked men who didn't pound on their chests.

Inside the castle, Trixie tried to close the door and almost dislocated her shoulder. "Motherfucker." She rubbed her sore joint. Little Angie had swung them open so easily. "I don't think I'm strong enough to close the doors," she shouted. Her voice echoed back and sent a shiver down her spine.

This was how horror movies began. She hesitated to take a step forward. Was she really going to be that girl? The one who went looking for the monster in the dark?

She shook her head. Angie wasn't a monster. She was a dragon—a self-proclaimed nice dragon.

"Angie?" she sighed. She had hoped the kennels would be stacked by the front entrance so she could just load them and go. A girl could dream, couldn't she?

One careful step at a time, she left the safety of the sunlight. Hands held out in front of her, she felt her way forward, hoping to encounter a light switch and a map. For all her bravado, she couldn't afford to lose her job. The hours were shitty but it paid better than any other job she was qualified for and she didn't qualify for much. She and Ruby needed a roof over their heads and food in the fridge. Electricity was optional some months.

Trixie's fingers trailed over cold stone until they hit a gap in the wall. She stumbled forward and caught herself on what felt like a banister. Stairs. Great balls of fire, she'd almost gone head over heels down a flight of stone stairs. That would have killed her for sure.

A faint sound caught her attention. It sounded like singing. "Angie?" Her whispered question was barely audible.

"Hello?" someone whispered back. The voice seductive and very male.

"I'm looking for Angie." She descended slowly in her blinded state.

"Why? She's such a bore."

Trixie paused at the bottom of the long and deep stair well. A high stone archway stood above her head. She could see faintly because a light flickered far ahead. It illuminated just enough for her to perceive she was in a large room. Heavy darkness surrounded the bubble of light. This was where a smart person would turn around, and she was a *very* smart person. She twisted, one foot on the step, ready to run.

"Do not go." He sounded so disappointed. "I'm so lonely. Eoin is too occupied with his new mate to talk to me anymore."

"I'll let him know."

"Are you a thief?"

"No, why?"

"You keep whispering. Are we going to exchange secrets?" Though he whispered, she could still hear him.

He was right. Why the hell was she whispering?

Okay, time for a reality check. She wasn't starring in her own horror movie — she was in a dragon's castle. That housed a gargoyle, but he hadn't been evil. He had only made Angie blush with a whistle. It was actually kind of funny. What the hell, when in Rome… "Do you happen to know where the cat kennels are stored?"

"Yes."

She took a step toward the light. "Where?"

"It's a secret."

She gave her ponytail one sharp yank, then glanced up the staircase.

"Come on, little mouse. A few minutes of conversation in exchange for information."

She squared her shoulders and cracked her knuckles. Little mouse, her ass. She'd grown up in the worst part of New Port and still fucking lived there. Murder, drugs, and theft were her playgrounds. She and Ruby got through it together. A little dinged with a few rough scrapes, but all limbs intact. Still walking, still talking. Some weirdo in a castle basement *did* scare the crap out of her, but she wasn't going to let him know it. The best way to become a victim was to act like one.

Damn it, she should have left as soon as she'd heard her voice echo.

Stupid her.

CHAPTER TWO

Trixie crossed the empty alcove, her footsteps echoing against the stone floor. The room reminded her of a dungeon that she'd seen in a few movies, and those movies could have used a few pointers from this place. The light guided her into a long hallway. It flickered through a door at the end.

Stopping at the threshold, she noted the rusty iron bars that must have been the door. Oh. So, it *was* a dungeon. *Okay, dipshit, you walked all the way here of your own free will.* No one to blame for this mess but herself.

The door was ajar. A good sign, right? She peeked inside.

Someone sat on the floor by the lit candle stand. A candelabra? People still used those? Well, she guessed the dragons did. She just assumed the place had electricity. Might be that was why she couldn't find a light switch. And…she was rambling in her own head.

There *was* a man. Ink black hair streamed from his bent head, pooling on the floor around his hips. He rested his arm on his knee covered in thread bare clothes. Lifting his face, he ran his midnight gaze over her from head to toe and back again. He rose to his feet in a smooth move that spoke of a very masculine strength. He held out his hand. "Viktor Petrov at your service." His distinct Russian accent was clear enough for her to understand him easily.

"I'm Trixie." It felt impossibly right to place her palm against his and allow him to kiss the back of her hand. She found herself the sole focus of Viktor's perceptive near-black eyes, the eyes of a man who was used to stripping away souls, unearthing the most deeply buried truths.

"A pleasure to meet you, Trixie. Please, come join me." He gestured to the dirty floor as if it were a posh love seat.

"Umm, I'm good." She stood there, still stunned at the sight of this gorgeous man a couple of inches from her. Her inner vixen purred.

God, when had she developed an inner vixen? But this guy could make nuns break their vows.

"As you wish." His lips formed a perfect seductive smile. "I am happy you did not run." He ran his fingers through her hair, catching a few knots in the process. "Lovely shade of pink. Neon, is it?"

"You know your hair dyes." That was the exact name of her color.

"It is my duty to know such things. I am an artist." He came closer. Though Viktor was beautiful, what saved him from crossing the line into a more delicate prettiness was the stubborn hardness of his jawline, the unflinching expression in his stare.

Then she noticed a metal collar around his neck.

Cotton candy hair. Viktor bet she tasted just as sweet. His fangs ached as well as other parts of his body. He had been alone in this dungeon too long, to the point of looking forward to Eoin's short visits.

"Are you a present?" Viktor scanned her beige one-piece jumpsuit. A zipper ran up the center and there were various stains on the material.

"What's that supposed to mean?" She quirked her head, possibly insulted. He was not sure. His mind still rang with the echoes from endless nights of bloodlust and, to be honest, human women… Well, women in general, confused him when he was sober. They said *no* when they meant *yes* and *yes* when they meant *no*. Then changed the rules and said *no* when they meant *no*. Or was it purple?

Wait, what was he thinking about?

He scratched his chin.

Dinner cleared her throat. "What did you mean by a present? I'm not a delivery person, if that's what you meant."

Honesty would probably send her running, but lying was too difficult of a concept for him to grasp yet. His mind was a honeycomb of instincts and his brain was oozing out of the holes his hunger had caused. "Sometimes Eoin hires professionals to feed me, but they tend to dress more—" He couldn't think of the word.

"Professional," she offered. Her eyes were wide, not with fear, but with wonder.

Viktor smirked. "You *are* good." The innocence was believable and adorable. She was a very good actress. He would have to get her business card. She struck all his bells with just the right tone, and after hundreds of years, his bells were so cracked he was shocked by his reaction. "I wanted to say more seductive, but this outfit…" He rubbed the thick material between his fingers. "It works for me. Modern working girl, not afraid to get dirty." He leaned in and inhaled. Under the usual city smells, he scented strawberries, coffee, and canines.

They jerked away from each other simultaneously.

"I'm not who you think I am." She edged toward the door and out of his range. "You said you knew the location of the cat kennels."

He opened his mouth but nothing came out. He scratched his head and marched back to where he had been sitting. "You were serious? You are looking for what again?" She smelled strongly of canine. Not wolf. Their scents were close but someone with an acute nose could tell the difference easily. It was like the variance between grapefruit and oranges. One was tart, and the other sweet and tasty.

"Cat kennels." She spoke slower as if he had cognitive trouble, which in some way he did — *had*. He was better. She used her hands to make a box shape. "Small cages in which to carry small animals."

"Eoin did not send you?" Maybe he was not as recovered as he had thought. "Are you real, Trixie?"

She dropped her hands. "What the hell is going on here? Of course, I'm real. How long have you been down here?"

"A few days? Maybe weeks. It is difficult to remember." Viktor grinned and closed the distance between them. That familiar smell could only mean one thing. "Are you a weredog?" He and Eoin had had a running argument of their existence. He believed if the wolf variety existed so should the other. With all the other were-animals in the world, why not dog? Yet the dragon kept pointing out the obvious. Where were the dog packs if they existed? Viktor believed they were too evolved to require packs, or too rare.

"No," she dragged out her answer. "Why would you think that?"

"Your smell. Why do you smell so much of dog?"

She winced. "It's my job. I'm an animal control officer so I deal with lots of dogs."

He sighed. One day he would prove the dragon wrong, but today was not the one.

Trixie gave a small laugh. "You look so disappointed. Do weredogs even exist?"

The sound of her amusement was pure sunshine. "Yes, but I have yet to find one." He winked. "Come into the light. I want to see you better."

She glanced at the open cell door.

"I will not hurt you. The thought of being alone again is threat enough to guard you against harm." He held out his hand and noticed the dirt under his nails, the threadbare material of his clothes. Prince Charming, he did not resemble.

Ignoring his hand, she circled him. Her gaze focused on his collar.

Viktor twisted to follow, the chain connecting him to the wall dragged across the stone floor.

Her gasp echoed within the dungeon. "You're chained up like an animal." She crossed to the silver infused hardware affixed to the thick wall of his prison and tugged.

He gave her an incredulous stare. "If I cannot break these bonds, then neither will you." He peeled away her fingers from the chain, noting she had scraped her hand. She was sweet. He kissed her palm and licked her wound, her taste an ambrosia. So very sweet. He moaned as the flavor coated his tongue. Her innocence was not an act. "Virgin," he murmured.

She yanked away. "How did you know that?" She tucked her hands under her arms.

Viktor stared at his empty palms. The sound of her pulse was a song in his ears, her taste lingering in his mouth. He wanted more. He wanted it all. A tremble shook his hands. He could not do it. He had fought too hard to regain what was left of his sanity. No matter how tempting the morsel. Or her rarity.

"Hey," she whispered and cupped his face. She drew his chin up until their gazes locked. "I'm going to help you, okay?" She traced her fingers along the collar.

Help *him*. He was the most dangerous creature in the city, bar Eoin. She was the one who needed help.

"I can't even see a seam. How was it put on?"

"Eoin welds it shut."

She slowed her assessment. "He welded while you were wearing it?"

He nodded and took advantage of her proximity to smell her hair. *Now* he smelled the human. Her outfit had thrown off his senses.

"Didn't it burn you?" Her eyes were wide again. Blue eyes, like the sky and the sea.

"Yes." He could barely speak. His fangs had fully extended. "You should go now."

"But—but…" Her gaze fell upon his mouth. "Big teeth."

He pulled back his lips so she could see better.

She swallowed visibly. "Vampire?"

He nodded, waiting for the screams. Maybe, if he was lucky, she would find a stake and end him. He deserved nothing less.

"You exist?"

He blinked.

"I mean, I always suspected but you never came out with the other supernaturals." She eased back toward the exit. "Is that why you're locked down here? Because you're a vampire?"

"No." He leaned against the wall, holding the chain. "I am here of my own free will."

She stopped in her tracks. "You *want* to be chained down here?" Her reaction was adorable and her concern awoke a slumbering desire.

Viktor had not liked someone in a very long time. Trixie made it difficult to dislike her. "Not anymore. I was a danger to the city." And a bigger danger to her. He destroyed everything he cared about.

"And now you're not?" she asked, still not moving away like she should.

"You are still alive, are you not? I think, maybe, I can be trusted to go free again." He stalked toward her, growling low in his throat, reminding her monsters still hid in the dark. "If you see the dragons, please let them know I would like to go home."

She spun on her heel and ran.

He let her escape and shouted after her, "Sorry I lied about the kennels."

CHAPTER THREE

Breaths bursting in and out, Trixie ran up the stairs, taking them two at a time with her long legs. Her brain had become an old LP record skipping. *Vampire, vampire, vampire…* Instincts as old as man drove her forward and away. That's all she focused on. Getting away.

A light framed the top of the spiral stairwell and she burst through with a gasp.

"Trixie?" Angie stood in the hallway, a cat kennel in each hand. She peered at her as if she'd grown a second head. "Are you okay?"

She leaned against the wall, staring at the stairwell, half-expecting Viktor to jump out. But Angie was a fire breathing dragon. She'd be able to fight him off, right? She blinked at the bright lighting. "You have electricity?" Why was Viktor using candle light and sitting in the dark?

Angie's eyebrow quirked. "Yeah, we're not barbarians." She passed Trixie, heading toward the exit—she hoped. The dragon tossed her a weird look. "What were you doing in the basement?"

Once outside, the sunshine melted Trixie's terror away. Her encounter with Viktor suddenly felt like a nightmare she couldn't quite grasp. Had she really met a vampire? She glanced at the castle wall with its winking gargoyle. "Don't you mean dungeon?" she asked in a whisper, not able to take her eyes off the building that contained all the things that would haunt her forever.

Angie dropped the two kennels next to a pile by her truck. She spun around, pinning Trixie with her glare. Her eyes no longer looked human, the pupil suddenly slit like a cat. "Damn it, you should know better than to snoop in someone else's home."

Heat bloomed on Trixie's cheeks and she pressed her hands to her flaming skin. "I know. I know. But I got *lost*." She shouted that last word.

The dragon sighed and her eyes shifted back to human. "Did you meet Viktor?"

She nodded, fighting tears. "Why don't we know about them?"

Angie drew closer, hands extended.

Trixie's back hit the truck's side before she knew it, heart thumping a mile a minute.

Angie slowed. "I'm not going to hurt you. I just want to make sure he didn't bite you." She pushed her hair away to examine her neck, then pushed the sleeves off her wrist. "You look unscathed." She sounded surprised. "Tell me what happened."

Trixie looked at her torn running shoes. "He said he knew where the cat kennels were."

"Didn't your mama explain about stranger danger?" The dragon huffed, hands on hips. "That was so dangerous, Trixie. He could have killed you." She slapped her own forehead. "Fuck, if he had. How would I have explained that to Ken and Betty?" With inhuman strength, she hugged Trixie tight. "Don't ever do that again, you understand? He's dangerous." She set her back on her feet.

Trixie coughed, air returning to her squeezed-empty lungs. Viktor wasn't the only dangerous creature here. Her ribs would ache for a few days after that hug. "Is that why he's chained to the wall?"

Angie rubbed her temples. "Eoin is going to kill me." Then she grabbed Trixie by the shoulders. "You can't tell people about Viktor, or vampires."

Trixie sank to the ground, her legs refusing to support her anymore, and Angie followed. Trixie's stomach rolled. The dragon looked like how Trixie felt.

"Why?" she whispered. A shiver ran through her body and she rubbed her arms. "I mean, we know about shifters and magic and witches. Why not vampires?"

"Did you flunk history class in high school?"

Trixie shrugged. "Maybe." She hadn't attended often. She'd worked at a sandwich shop to help support herself and Ruby. Food had seemed more important than history at the time.

"Shifters didn't have much of a choice. We were discovered instead of coming out. Medieval times were bloody for both our kinds."

"I know. I watch television. I'm not totally ignorant." She pressed her lips together and glanced at Angie. "Sorry, I didn't mean to snap. I've been up all night at work."

"And then you met your first vampire." Angie flung her arm around her shoulder in a side hug. "And lived." She leaned her head back on the truck. "You really can't go public with this, Trixie. It would be chaos."

"As if anyone would believe me." Angie was right, though. Trixie could imagine human reaction to discovering vampires really existed. Look how she'd reacted and she was a laid-back person. "They'd probably hospitalize me."

"There's that. Or there's the repercussion that the vampire community might want to silence you. Permanently."

"That's comforting." She closed her eyes. What would keep Viktor from finding her to do just that once Eoin let him go? There couldn't be many pink haired Trixies in New Port that worked for the animal control office. "Shit."

"Don't worry about the vampires. I'll have a talk with Eoin. He'll vouch for your safety and no one screws with my mate."

She gave Angie a watery smile. He was only one dragon. He couldn't watch over her every night. Trixie's days were numbered. If the vampires wanted to ensure her silence, they'd want a permanent solution. She climbed to her feet and started loading the kennels. She needed a beer or six and a long, hard sleep.

"Viktor asked me to tell you that he's ready to go home."

Angie snorted. "We'll let Eoin be the judge of that. Those two have been doing this for decades. Viktor goes crazy and Eoin locks him up for everyone's safety. Personally, I think Viktor needs to retire from being a vampire."

"Retire?"

She ran her finger across her throat. "He's a menace to society. I don't care what either of them say. Viktor has killed too many people to deserve any more chances at rehabilitation."

"Oh." He hadn't tried to hurt her though. She kept that to herself. Angie sounded like she already made up her mind. Trixie slid behind the wheel of the truck and started the engine.

"Thanks for lending us the kennels. The cats are great at keeping the rat population down." Angie gave a weary smile. "And keeping Eoin entertained."

Trixie waved and put the truck into drive. She couldn't leave the castle fast enough. She wished her vehicle could hit warp speed. It really didn't take long to return to the animal control central dispatch, it just *felt* like an eternity.

Boss-man held out his hand for the keys. "Back already with the kennels?"

"They are in the back of the truck." She pointed with her thumb over her shoulder. "See you tonight."

"About that, Trixie." He crossed his arms and glanced at his feet. "I can't let this slide. I've let too many things slip, like the missing tranquilizer darts from your gun and the personal use of city equipment."

She pouted. "Come on. You know I only mean well." She pressed her hands together. "I'm your best worker. I'm never late and don't call out sick." She was the only one who took this job seriously. Half the time the other two trucks working the night shift were at some rest stop.

"I know, I know. That's why I'm only suspending you for the rest of the week." He leaned forward. "I have to make an example of you. Otherwise, everyone will start doing this shit and I'm going to lose my job."

Breathing a sigh of relief, she nodded. "Okay, I can handle that."

She wouldn't argue. He had a point about those darts. If he investigated a little harder, he'd find out she'd shot the beta leader of the city werewolf pack right in the ass. Twice. Then boss-man would really have to fire her. Time off, even without pay, would be welcomed. It would give her time to sort out this vampire stuff. She wasn't sure what to think or how to feel. A few hours of sleep would help sort that out she hoped.

She tossed her smelly work suit in her locker and ran for the city bus.

Nothing like public transit after the longest and scariest night shift of her life. She stood in the aisle even though there were seats available. If she sat, she'd fall asleep and wake up across town or worse.

Her phone beeped. Ruby was texting her. She smiled at her message.

I don't think I have enough limbs to accomplish those sexual acts, she texted back. *I'm on the bus doing my impression of the walking dead. Be home soon.*

The zombie reference reminded her of Viktor. Were vampires dead or were they born like shifters? And even though Angie had tried to explain why vampires lived in secret, Trixie still didn't understand. Yes, the shifter exposure had caused a war, leaving many dead, but humans lived side by side with supernaturals now. What was one more type of creature in the grand scheme of things?

The bus let her off in front of her apartment building. Built in the late twenties, the structure was of solid brick. Chipped brick now, with rusty metal fire escapes that were barely attached to the wall. Even the pigeons didn't trust them enough to perch on the railings. Beggars couldn't be choosers though. The place was cheap and didn't have bugs.

That last part made it a palace in her opinion.

She entered and climbed to the top floor where she found Ruby waiting in the hall.

Her hair in curlers, Ruby wore a short faux-silk robe and fuzzy purple slippers. She handed Trixie a cup.

"No coffee." She sniffed the contents and smiled.

"There's more whiskey in the cupboard. Thought you might need it." Ruby sauntered back into their home and plopped onto the worn but comfy couch. "Did you lose your job?"

She grimaced. Her sister had an uncanny way of *knowing* things. Ruby called it a *lucky guess* because if she had real powers, she'd have won the lotto by now. Trixie thought there was more to it though.

"No." She sat next to Ruby and took a long drink, then promptly wheezed for air. Wow, that was cheap whiskey. "I've been suspended for the rest of the week. Without pay."

"Don't worry about it. We'll make ends meet. We always do." Ruby rubbed Trixie's shoulder and took a closer look at her face. "Stop it. You're worrying too much."

Sure, she was, but not for the reason Ruby thought. Trixie's mind had returned to the castle. More specifically, to the person in the dungeon. Angie had assured her Eoin would protect her from any vampire backlash if they discovered she knew they existed. The only way that would happen was if Viktor told anyone, because she had decided to keep her mouth firmly shut. Not just for her safety, but for Ruby's. If someone wanted to make Trixie suffer, all they had to do was hurt her sister. It wouldn't take a genius to figure that out.

What was she going to do?

She glanced at Ruby and held up her cup. "Thanks. I really needed this."

"And some sleep." Ruby leaned against her shoulder and turned on the television. One of the local morning shows discussed the increasing crime rate in Riverbend, the city closest to New Port, and how the local wolf pack might be involved. Trixie had met their alpha at Betty's wedding. This news didn't surprise her.

She finished the contents of her cup and let it warm her from the inside out. "I met the most beautiful man this morning," she murmured.

Ruby made a sleepy noise.

"Too bad he's a murderer." Trixie promptly fell asleep.

Annie Nicholas

CHAPTER FOUR

The bag of expired packed red blood cells in Viktor's hand was cold and lifeless. Eoin had procured it from the local blood bank. The hospitals would be forced to destroy the bag anyway.

"Yum yum, old blood. You know how to make a friend feel special." He bounced it, the fluid thick and dark red.

"It's all I could obtain. Your usual sources refuse to come to the castle and I had business elsewhere then New Port today."

"My sources would come if you did not insist on scaring them each time." He bit into the bag and drained the contents in a few gulps. It tasted like chemicals. The blood banks spun the cells free of plasma so it was more concentrated for transfusions — less fluid more hemoglobin. They also added preservatives to keep the blood from clotting. This was a vampire's equivalent to a Twinkie. It eased the hunger but he distrusted its nutritional value.

"Their choice of business makes me question their character. Do I want them to feel comfortable? I think not. I have a mate to think of now. Her safety comes first."

It was interesting to watch Eoin's evolution from terror of the skies to lovesick puppy. Yet he managed to maintain his fearful reputation. The dragon seemed more unstable when it came to Angie's happiness.

"Why do you have cat kennels?" Trixie still plagued Viktor. No matter how hard he tried to forget, his thoughts circled back around to her. Was it bloodlust or just lust?

Eoin watched from the other side of the room, arms crossed while he leaned against the wall. He shrugged. "I adopted some cats to take care of the rodent population. Angie hates rats and mice."

"Cats? You have pets now?"

"I'm surprised you haven't seen them. They're inquisitive creatures."

"They are also intelligent. They know not to come down here."

Eoin grimaced. "Unlike a certain human girl."

"Trixie." Would he seek her out once he was set free? No, she was better off if he stayed away.

He had to stop fooling himself — of course, he would hunt her down. What he would do with her was what concerned him.

"How much longer do you plan on keeping me here?" He tugged at the silver infused titanium collar welded around his neck. He had yet to break it. This was his fourth time being locked in Eoin's dungeon for killing.

It was in his nature to hunt humans, but vampires did not need to kill to feed. Eoin and the others just assumed he was an asshole. Older supernaturals had all killed people. Those had been different times. Dragons, vampires, and shifters had all eaten humans at some point in history, hence Eoin's tolerance of Viktor's slips. It was only in present time that they were expected to respect human authority.

Viktor didn't kill out of malice though. He was ashamed to admit he had control issues. It didn't take much. The vampire council understood and turned a blind eye to his indiscretions. He, on the other hand, could not ignore the fact that while others had changed with the times, he was locked in bad habits.

For one hundred years, he had tried to stop killing. Most of the time he did a good job at keeping his prey alive, but most wasn't good enough.

"I set you loose too soon last time. It's only been a decade since the last time you were chained in my dungeon. You shouldn't have slipped and killed someone so soon." The dragon eyed him from head to toe. "You're running out of skin for your victims' names. What then?"

"I did not harm the girl. She stood right here by the wall and I did not lay a finger on her." Except to touch her hair. Odd that he would want to do that before tasting her soft skin.

Eoin pushed off. "I only have your word on that. She could have been standing outside your reach the whole time." He shook his head. "No, when I make a mistake someone suffers for it. A few of those names I carved onto your flesh are just as much my responsibility."

Viktor bared his fangs and snarled at him, proving the dragon right. Again. He was not ready. Hunger rode vampires unlike any other supernatural that existed. Let their control slip just a little and it took over. Unfortunately for him, his hunger threshold was unpredictable. He envied those who had been taught the proper ways of feeding as fledglings. He, instead, had been abandoned as a wild animal and regret was his constant companion.

He tossed the empty bag of blood at Eoin. Residual droplets flew in the air, landing on his friend. The dragon did not comprehend Viktor's complicated past or what drove him. Only a select few of his kind knew and even *they* were losing patience with him.

Eoin grabbed him by the throat. "If I let you out, I'll only have to carve a new name into your hide tomorrow night. It's too soon, Viktor. And you know it, so stop giving me and Angie a hard time."

"Your girlfriend would taste better than this bagged shit you bring me." He managed to force the words past Eoin's constricting fingers. Why did he antagonize the black dragon of New Port? Because he was the only one strong enough to kill him. They had been friends since Eoin had moved into the castle. The dragon trusted Viktor enough to let him ink his skin use it as his personal canvas. The tattoos Eoin bore were some of Viktor's best work.

"Leave Angie out of this. If she had it her way, you'd already be a pile of ashes in my sunny courtyard." Eoin tossed Viktor against the wall and a few of his ribs broke. "You touch her, I'll drop you into the deepest hole I can find and forget you ever existed. Death is too good for you."

Viktor sank to the ground with his back to the cool wall and tore the stained shirt off his back. He examined his flanks. No bones poked out. He had to be sure. They were a bitch to reset if they healed that way. "I thought we were friends."

"We are." Eoin squatted so they could be eye to eye. "That's why you're still alive." Eoin wiped the blood splatter off his face.

"Angie hates me that much? She does not even know me."

The dragon frowned. "It's not you as much as what you are. She tolerates your being here because you told me about the magic tattoo shit that Ken's mate had inked on her arm."

"It makes me happy that my plan worked. How long did it take for the effects of the magic spell to fade?" He had met Betty by accident. Like Trixie, she had stumbled into his cell. The little shifter had black magic needled into her skin.

Werewolves. All that strength and passion yet so little brains.

"She shifted a few hours later."

"Dark magic." Viktor leaned forward, grinning at his oldest friend. "We should hunt down this witch like the old days."

"Oh yes, we should. I'm sure the evening news would love to cover a witch burning."

"You grow boring as you age. You worry too much about the media."

"You don't worry enough." The dragon rubbed his jaw. "I also don't think the spell was intentional."

He sat up straighter. "What do you mean? How do you accidentally cast a spell? Magic doesn't work that way."

Eoin tossed him an annoyed look. "I know how magic works." He sighed. "We agree that the symbol is the source of the spell and not the ink?"

He nodded.

"Well, Betty admits to choosing that design. No one forced it upon her."

"Choosing? From what?" A sinking sensation in his gut.

Eoin's expression darkened. He looked more his dragon self than human. "A book the artist owned. She offered it to Betty to flip through since she hadn't decided what she wanted inked. I don't think this artist is aware of what they own."

The sound of Viktor's hand smacking his own forehead echoed within the prison cell. "They are using a spell book for tattoo art choices?" Oh, the havoc this person could cause. It would be Salem all over again.

Eoin chuckled. "Apparently."

"This is not a laughing matter. It is a miracle they have not summoned Gozer The Destructor."

"Gozer? You watched the DVDs I gave you last Christmas. I thought you avoided modern entertainment."

"I was bored." He liked television and movies, but it was a past time enjoyed better with company. Watching those DVDs only confirmed his belief. Books were a better way to spend time alone.

"She's a tattoo artist, not Merlin. Tone down the dramatics." Eoin straighten to stand.

And he followed. "I am Russian. Drama flows in my veins. You should take this more seriously."

"Not my territory." The dragon shook his head. "The artist is dhampir, by the way."

Viktor pinched the bridge of his nose, staving off a growing headache. Dhampir were rare. Half-human, half-vampire. They also fell into *his* jurisdiction. "Trouble in Riverbend tends to flow into New Port." The cities were only two hours apart and both were considered Viktor's hunting ground by vampire law. He did not understand why Eoin only wanted one city.

"I'll send a message to the local wolf pack alpha if it will make you feel better."

"I would feel better if you released me and let me take care of this. Riverbend's vampire nest answers to me, after all. That includes dhampir. Plus, the nest leader is a huge pain in my ass."

"No, you're not ready to leave." The dragon pulled out a set of dice. "Want to play? I'd like to win back some of my dignity."

Viktor sighed and returned to his spot against the wall. "You have no luck, friend."

Eoin would not release him. Long ago they had made a deal. Eoin would lock him away for everyone's safety when Viktor asked, and not let him free until he deemed him sane. Viktor had asked for this fucking chain.

Later that evening, Trixie sat on the edge of the tub and watched Ruby prepare for work. The diner had a retro theme so she wore a uniform. Short skirt and a button-down blouse with a small waist apron. Ruby piled her long, curled hair in an old fashion hair-do. "Sammie's making the fish special tonight. You want me to bring some home?" She spoke around the hairpins in her mouth.

"Sure, I'll eat anything." They couldn't afford to be picky eaters. She rose to her feet and came around behind her sister to help with stray curls. Ruby always tried to look her best. She said it was for the tips, but Trixie had seen her put this much effort just to go grocery shopping. Trixie wished she could look so put together and beautiful. She was lucky to apply mascara without poking herself in the eye.

"Thanks." Ruby took the stray strands and artfully added them to the pile. Turning her head, she examined her refection. "Perfect. When is Betty returning from her honeymoon?"

Ruby and Betty had met through her. They liked clubbing together and dragging her along. "Uh, next week I think. Why?" She doubted the newlyweds would want to go dancing with them.

"I want to see if she'll introduce me to Ken's dad."

"The alpha? He's old enough to be *your* dad." She swatted Ruby's shameless ass.

"Dads are never that hot, and he's rich, so if he wants me to call him daddy, I'd be fine with it."

Trixie gagged. "You're nasty."

She kissed Trixie's cheek, leaving a red lipstick mark. "Life is too short to be anything else. Now, what are your plans tonight?"

"Steal a car, take it for a joy ride to the dragon's castle, and stake a handsome vampire in their dungeon." She gave Ruby her million-dollar smile. There was no point in lying. Trixie had learned to tell Ruby her crazy plans without hesitation—that way her sister never believed them.

Ruby patted her cheek. "That's my girl. You have my number if you need bail money."

"Yep." See, Ruby hadn't believed her when she was being honest. Deadly honest.

She'd decided this morning that the only way to ensure her and Ruby's safety was to take out the one person who would care that she knew vampires existed.

She followed her sister to the apartment door and locked it once it closed.

Pressing her back to the wall, she scanned her home. What could she use for a stake? Yes, she was planning murder. The murder of a dead man who killed people. Angie had admitted Viktor was a bad person. Dragons didn't lock up nice, law abiding citizens or their dungeons would have been full. The only occupant she'd seen was one badass vampire.

Who she had no idea how to kill. The only information she had on the subject came from movies and books. Some vampires walked in the sun and sparkled, others spontaneously combusted in the light. Some vampires were born as vampires, and so on. But the one thing most had in common was a wooden stake through the heart. Was it a myth? Maybe. Pretty much anything could be killed when you stabbed in the heart. It was a chance she'd have to take because Eoin might be letting Viktor out soon.

She searched her apartment for anything wooden and long. The only thing resembling a stake was a wooden baking spoon. With a knife, she carved the end of the handle to a sharp point. That would do the job.

How did she plan to kill a vampire who was both faster and stronger than she? He was chained to a freaking wall. It wasn't like he could run away. Now, if she reached the castle only to discover he'd been let loose, all bets were off and she'd leave the city with her sister in tow.

Trixie pulled on a windbreaker — the top of the mountain was cooler than in the city — and caught the bus to downtown New Port.

Stealing a car was easier than most people thought, especially in this neighborhood. She'd been doing it since before owning a driver's license. She had left that life behind after her first stint in juvie, but there was no other way for her to travel to the castle. No *free* way. She hadn't the cash to pay for a taxi. Once she was done with the car, she'd leave it close to where she'd stolen it so the police could return it to the owners, with a little gas missing. And maybe a sorry note.

A jimmied lock later, she bent under the steering wheel of a later-model vehicle. The older cars were the easiest to steal. The less computerized the better. She hotwired it to start. Just like riding a bicycle.

She drove to the castle. Her palms sweated and her heart drummed. The larger the stone building grew ahead, the less confident Trixie felt. Trixie, vampire slayer, didn't have a ring to it.

Then Ruby texted her. *I'm going to work a double tonight. Don't wait up.* She was pulling extra hours to make rent and bring home food this week because Trixie had screwed up. Not to mention, Ruby didn't know her life was in danger *because* Trixie was nosy. Trixie wanted to tell Ruby everything. She *wanted* Ruby to talk her out of this.

In the end though, Trixie knew she'd regret either decision. If she didn't kill Viktor, she was pretty sure they'd be on his dinner menu. If she killed Viktor, she'd be no better than him. Given this choice, she picked being a killer.

Contrary to everything she had done in the last twenty-four hours, she wasn't a total idiot. She parked the stolen car along the road out of sight of the castle. Though she had a checkered past, breaking and entering castles were not on her resume. She'd had a hard time finding a light switch this morning so she highly doubted that they had a security system.

Creeping along the tree lined road, she kept an eye on the sky for Eoin or Angie. Moonlight lit the stone structure as thin clouds streamed past the bright orb. The stone gargoyles didn't move and she couldn't tell which were real. In the distance, a wolf howled.

Her spine snapped straight. "Are you kidding me?" The werewolf pack must be out hunting. She hoped. Shifters wouldn't hunt humans but the real wolves weren't as discriminatory. She caught her breath and waited for her heartbeat to slow. She didn't want to do this.

She pocketed her spoon/stake and wiped her hand down her face. What else could she do to protect her family? Doom settled on her soul. She could make a deal with Viktor. He wanted out. That would mean she'd have to trust the word of a self-proclaimed crazy vamp.

She hung her head. Maybe there was something else he wanted? She ran her fingers over her throat. Standing outside wouldn't solve her problem. She had to go speak with him. Worst case scenario, she'd pull out her stake.

The place appeared quiet. Nothing moved. She raced across the courtyard to the front door. She pushed. It was unlocked, because who would be crazy enough to break into this place? Once it was open enough, she slipped inside the blinding darkness. She'd had the forethought to bring a flashlight but the narrow beam was swallowed by the enormity of the place.

One careful step at a time, she left the safety of the exit. She held her hand out, hoping the light would encounter a wall to guide her back to the stairwell. Blinking didn't help her eyesight, but that didn't stop her from trying.

The light brushed over the stone wall and she breathed a sigh of relief. According to her memory, she only had to follow this hallway and the stairwell would be on her right.

The walk seemed longer but she knew it was her imagination. She kept her hand to the wall as a guide and used the flashlight to search for the stairwell entrance. Quiet blanketed the castle. It was eerie for a city girl used to background noise.

Light illuminated the stairs and she grinned in triumph. Her fingers brushed over a rough, irregular surface. She twisted toward the wall with her light and came face to face with a gargoyle.

He was stone still.

She jumped. She couldn't help it. The reflex was a kneejerk to weird shit.

"You shouldn't be in here," he said, his voice ground like gravel.

She stumbled backward.

"Watch the stairs!" he shouted. His outstretched clawed hand grabbed for her, stone wings spreading behind him.

Her next step met only air.

This was going to hurt.

Annie Nicholas

CHAPTER FIVE

A gravelly, male shout echoed in the dungeon.

Eoin spun from his and Viktor's dice game. "What was that noise?"

"No, no. I am winning for once. Do not distract me." Viktor rolled a losing set. "*Xyёвo.*" He swore in his native tongue.

The sound of flesh meeting stone reached Viktor's ears. The thud was followed by the crack of bone.

The dragon strode out of the jail cell.

Viktor kicked the dice away. Maybe Eoin hadn't seen.

A faintly familiar scent reached his nose. He sat up straighter. Oh no…

Trixie.

He sniffed his arms and hands, hoping it was residual from their encounter but only smelled his overwhelming stench. He was getting better if he desired a shower.

Eoin's gasp reached his ears.

Viktor rose, stretching his chain to its limit. Trixie's scent was stronger and it was tinged with her blood. *Her blood.* She was hurt. "Eoin," he called out. "What has happened?" He pulled at his collar.

"Angie!" Eoin's roar made the foundation of the castle rattle. "Call nine-one-one."

Panic pierced Viktor's heart. The human emergency system? Trixie must be hurt badly if the dragon wanted to involve the human authorities.

Viktor paced back to where his chain was attached to the castle wall and gripped the metal with both hands. Placing his feet on either side of the stone block, he pulled. He couldn't break the chain but he *could* break the castle. He'd just never had enough incentive to try. Technically, he could just end up ripping his arms off.

Trixie's weak groan reached his ears.

With one muscle screeching pull, he yanked the anchor stone free of its masonry. The foundation groaned and the wall cracked as the stone clattered to the floor.

"What the fuck?" Eoin shouted.

Viktor lifted the stone, bigger than his torso, and set it on his shoulder. The weight staggered his footsteps and the chain dragged over the floor, but he managed to leave his prison and see Trixie's prone body at the foot of the stairs. Her neck bent at the wrong angle.

She still breathed and he heard her heart stutter. Time was not on their side.

He dropped his burden next to the stunned dragon, who stared at the block of stone at his feet. Blood trickled down Viktor's arm where the stone had scraped over his skin. It dripped from his fingertips, landing next to Trixie. Viktor stared, unable to think clearly.

She had been so kind to him. Genuinely worried about his imprisonment. He had scared her away because she had kindled unwanted desires. Dangerous needs. Here she was, at his feet, dying.

He dropped to his knees.

Angie came racing headlong down the stairs. "Is she dead?" Tears streamed along her cheeks and she pressed her hands to her mouth.

"She still has a pulse." Eoin glanced over his shoulder in Viktor's direction.

Angie stared at her cell phone. "There's no reception down here. I have to go outside."

The tabloids would explode once news of a human girl dying inside of the dragons' castle was leaked. Viktor cupped Trixie's cheek and her eyelids fluttered open. "You are dying," he whispered in her ear. She smelled of lilacs in spring. His old home in the country had had lilac trees bordering the east part of his lands. At night, they perfumed the air, but they bloomed for a very short time. Much like this girl. "But I can stop that." He pulled away and saw the understanding of his offer dawn in her eyes. At that same moment, he realized what he had just offered her. He would be her sire, be responsible for her actions. Never once had he been tempted to make another vampire.

Her pulse slowed and her eyes widened.

Then he realized she could not move. Or answer. "Blink if the answer is yes."

Her lids closed and her heart stuttered.

"Fuck it." He bent over her. Sharp fangs slid into her young skin like butter. The coppery flavor of her blood caressed his tongue. His mouth watered and he moaned at her exquisite hot iron pulse. Live blood flowed into his body. Pure heaven to his dulled bagged-blood senses.

Fingers tangled in his long hair, dragging him off Trixie. Eoin used the strands like a rope as he pulled him to his feet. "I can't believe you." Pure disgust in every word.

"She's dying." Unable to resist, he licked his lips clean. "I could save her, you idiot."

Angie knelt next to Trixie's broken body. Sorrow-filled noises worked their way out of her throat. "You can fix her?"

Eoin released his hold on him. "You'll bind her to you?"

Viktor returned to draining Trixie. Time was of the essence and he had none to spare answering either of the dragons' asinine questions. Her heart barely beat. He drank his fill and then some more. Like all creatures, creating life came with a price.

Veins filled to bursting, he could barely move as he finally withdrew from Trixie's throat. He bit into his own wrist and let his blood trickle into her mouth.

She would belong to him forever.

Angie jumped to her feet. "It was that gargoyle. I heard him inside the castle again." She stormed up the stairs.

Eoin hesitated at the bottom, tossing Viktor a concerned glance.

"Go, I have this under control." He had witnessed enough births to know what to expect. Having the dragons gone would help save what was left of his dignity.

Angie's shouts carried through the stone. Things crashed against the walls far above him.

Eoin took the steps three at a time.

The wound on Viktor's wrist kept closing and he had to repeat the bite four more times before her lips sealed around the tear. Cross-legged, he propped her against his chest and let her drink. Once she was feeding on her own, his head spun at the sudden drain. Fire coursed through his veins. He grimaced at the burn.

Trixie's neck made sickly cracking pops as it realigned and healed.

His chest constricted and his gut cramped. He closed his eyes and rocked her in his arms. She had to drink it all back. The muscles in his back spasmed and he cried out.

The shouts above had turned into roars. The foundation shook and stone dust fell upon them as a blast hit the castle walls. Was Angie attacking her home? No, she was after the gargoyle and had bad aim. The foundation shook again. That woman had a temper.

Trixie went limp in his arms and he lay next to her on the floor. He was too drained of energy to do anything else. Before his eyes, Trixie's skin smoothed into creamy porcelain, her freckles highlighted by the contrast. Her pink, over-treated hair relaxed into thick waves around her head. Her chest rose.

He shot their environment a distasteful glance, hating to have her wake in a dungeon. It could be worse. *He* had been born on a moonlit battlefield surrounded by his fallen brothers. Alone. He pressed her hand to his lips. Unlike him, she would have a teacher. Or *teachers*. He was a bad example for a vampire. That did not mean she had to be. The local vampire nest would raise her better.

Trixie shivered. The cold floor under her back sucked away her body heat. Rolling onto her side, she groaned as her stiff muscles protested. She was lucky all she had were bruises from that fall. She rubbed her sore neck—she should have broken her... She blinked her eyes open and listened to the distant dragon roars.

The clink of metal on stone caught her attention.

She rolled over onto her other side.

Viktor sat watching her, his liquid silk hair falling like a veil as he leaned forward and plucked the wooden stake out of her pocket. He quirked an eyebrow at her weapon.

"I can explain." She tried to sit but her arms didn't want to support any weight and she only flopped into his lap, face first. Mortified, she squirmed and only managed to rub herself hard into his crotch. "What is wrong with me?" Her voice came out muffled.

He cleared his throat and pulled her into his arms. "You sustained a serious injury and are still healing."

This close to his face, she noticed how perfectly shaped his lips were and how sharp his fangs appeared.

"I fell down the stairs." She glanced at the stone spiral staircase. No wonder she felt like road kill. She must have knocked herself out. "The gargoyle startled me."

"The dragons are attempting to barbeque him as we speak." His statement was followed by an explosion outside.

"Oh no! He didn't do it on purpose. We have to stop them."

Viktor gave her an amused look. "I am not stepping outside while the dragons are this upset. Vampires are quite flammable. Gargoyles, not so much."

"I didn't know that." She flexed her arm. "How long was I unconscious?" Maybe she had a concussion? It didn't explain why her limbs were acting so weird.

Viktor remained quiet, twirling the stake in his free hand. "You wanted to stake me?" Then he spun it to the spoon side. "Or bake for me?"

"It was only a precaution." No matter how brave she had sounded in her head, she wouldn't have been able to kill Viktor. She couldn't even kill a spider. She carried them outside before Ruby pulled off a shoe. "I wanted to talk to you. The stake made me feel safe."

He shook his head. "Too thin. It would have broken before penetrating my heart."

She stared at her legs, trying to bend her knees and failing. "Something's wrong, Viktor. I'm scared. Maybe we should call an ambulance." She'd figure out a way to pay the hospital bill.

"You are healing. Give it a little more time and you will feel better."

She eyed the vampire who didn't seem to be playing with a full deck of cards. "Why don't we let a doctor examine me anyways?"

"He would just pronounce you inhuman." Viktor cupped her face. "Remember, Trixie."

Frozen fingers of fear gripped her spine. She recalled the fall, rolling backwards head over heels, landing awkwardly with a sharp crack. She touched the spot where it had hurt but now didn't. She *had* broken her neck.

Then Viktor's face had hovered over hers, concern and fear in his eyes. He had whispered urgent words in her ear.

"You offered to keep me from dying." After that, things had gone dark.

"I made you vampire. I am your sire. Did I do wrong?" His long elegant fingers traced the freckles on her face. He seemed mesmerized by them. "I tried to give you a choice but you were fading so fast."

"What kind of choice was that? Of course, I want to live."

In the distance, she recognized Angie's voice. "I can't believe we lost him."

"Angie?" she called out.

Silence was her answer.

"Angie?" she shouted louder.

Footsteps echoed toward them as Angie descended into the dungeon, out of breath and eyes wide. "Trixie!" She hugged her tight. "It worked. You're alive."

"Depends on your definition of alive." She patted Angie on the back, her arms seeming more coordinated already.

A man with dark stubble on his head and piercing blue eyes followed at a more leisured pace. His eyebrows rose. "That was fast."

"Who are you?" She was losing track of all the new people.

"This is Eoin, harbinger of smoke and fire. My warden." All this time, her *sire* kept stroking her hair, as if she was his new pet, and while the *black dragon of terror* stared at them. "She's weak and will need to feed soon."

Trixie tried to stand and prove Viktor wrong but only managed to hop in his lap. "Maybe we should get a second opinion, like a doctor or something."

"No." Angie and Eoin spoke in unison and glanced at each other.

"Ah, they finally agree on something," Viktor whispered in her ear.

Her heart thrummed like a hummingbird. *A vampire...* "How come I can still feel my heartbeat?" She pressed her hand over her chest.

"Because you are not dead. Just not human anymore." Viktor took her hand and set it over his beating heart. "See?"

She opened her mouth but nothing came out.

Angie leaned forward. She was so close and smelled like barbeque popcorn. Trixie's favorite. She inhaled deeply. Her stomach growled and her teeth ached. A sharp pain pierced her gums and she clapped her hand over her mouth. "Ouch."

Viktor gently pried her hand away and examined her teeth. He smiled with full fang exposure. "Very nice."

She fingered her pointed teeth and glanced at Angie.

"Not her." He shook his finger. "Dragons' blood burns. Shifters hold no nutritional value. Only human blood will sustain you." He glanced at Eoin. "Do you have any readily available? You can call my people if you do not."

"You know I don't like your people." Eoin scowled. "I have some saved for emergency. I'd say this qualifies." The dragon climbed the stairs and returned shortly with two bags of blood.

Viktor bit the corner off a bag and held it to her lips. "Drink. It will make you stronger."

The smell of it hit her senses like a sledge hammer. Hunger tore through all pretenses of civility, shredding away the remains of her humanity. The next thing she knew, she held an empty bag in her hands.

Angie stood behind Eoin, peering over his shoulder with wide eyes.

Trixie wiped her mouth, smearing red along the back of her hand. "Don't you dare judge me."

Eoin threw back his head and laughed. "You should see Angie eat in dragon form. I thought she was going to choke."

Angie smacked his shoulder. "We were never to speak of that again."

Something akin to envy crossed Viktor's face as he watched their exchange. He was lonely. He'd admitted it to her this morning when they first met and he'd lured her into his cell. She didn't think it came only from his being held captive. That deep of reaction developed over time.

She fingered the collar around Viktor's throat, worry a constant gnaw in her gut. "Are you going to chain me to a wall?" *What* was she going to tell her sister? *How* was she going to tell her? Ruby was going to come home from work and never know what happened. She hadn't taken Trixie's plans for the evening seriously.

Viktor's smile widened. "I am growing weary of chatting to myself."

"You need to keep that kind of crazy talk to yourself from now on." Trixie poked him in the chest. "If I wasn't so weak, I'd be freaking out on your ass."

He held up the stake. "And use this?"

"No." She crossed her arms and turned away. Tears burned in the back of her eyes. Nothing had gone according to plan.

Angie stood. "No more vampires chained in the basement."

"Dungeon," corrected Eoin.

She glared at him. "Or gargoyles on the castle. I'm going to fry his prankster ass."

"Once you catch him." Eoin eyed Trixie. "Can you walk?"

She tried to move again but weariness weighed heavily on her limbs. Her head spun with the effort to stand and she leaned against Viktor. "Worst day ever."

Viktor's smile faded. "Vampire births are always tragic." He lifted her chin and kissed her forehead. "Yet it is your new birthday."

"You're crazy." In a sweet way, he was trying to console her. He was the only one who knew what she was going through.

CHAPTER SIX

Angie helped Trixie to her feet and led her away from the dungeon. "I can't tell you how sorry I am. That damn gargoyle has no boundaries." She paused to glare at the men. "Viktor, shower before coming upstairs." Angie supported Trixie under the arm as they climbed the stairs, passing the main floor and going higher in the spiral. Trixie realized they were in one of the towers.

Viktor had been right. The blood made her stronger. By the time they reached the second floor, her legs responded like normal and she leaned less on Angie. That wasn't the only thing though. The scent of cool, forest growth caressed her nose and the dark halls glowed with pale moonlight filtering through a slit window. Trixie saw everything. She heard everything. She could *count* the chips in the stone stairs, the frogs singing outside in the pond. She *heard* every leaf shudder in the breeze. She could feel the animals in the deep forest, scurrying, hunting, doing dark things. She'd never felt so alive, so in touch with her surroundings.

Trixie stared at the walls, mesmerized by the web of cracks within the stone. Fingertips tracing the pattern, she slowed to a stop. It was magical. How had she missed this before?

Angie stopped with her. "Are you tired? We could sit on the steps and let you catch your breath."

Her breath? She *was* breathing. Being a vampire wasn't like the movies. She wasn't dead. Angie's barbeque popcorn scent drew her attention away from the wall. Under it,

Trixie also smelled brimstone and cloves. Sweet and spicy like cinnamon candies. She leaned closer. "You smell great."

The white dragon, the friendly one, retreated and Trixie followed.

She couldn't stop her legs. It was if her body had an autopilot and she didn't know how to shut it off. Angie smelled so good and Trixie was still hungry. She only wanted a little taste.

"Easy, Trix." Angie grabbed her by the shoulders with strength Trixie wouldn't have guessed the small dragon possessed. "I'm not on the menu, remember? You'll burn if you drink my blood."

Trixie blinked and managed to stop. "Right."

"Let's find you a snack." She shouted down the stairs, "Eoin, bring more blood." Then dragged Trixie farther up the stairs to what seemed like the top of the tower. "Now."

"I'm okay, seriously." Trixie rubbed her forehead and fought past the fog in her mind. "I need to adjust. Can't I just go home?"

"I know, but honey, Viktor's been a vampire for a really long time and he's been chained in the basement for a reason. Controlling your hunger isn't as easy as it might sound. Or so I've been told repeatedly. So, let's take baby steps before I set you loose on the unsuspecting population of New Port."

Trixie pictured New Port in the midst of a blood bath with her as the serial killer. She stopped fighting Angie.

The dragon pulled her inside a room where all the furniture was covered in dusty sheets. "We don't have guests often."

Trixie crossed the room to the farthest side. "Lock the door." She didn't trust herself. Dark suggestions whispered in her thoughts. They consisted of shadows and blood and screams. It was difficult not to listen since it had no voice, but came from something deep within her.

Angie paused in removing the coverings and tossed her a concerned look. "You bet." And she closed and locked the exit. "I'll open the windows to let in some fresh air though. The dust is thick enough to build castles." Fresh air blew inside the room. "Trixie, did I forget to give you a kennel?"

An ornate mirror hung over the mantel of the fireplace. Trixie stared at her reflection. "No, why?"

"I'm trying to figure out why you're here. Inside the castle."

"I came back to talk to Viktor."

"Why would you want to do that?"

There had been so many good reasons at the time. "Doesn't matter now does it." Turning her head slightly, Trixie examined what used to be damaged, over-processed hair with split ends. The pink strands now poured over her shoulders in soft, thick waves. Her pale skin glowed and her freckles, which she hated, made her appear exotically spotted. The blue of her eyes sparkled like they were made of sapphires. Flawless. Even the scar on her chin that she'd had since forever had vanished.

This was the best makeover ever.

"Do you have a scale?" she asked Angie.

She set the last of the dusty sheets in a corner. "What for?"

"It looks like I lost some weight. I just wanted to confirm it." She examined her butt in the mirror. Those stubborn fifteen pounds she'd been struggling to lose seemed to have melted away. "I look good for someone who just broke her neck."

Angie made a strangled noise, hands clutched to her chest.

"I didn't mean to upset you." She patted Angie's shoulders, doing her best to keep her distance. "Really, I'm not mad, just disoriented. I mean, I'd be dead if Viktor hadn't turned me." She took a shaky breath. "I like being alive." Even to her own ears, it sounded like she was trying to convince herself more than Angie.

Angie shook her head. "Everything will be different for you now."

The dragon meant Trixie wasn't human anymore. The rules had changed in the blink of an eye and she wasn't even sure what those rules were. She assumed no more daylight. She sat on the edge of the loveseat. No more food. She'd have to figure out how to obtain blood. And the worst thing, vampires lived in secrecy and she sucked at lying.

Trixie massaged the bridge of her nose. Apparently, she could still have headaches. She'd come here tonight to ensure Ruby's safety and had made things worse by dying.

"Shifters live in the open alongside humans. I know I asked this before, but why not vampires?" Trixie clutched her stomach, which was twisting in knots and not because she was hungry. She had a sister and friends that she wouldn't give up. How did she do that without telling them what she was?

Angie rubbed her brow. "Vampires *feed off* humans. Do you really see the citizens of the world rolling out the red carpet for vampires?"

When Angie put it that way… "I guess not." Trixie leaned back in the chair, pressing the back of her arm over her eyes. She wasn't thinking straight. Those whispers were growing harder to ignore. "Where's Viktor?" He dealt with this all the time. He had to have answers she needed so she could make these strong urges go away. "I thought Eoin was going to bring him."

Angie scooted to the locked exit, her steps fast. "I'll go check. Wait here." She left and Trixie heard the lock tumble back into place. Angie was afraid of her.

Good, Trixie was afraid too. Especially since she recalled that bag of human blood with such yearning. With such lust.

"I do not understand why you are so upset." Viktor sat upon the cut stone he had pulled out of the cell wall. The one his chain was attached to. "I am sure you can afford to reset the block. I did not even crack it."

Eoin spluttered, "I don't care about the fucking wall. You *made* a vampire."

Viktor hid his smirk by staring at his feet. It was not often he witnessed Eoin flabbergasted. "Oh." He shrugged. On the outside, he fought to remain nonchalant. If he allowed himself to truly consider his actions, then they would both be shouting and pacing the dungeon like lunatics. One crazed supernatural at time seemed prudent.

The dragon crouched in front of him. "For as long as we've known each other, I've never heard you mention creating another of your kind." He ran his hand over his face.

Viktor shrugged again. How could he explain the urge to save Trixie when he did not understand it himself? Maybe he had been alone too long. Maybe he'd liked meeting a nice girl for once. Maybe she deserved better than a stupid death from falling down the stairs. "I righted a wrong." She had come to stake him. That took balls. Maybe he liked girls with balls?

Eoin snarled. "What am I supposed to do with her?"

"Nothing." Angie came barreling down the stairs with her usual stormy presence. "And why hasn't he showered yet? Stop gossiping and move. He's her sire. He needs to teach her about being a vampire."

"Not a good idea," Viktor spoke before Eoin.

His old friend gave him a weary smile. "Will the New Port nest take her in?"

"Wait. Don't tell me you're going to let him get away with this?" She crossed her arms, tapping her foot. "Viktor has a responsibility to Trixie."

Viktor shook his head. Angie did not know him and did not understand what a mistake that would be. "I am a terrible person, especially for modern culture. I would only lead her astray."

Angie's eyes narrowed. "Viktor, you're a little eccentric but you saved Betty's mating and now you saved Trixie's life. Not so bad in my books. Stop with the self-pity shit. This is serious."

He gestured to the names covering his body. "They would not agree."

The dragon snorted. "Most of those names came from long, long ago." Eoin, for some reason, believed in Viktor's redemption, otherwise the dragon would have killed him. Instead, he helped Viktor by chaining him in a cell so he would not kill other innocent people.

"Enough." Angie clapped her hands. "Trixie has a million questions and she's hungry again. And starting to freak me out. Your stay in the dungeon is over." She handed Eoin a key. "I placed her in the room at the top of the tower. I'll go get the blood in the kitchen fridge."

"Are you sure about setting me free?" Viktor slowly rose to his feet, hope a fleeting flicker of smoke. "I do not want to kill again." His sanity was returning, it seemed.

Eoin rested his hand on Viktor's shoulder. "My friend, that's the first sane thing I've heard you say in weeks." He glanced at Angie. "I'm not ready to set him free though. We can move him closer to Trixie and chain him there."

"Still with the chain?" She set her hands on her hips. "I'm starting to think you guys are enjoying this too much." With a shake of her head, she ascended the stairs.

"Trixie might be good for you." Eoin undid the lock holding the chain to the stone. "A much-needed distraction."

"How so?" Viktor followed his jailor out of the dungeon.

"You could teach her to be the type of vampire you aspire to be." Eoin tossed him an amused smile. "She's quite a stunning vampire."

Viktor growled and yanked the chain from Eoin's hand, refusing to be led like a pet dog. "You are mated." All vampires were beautiful. Otherwise they would starve. It was a predatory evolution.

"Doesn't mean I'm blind." Eoin chuckled. "I saw the way you looked at her. You're not unaffected."

They climbed to the first floor where Viktor was given access to a shower. The first one he'd had in weeks. He rattled the chain. "What about this?"

"It won't rust. You have five minutes. Don't waste it."

"You are an asshole." He stripped and turned on the hot water. The hot water was blinding joy, but he couldn't soak in its glory. He washed and had barely rinsed when Eoin tugged on the chain.

"I brought fresh clothes."

Viktor dried then exited the shower. He found a clean pair of pants folded on the sink counter top. "Just pants?" Fresh skin felt wonderful.

"That's all I have that will fit you."

Viktor *was* slenderer than the dragon. Exiting, he scowled at Eoin before the dragon led him higher in the tower.

Old tapestries still clung to the walls, unlike the more habited parts of the castle where the walls were mostly bare. "I have never been here." Viktor twisted around for a better look. It was rare for Eoin to allow anyone in the older areas of his home.

"This is the South Tower. Angie wants to reclaim this part since the windows are mostly intact."

"For now." He chuckled. Dragon roars tended to shatter glass and both had hair trigger tempers.

Eoin tossed him a warning glare. "I'm not allowed in this area as dragon."

"Ah." Eoin, unofficial ruler of New Port, smote by a small, feathered white dragon. Viktor kept this to himself since he did not truly have a death wish.

Eoin pulled out the key Angie had given him and unlocked the thick wooden door.

Viktor frowned. Blood trickled over his fingernails where they cut into his fisted palms. "I thought you said she wasn't a prisoner." Trixie should not suffer for his mistakes.

"She's a new, hungry vampire and there is an unsuspecting city just miles from here. She'll remain under lock and key until you or someone else takes responsibility for her education. She needs to learn the basics and the laws at least." He fiddled with the old lock.

Angie arrived behind them, a bag of blood in hand. "What are you doing?"

"The lock is stuck," the male dragon grumbled. "I'm trying not to snap the fucking key again."

"Lift the doorknob a bit." She shoved the blood into Viktor's hands and pushed her mate aside. "You're going to break it if you keep trying to force the turn."

Viktor squished the bag in his hand, watching the ruby fluid in fascination as the plastic stretched. This wasn't the concentrated blood bank crap Eoin had fed him. This was whole blood, probably bought off the black market. "Where was this earlier?"

"This was your next meal. The bag I gave you today was expiring so you had to have it today." Eoin spoke absentmindedly.

Some vampires disdained modern ways. Viktor wasn't one of them. He loved the convenience of bagged whole blood, even if the taste was a little off. There were some entrepreneurs, otherwise known on the black market as blood mongers, who catered to his kind. They didn't tamper with the blood and added only a touch of preservative to keep it from clotting. They even delivered, except to the castle. "Wait, how did you obtain this?"

"I have them deliver it to Angie's shop." The dragon winked at him over her head. "See, I try."

The lock clicked and the door swung open.

Viktor stepped inside ahead of the dragons, blood in hand. He desired to see the changes the earlier meal of blood had on Trixie and offer her another. Just past the threshold, he came to a halt. The room was empty. "Wrong room. She is not here."

Angie pushed past him and spun a slow circle. "Where'd she go?" She rushed back into the hallway. "Trixie's gone," she hissed at Eoin.

"Search outside and I'll check the castle." The black dragon pointed at Viktor. "You stay here." Both dragons raced off, leaving him alone in the room, carrying the long length of chain connected to his collar.

He smiled. Dragons were so excitable. The windows in this tower would not stay intact long. He crossed the room and pulled open a curtain. The old wooden frame encasing the glass was open. "*Хуёво*," he muttered under his breath. Trixie was too young to fly. Hell, *he* was too young to fly, but she did not know this. He scanned the ground below. The fall would not kill her but her bones would shatter and it would hurt like hell.

Except the lawn was empty and crater free. He punched the window frame, cracking the old wood. Had he already lost her? That had to be a record.

He wrapped the long, heavy chain his bare torso, since he could not snap it free of the collar, and he did not want to trip over it. Then he leaped out the opening.

The weight of the chain sped his fall and the impact left his knees aching. Where was she? He glanced at the smooth wall of the tower. The climb down would have been very difficult for an amateur. She surely would have fallen.

The sweet scent of her blood drifted in the air—faint and floral. He would have missed it if not for her blood already caressing his veins. He followed the song it sang until he found a drop congealed in the dirt.

Only a drop?

Falling from that height, she should have been bleeding out. He knelt next to the spot and rubbed it between his fingers. He was missing something obvious.

Closing his eyes, he rewound his memories, replaying the last day since he'd encountered Trixie. Her curious expression when she'd first laid eyes on him, the smell of her attraction, the sound of her body impacting the bottom of the stairwell. The taste of her blood, Angie's screams, roars and fire balls.

He opened his eyes and scanned the castle walls. Angie had been after a gargoyle. Blamed him for hurting Trixie, but gargoyles weren't predatory. If anything, they were pranksters. Thieves.

He gnashed his fangs. Trixie had been stolen from *him*.

CHAPTER SEVEN
(Earlier that night)

The lock clicked in place. Trixie didn't blame Angie for not trusting her. Hell, *she* didn't even grasp what was going on. She rubbed her completely healed neck. It didn't even ache anymore.

She was a vampire. A lady of the night. She snorted and returned to the mirror for another look at this stranger with her face. Opening her mouth, she examined the baby fangs. She hoped they grew bigger. They made her look kitten-like.

And what was up with the hair? She ran her fingers through the thick waves. Anyone who dyed their hair a vibrant color like hers understood that damage was an issue. She usually did intensive oil treatments but had never gotten these kinds of results.

She traced the reflection of her pale face. Dammit, where was Viktor? She had a bazillion questions. Patting her pockets, she searched for her phone. Ruby would be home soon and Trixie needed to talk to her. Her sister always knew how to wiggle out of trouble and Trixie sure could use her problem-solving skills.

The cell phone screen was so shattered she'd slice her fingers if she tried to swipe it.

Someone cleared his throat behind her. She spun around, expecting to find Viktor. Instead, she came face to face with the gargoyle that had startled her. Or at least, she thought it was him. They all kind of looked alike.

He climbed into the room from the open window. "I'm glad to see you're okay. I didn't mean for you to fall down the stairs. The way the dragons are reacting, I thought I had killed you."

She stared at his massive bat-like wings and huge horns protruding from his head. Up close, he looked more like a demon. It was difficult to respond with her heart in her throat.

He tilted his head as if perplexed. "You are okay, right? You look a little pale."

"It's you." All she had wanted this morning was to retrieve the cat kennels and not lose her job. That seemed so important then. Instead, she had lost her humanity and the life connected to it because of this monster in front of her.

He patted his chest as if checking. "Yep, it's me." He chuckled.

"Enough with the jokes." She crossed the room, confident that, as a vampire, she trumped gargoyle in the supernatural pecking order. Fury sharpened her vision and she had lots of fury. "Asshole, I *did* die because of you."

His eyes went wide and he gently poked her with a claw. "You're not a ghost."

She stumbled from his strength. "I'm a vampire." Rubbing the sore spot he left, she eyed his big muscled arms.

Okay, so maybe he trumped her after all.

"Oh." He sounded so relieved she almost laughed. "Then no harm done."

"No harm?" Her voice rose to an octave that only dogs and, apparently, gargoyles could hear. "I fell down those stairs and died. Like a few hours ago, I was human. The resident vampire chained in the dungeon turned me." She hiccupped. How would she keep her job? She glanced at the midnight sky. Sure, she worked the nightshift but she still had to get home in the light of dawn. "Nothing is ever going to be the same again. I can't even call my sister." She tossed her broken phone at the gargoyle.

It bounced off his rock-hard head and he didn't even seem to notice. "You're crying blood."

"What?" She spun to look at the horror show in the mirror. It only made her cry more.

"Don't..." The gargoyle hugged her. It was like being crushed by stone. "I can fly you home if you want." He stroked her hair, snagging it on his rough stone hands. "Just stop crying. You're kind of grossing me out."

She slapped his shoulder, yet a laugh still bubbled past her sobs. "I hate you."

"I know. I hate me too."

She wiped her face. Ruby would know what to do. Maybe they could run away together? Maybe she'd want to be a vampire with her? All she knew was that she had to get away from the castle of angry dragons and sexy vampire. She couldn't think around them. They wouldn't let her. "You'll fly me home?"

"Sure." He scooped her into his big arms and carried her to the open window. "Where to?"

She pointed toward the city. Her bloody tears wouldn't stop even when he leaped through the window and flew. Regret weighed heavy on her heart. Instead of enjoying her first flight in the arms of a gargoyle, she kept thinking of how her sister would take this news. Yes, she knew she shouldn't tell Ruby about vampires existing, but there was no way she could keep it a secret now. Her sister was the jam to Trixie's peanut butter. She was not going to disappear mysteriously. She *would not* leave Ruby wondering what happened to her for the rest of her life. That would destroy Ruby faster than knowing the truth.

They'd figure this out together.

Maybe with Viktor's help. No more dragons. And she had to keep her hands off Viktor. Fuck, that would be impossible.

Bleary eyed, she searched the city below for a familiar landmark. It wasn't easy giving directions from a new vantage point. "Umm, that looks like the bar district. I think my building is that way." She pointed east, or what she thought was east.

"Don't you know where you live?" The gargoyle angled their trajectory with a lazy turn.

"Not from the sky. It's not like I can see the street signs from here."

"Are you sure you're a vampire?"

She shifted her weight in his arms. "What is that supposed to mean?"

"The vampires I've met would be able to read them from this distance."

"I'm not even a day old." She stared at the street corners, looking for a sign. Her vision telescoped. With a yelp, she grasped his shoulders as the world spun. "Whoa, it worked." She shook her head, trying to regain her equilibrium. "How does that work?" Trixie's eyes had been normal a few hours ago, but now she had superhero vision. "I can get in a lot of trouble with this new toy." She scanned the windows of the surrounding buildings.

The gargoyle placed his hand over her eyes. "Use your powers for good." His smile was full of mischief though.

"What's the fun in that?" She refocused her new found binocular vision on the street signs and found her bearings. She recognized the buildings and neighborhood now. "We're going the right way. Not much further to go." She pointed in the distance. "See that rain collector on top of that building? I live across the street."

Soon, she would see her sister. Ruby should be home by now from her double shift and most likely pissed to all hell that Trixie was missing and not answering her broken phone. Wait until she explained why.

Trixie cringed inside and wiped her tear streaked cheeks clean with her sleeve. Red stained the material. Gross.

The gargoyle landed on her three-story brick building smooth as butter and set her gently on her feet.

"Do you have a name?" she asked, tired of thinking of him as *the gargoyle* since he seemed nicer than most humans she'd met.

"You can call me Nick." He scuffed his clawed toe on the surface. "I'd stay and help but I suspect the dragons will continue their hunt for me. I'll just be putting you in more danger."

"Vampire." She gestured to herself. "Am I not immortal?"

Nick chuckled, his cheeks developing twin adorable dimples.

"You are very flammable though." A familiar accented voice spoke from thin air.

She jumped. And spun a slow circle. "Viktor?" Was he smoke like she'd seen in the movies? Now that was a super power. "Where are you?"

A set of long, elegant fingers gripped the edge of the roof. Viktor climbed over the top. So not magical, just fast as hell. And he had scaled her building shirtless with the heavy chain wrapped around him. He stunned her with his beauty again, even with his just-broke-out-of-a-dungeon fashion statement. Hip length, midnight hair blew in the wind, exposing his chiseled muscle torso. Sweet mercy, he didn't have an ounce of fat on him. His barbarian hotness weakened her knees.

Nick pressed a clawed fingertip to her chin and clicked her mouth shut.

Suddenly, Viktor was so close she gasped. He moved before she could finish a blink, which made it appear as if he teleported the short distance. He gripped Nick's wrist, squeezing so tight the gargoyle moaned. "Thief." The vampire bared his long fangs. "Did you really think you could take what is mine?"

Nick fell to his knees, his eyes wide and mouth open in soundless agony. The gargoyle easily outsized Viktor in mass and he had carried her across the city as if she weighed nothing.

"Trixie, take the chain and wrap it around him." In a graceful move, Viktor had both of the gargoyle's arms behind his back.

Her hands fluttered uselessly for a second. For the last twenty-four hours, she'd been in a constant state of confusion and indecision. She fisted her hands and glared at both males. "What did he steal?" Had Nick used her as an excuse to take something from the dragons?

Both stared at her as if she'd spoken in tongues.

"I owe her a blood debt," Nick explained to Viktor. "I can't say no to her."

Viktor's gaze darted to her. The intensity so fierce she stepped back. "She's mine so her debt is also mine. You will have no more contact with her. I know your kind too well, gargoyle."

His? She belonged to no one. She tried to respond but her thoughts raced so fast all that came out was a mangled version of rap. Vampire. Gargoyle. On *her* roof. Blood debt?

Hmm...blood. Her stomach growled. She never had received the promised snack before leaving the castle. That might not have been the wisest idea. She clamped her hands over her abdomen. "I'm what he stole? I don't belong to you, Viktor." She backed away toward the roof entrance to the building, praying it was unlocked. "How do you know where I live, anyways?"

"*This* is where you live?" He scanned her neighborhood as the flashing lights and sirens of a police car sped by. He frowned. "Quaint."

Viktor shrugged off the chain, giving her a full access view of his tattooed body. He had those side ab muscles that led to his groin, which she had no real name for except Trixie's Achilles heel.

The chain was still attached to his collar as he used it to secure Nick's arms. The vampire tugged at the restraint and seemed satisfied. "I tracked your tears." He stalked her as she retreated.

Nick, unfortunately, was dragged along.

Her back hit the door.

Viktor ran his thumb under her tearstained eyes. "I am sorry, but together we will make this right for you."

"My tears." She jerked from his scorching touch. It set off alarming signals in her body. Something she had thought was missing in her genes. That sexual craving everyone else experienced hadn't existed until she'd met Viktor. She would have blamed in on the vampirism except she'd desired Viktor when she'd first encountered him, when she had still been human. "How the hell do you track tears?" She wanted super x-ray vision to see other people's shed tears. What other things would she be able to do?

"The scent of your blood is mingled in them. You are my fledgling. We are bound now. Tracking your blood is easy."

That wasn't alarming. Viktor, crazy vampire, will *always* know where she was. Suddenly, coming home to Ruby sounded like the worst idea she'd ever had. "How are we exactly bound?" If he said *bride*, she'd have to steal the stake in his pocket and stab him. Even if he did have *sex-god* stamped on every inch of his delicious skin.

"I'm your sire. My blood is in your veins."

She pressed her fists to suppress the constant ache in her gut. It was worse than a bride.

She was a slave.

CHAPTER EIGHT

"You need to feed." He kicked open the roof door. "Show me to your home."

"That probably wasn't locked." Trixie didn't move. "What about Nick?" The gargoyle was responsible for her fall, but she didn't punish people for accidents. If she did, then she should be on the country's most wanted list.

The gargoyle raised his eyebrows.

"The dragons will figure out what happened. They'll follow the trail here like I did and retrieve him."

Nick's gray skin paled. "I wronged *her*. Not *them*. She has blood rights and should dictate my punishment."

Viktor shook his head. "Your foolishness caused her death, but it was under *their* roof. She was a guest and you broke guesting law." His hard glare softened for a second as it landed on her. "Trixie's soul is too gentle to meet out proper punishment." He jerked Nick to his feet. "The dragons get you."

"I've had enough of you, Viktor. If anyone has—has blood law then—"

"Blood rights," Nick corrected.

"Rights, that's me." Sounded like she had to learn a whole new legal system. She hadn't done to well following human laws. After what she had witnessed in the last few hours, she'd say supernatural punishment was much more medieval. "I'll decide what happens to Nick."

She couldn't believe she was defending him, but she knew what it felt like to be punished for things out of her control. Like those cat kennels.

Viktor's eyes danced with amusement. "What do you know of gargoyles?"

She set her hands on his, the one holding the chain. The zing that traveled through her fingers must have been from that blood bond between them. It was too strong to be anything else. "Nothing, but the dragons might kill him." She *did* have a soft soul and there was nothing wrong with that.

"He killed you."

"Not on purpose." She tugged on Viktor's fingers, trying to pry them open with no luck.

She managed to only make him more amused. "Gargoyles are notorious thieves."

"Not all of us," grumbled Nick.

"What about Venice last week? Do not tell me a gargoyle was not involved in that girl's disappearance." Viktor's amusement faded as he stared at the kneeling Nick. "Humans might not suspect but the rest of us know." The vampire then raised his hand until he could kiss Trixie's prying fingers.

She jerked away as if branded. "How could you know anything about Venice? You've been locked in the castle basement."

"Dungeon," he corrected. "Eoin keeps me apprised of world events and I am his guest. Not truly a prisoner."

"And I don't truly belong to you. Give me that chain. Nick owes me, not you." She held out her hand. It trembled, but she didn't back down. The dragons might kill the gargoyle. She wouldn't be part of that.

Viktor glanced from her to Nick and handed over the chain. The gargoyle smirked.

That was easy. She stormed off the roof to her third-floor apartment. Footsteps dogged her heels. She glanced over her shoulder. Viktor followed behind Nick. "You're not welcome in my home," she stated.

Viktor traced the collar around his neck in that slow, seductive way he had. He ran his fingertips over the chain still locked to it. The same one restraining Nick. The same one she held.

Well, fuck. She'd walked straight into that one.

"It is not safe for you to be alone." The vampire looked way too pleased.

"I'm fine."

Her apartment door swung open and Ruby stood in the opening, hands on hips in full redheaded fury. "Where the hell have you been? Why haven't you been answering your phone? I was about to organize a search party and..." Her gaze fell on her companions and the chain. "This is new. Got something to confess, Trix?"

Even though her sister only wore a thin T-shirt, sans bra, and a thong, Viktor's gaze never left Trixie. Nick's was totally absorbed by her sister.

Viktor bowed. "May I come in?"

Ruby's mouth hung open as she backed out of the way. Her stare was locked on Nick. "What are you?"

Viktor passed between them, dragging Nick along in the process.

Trixie sighed. "He's a gargoyle." It seemed like inviting a winged monster and a murderous vampire into their home didn't bother her sister.

Ruby gave her a critical eying. "You look great. What have you been doing all night? Why didn't you call me? You know how I worry."

She showed her the trashed cell phone. The one Trixie had no insurance on or money to replace.

Ruby grimaced. "We'll figure it out. I know a guy who knows a guy. I'll get you a working one."

A stolen one. Trixie didn't like her dealing with the guy who knew a guy. Ruby came home with bruises after those visits, though she waved them off with poor excuses.

"Don't bother." Trixie followed her sire's path into the living room. "Viktor offered to replace it."

The vampire raised an eyebrow, his gaze taking in the broken phone in her hand. "It is of no consequence."

"No consequence at all." Ruby tilted her head, a flirty smile on her lips. "And who might you be, Viktor?"

"Master of the city. Your roommate is in danger if you stay here without supervision." Viktor did what appeared like a security check of the apartment.

"Ruby, meet Viktor, master of the city, and Nick, gargoyle from the dragon's castle. Boys, this is my sister, Ruby."

Her sister raised a well-manicured, delicate eyebrow. "Why don't we have fun like this together? When we go out, all I meet are drunks and drug dealers." She smelled fried chicken and gravy and it made Trixie's mouth water.

The hunger pains grew much worse to point of her wanting to double over. "Did you bring home leftovers?"

"Yeah, it's in the fridge." Ruby followed their guests deeper into the apartment, her gaze tracing Viktor's form with open admiration. She tossed Trixie a salacious wink. "Is it Christmas already?"

She fought a groan. Ruby would steal him away. No man could resist her sister's charm once Ruby focused on her prey.

The pang of jealousy was startling. Trixie didn't bother competing with Ruby when it came to men. None of them seemed worth the effort, but Viktor… Well, he wasn't a man. And she'd just rejected him on the roof, so where was this green-eyed monster rising from?

The galley style kitchen was attached to their living room. Only a counter separated the space, which they used as a dining table. Trixie went to the fridge and pulled out the Styrofoam box. Inside, she was surprised to find the fish special. "Why do I smell fried chicken?"

Viktor stood behind Ruby. He pointed at her in a silent response.

Trixie blinked. Was he saying Ruby was the source of that delicious scent?

"Do not eat solid food." He settled Nick on a stool by the counter before reaching across with his long arms and height to snatch the container from Trixie's hand. "It will make you ill."

"Hey." Ruby slapped the food out of his hand. "I brought that home for her and if she wants to eat it, then she can." She shoved the fish back into Trixie's hands.

But all she wanted was fried chicken. "We need to talk."

All three of them stared at her expectantly.

"I've talked enough to both of you to last a lifetime." Trixie pointedly stared at both men. "I meant Ruby. Alone." Her big sister, who always had her back no matter how terrible her ideas were. Cheerleader, roommate, and guardian angel. Also, the best shoulder to cry on.

God, Ruby was going to be so angry.

Viktor pushed Nick off the stool toward the fire escape. "We will wait outside for Eoin."

"Careful," Ruby called out. "The fire escape is old."

Nick leaned close to her sister and inhaled deeply. "You don't smell like chicken. You smell like—" He couldn't finish as Viktor gave the chain a sharp yank.

Ruby's eyes were round as she faced her. "What the hell is going on? And who's Eoin?"

Once both men were on the balcony, Viktor scanned the sky. "I see him in the distance. It will not be long, Trixie. Hurry to say your goodbyes."

Panic edged into Ruby's expression. "What's he talking about?" She pushed Trixie deeper into the kitchen. "Trix, talk to me."

"I'm in trouble." She took Ruby by the wrists, her sister's pulse hummingbird fast against her palm.

"You're hurting me." Ruby jerked her arms but couldn't break free. "Let go." Fear tinged her voice and made her scent grow crisper.

Trixie's fangs ached. She glanced at their hands. Ruby's fingers were ghostly white. She had stopped the circulation to her sister's hands. She leaned forward to sniff Ruby's throat.

Viktor seemed to materialize between them and untangled her hold on Ruby. "Not her. You are too hungry and too young. You might hurt her." He shrugged. "And never forgive me if I did not stop you."

Her fangs snicked back painfully and Trixie clamped her hand over her mouth. "Ouch."

But not before Ruby saw them. Her face paled. "Did I just really see that?"

"You can't tell anyone." She pushed Viktor out of the way. "No one can know."

Ruby glanced at the container from the diner. "I think I'm hallucinating. Maybe the fish was bad?" With her thumb, she shoved Trixie's upper lip open to examine her teeth. "Those better be fake, baby sister."

Trixie shook her head and pressed her lips closed. Her throat ached so much. She knew if she said one word, the waterworks would turn on and she'd cry blood all over her sister. Ruby was scared enough. Trixie didn't need to upgrade this to a horror movie.

Viktor scooped Trixie into his arms. "She is distressed. We cannot stay any longer. Once she is in more control, we will return." He leveled an icy glare at Nick. "She should not have come here in the first place."

Trixie turned her face against Viktor's chest, unable to look at her sister. Not because of shame, but because she saw her as fried chicken, of all things. With gravy. She had never been the kind of girl who wished for a knight in shining armor to swoop down and rescue her. Viktor wasn't exactly a knight but he did have a shiny chain and her best interest at heart. If she killed Ruby, she'd never forgive herself.

"Oh no you don't. Nobody is going anywhere until I get some answers." Ruby used her no-nonsense voice, which she didn't do often. "You, gargoyle, sit."

Trixie twisted around to see Ruby pointing at Nick, who was squeezing back into the apartment through the window.

He sat at Ruby's feet.

That was her sister. Worshipped by men of all races. Besides hair color and boob size, she and Ruby looked alike, and Trixie didn't have that female power to make a gargoyle heel at her feet on command.

"I died falling down some stairs a few hours ago." The words came out stiffly. "Viktor...brought me back to life by making me a vampire." He *had* saved her. She had to give him props for that, but she wouldn't *ever* belong to him. Nobody owned her, not even Ruby.

Her sister reached out then jerked her hands back to her side. Tears swelled in her eyes. "You mean I almost lost you?" As if unable to control herself, Ruby took a step closer.

Viktor kept their distance. "Stay where you are. Trixie cannot be trusted to control her instincts yet."

Ruby brushed away her tears. "So, vampires are real?"

Trixie fought the urge to roll her eyes. "In secret, for obvious reasons." She gestured between them and the fact that she had been about to feed off her sister. "You can't tell anyone, Ruby. It's important that you don't."

"Because…"

"We will kill you," Viktor answered for her and confirmed her earlier worries prior to falling down the stairs.

Wow, that seemed trivial now.

"Fine, whatever, I don't give a shit. I'll keep your secret." She folded her arms. "What do we do to help Trix?"

She met Ruby's determined glare and Trixie's heart swelled with pride. Her sister wouldn't abandon her. For a moment, Trixie had thought Ruby would be too afraid of the whole vampire thing. She knew she was, and *she* was the freaking vampire.

"We?" he asked. "*We* do nothing. Trixie will live with the local vampire coven. Once she is trained, she can visit."

Ruby's eyes narrowed, her lips tight.

Trixie knew this look. "Don't you dare call Betty or anyone in the wolf pack." Her best friend was on her honeymoon. "They can't do anything to change this."

Wind whipped outside the window, followed by a thumping beat.

"Is there a storm brewing?" Ruby shivered as a breeze blew through the open window.

Trixie cringed as she recognized the thumping noise for huge wings flapping.

Viktor nudged Nick with his barefoot. "To the fire escape."

The gargoyle stroked her sister's leg with a possessive hand before marching to the window, where a big green eye watched.

Ruby screamed.

The black dragon had that effect on people. He grinned, showing all his pearly white, sharp teeth. "Hello."

CHAPTER NINE

A clawed hand reached through the window. It wrapped around the chained gargoyle. "Got you, you little bastard." Pure joy.

Viktor's smirk did not last long as his charge squirmed in his arms until she all but fell to the floor. "Trixie." He tried to catch her but was yanked by the collar at his neck. Eoin was dragging him along with the gargoyle. "Wait," he shouted. "Wait a second." He spun to grip the chain and yanked Nick from Eoin's grasp.

Trixie stood frozen in front of her sister.

Ruby sat on the floor, side pressed to the wall and knees drawn to her chest. What was she wearing? Or not wearing? He had not noticed her half-nakedness until now. Her gaze, so full of fury a moment ago, was now pure terror and focused on his fledgling.

Trixie knelt in front of her. "We're not going to hurt you. The dragon is here for the gargoyle. That's all." Her tone soft and gentle as if speaking to a small animal. Supernatural creatures mostly lived in the open. There were a still a few closet shifters and, of course, vampires kept to the dark. Humans did not like being reminded of their fragility though. Her and Viktor's presence, with a gargoyle and a dragon, might have been too much for Ruby.

He had damaged Trixie's relationship with her sister. "This could have been handled better."

"You think?" Trixie shot back at him over her shoulder.

"I was not the one who jumped into a strange gargoyle's arms." If she would just give him a chance, he could help her on this journey. At least, until he could introduce her to the local vampire nest. She needed a little faith in him.

Ruby used the wall to help her stand and she sat on the edge of the couch, her gaze never leaving Eoin. "Why does he want Nick?"

The gargoyle sighed. "I killed your sister."

The flash of red in Ruby's eyes had Viktor moving in front of Trixie, but the redhead snatched the lamp next to her and smashed it on Nick's head. "You awful monster." She gestured to Eoin. "Eat him."

The dragon puffed out a chuckle. "Not yet, little warrior." But he did grasp Nick again.

"There is the problem of this." Viktor rattled the chain connecting him to the gargoyle. "It is time for it to come off."

"That's not part of the deal, Viktor. You shouldn't have left the castle either."

"My charge was in danger. You expected me to remain in that room and do nothing?" Trixie was his. If anyone should understand that, it was Eoin. She was a new vampire with wild urges and no one to help her control them. If he had not been here, she would have fed upon her sister, possibly killed her. "The only reason you knew where to find us was because I borrowed a cell phone on the way here to call you."

"I thought you said he'd follow the scent trail like you," Trixie whispered behind him.

"I did not want to leave it to chance. Eoin has been unpredictable since he mated."

"I *can* hear you." The dragon jerked the gargoyle closer, in turn making Viktor stumble forward.

Trixie rushed to his side. "Maybe we should do what the fire breathing dragon wants."

"You are not capable of carrying three people safely. You only have two hands." Viktor had many reasons for not wanting to return. Nothing nefarious, but he wanted to repair the damage done between Trixie and her sister. There was also that dhampir cursing shifters in Riverbend. Dark magic had a way of backlashing and Riverbend was part of his territory.

His fledgling's gaze had gone glassy as she stared at Ruby. Her stomach growled loud enough to rival Eoin's.

"She needs to feed. Let me take care of her before things grow out of control and you must chain *both* of us in your dungeon. I will return tomorrow night, you have my word."

Eoin released the gargoyle only to grip the chain directly linked to Viktor's neck and yank him against the window. He lost his hold on Trixie and she lunged for the only source of human blood in the room.

Ruby threw herself back against the couch.

Using his supernatural speed, he kicked Nick into Trixie's path. They went down in a tumble of wings and chain. The gargoyle pinned Trixie to his chest and dragged her back to Viktor's hold.

"You saved me," Ruby mumbled as she stared at the gargoyle in confusion. "I thought you were the bad guy."

Trixie's shoulders shook. She sobbed silently against Viktor's chest. He pulled her away and checked for injuries. Her face was a mess of blood-streaked tears.

"Enough of this." Eoin reeled both him and Nick to the open window. The dragon clung to the side of the building with his claws like a huge scaly cat. Traffic below had stopped and a crowd was forming. Eoin broke the collar around Viktor's neck with a well-placed claw. "On your word, Viktor. I've helped you because you asked, but don't expect my patience to be infinite."

He bowed as well as he could while holding Trixie.

The gargoyle blew Ruby a kiss before being dragged out by the dragon and carried away.

"What will he do with Nick?" Ruby stood on the far side of the apartment, arms wrapped around her body.

He shrugged. "Who cares?" He wiped Trixie's face clean with his hands. "Did I hurt you?"

"No." She glanced at Ruby. "I'm sooo sorry. I didn't mean to jump you. I—I…"

"Lost control." He finished her sentence. "It happens." Hopefully, she had not inherited his lack of will power.

Viktor scanned the apartment. Three doors led from the living room kitchen combo. Two of them bedroom and the third a bathroom. "Which one is your room?"

"We're staying here?" Trixie shook her head. "That's not a good idea. I already tried to eat Ruby twice. We—we should go to your place or that nest you mentioned."

Such a sweet thing. He caressed her beautiful, sad face. "But you did not hurt her. She will be safe as long as I am here to control you. I will protect you both."

The tears in Trixie's eyes dried. "You're going to control me? That sounds awful."

He ran his gaze over the silken strands of her shoulder-length hair, the bright color a contrast to his dark world, a beacon of joy. Those thick tresses tempted a man to fist his hands in the softness, tug her close, and sink his teeth—deliciously, carefully—into that full bottom lip. The curve of her waist and the flare of her hips a perfect place to grip.

"Like a master?"

"Yes." It came out husky.

Ruby's snort cut through the sexual tension. She no longer appeared afraid. "I'm going to make some popcorn and watch. This will be entertaining."

"I can't believe you're cracking jokes. This is serious shit, Ruby."

Viktor decided he preferred an angry Trixie to a sad one.

Her sister remained on the other side of the apartment, not cooking popcorn like she said she would. "Look, I'll be honest and admit that feeding you scares me." Ruby took a big, shuddering breath. "But the idea of you going off with Mr. Control Freak scares me more, so I'm willing to try." She tentatively crossed the room and glanced at him—he nodded—before grasping Trixie's hand. "Stay."

He separated the sisters before the contact was too much for Trixie.

She slid behind him. Her hunger was so strong it pulsed between their connection and began to drive his own insatiable needs. Shit.

"You are willing to feed her from your own vein?" He *had* to feed Trixie, because *he* did not have anyone here to control *him* if he lost his shit. Never having known his own sire, he had not realized how strongly connected he would be to Trixie. So now he had *both* their bloodlust riding his poor will power.

"No." Trixie dug her nails into his flanks. The sharp pain triggered dark desires of pink hair fanned on his silk sheets and her pleas for mercy a song in his soul. She tugged him away from her sister and his fantasy, plastering her slight body against his back.

He closed his eyes counting backwards from ten. Her hands were so soft. He bet the skin under her breasts was softer. Or better yet, the insides of her thighs...

"I'll hurt her," Trixie's desperate whisper broke his train of thought.

"If you need it, Trix. I don't mind," Ruby offered.

He opened his eyes, surprised to find Ruby close with her arm extended.

"I mean, you don't want all of it, right?" she asked.

Yes...

"Yes." Trixie echoed his thought. "This is a bad idea, Viktor."

He licked his lips. "Yes, I agree." Instinct made him want to drain Ruby. Share her with his Trixie. Feed his charge and care for her.

No.

Trixie would be devastated. He knew this in the core of his heart and the link that bound them. Her tearstained face had torn at him and he never wanted to see her cry again.

"I shouldn't have come here." She clung to him, needing his strength, relying on him like no other had done in centuries. "What should I do?"

Hunger was a palpable force in his veins and Ruby's poultry scent made it difficult to think. "Ruby, maybe you should back away now."

He stared at the ceiling—praying? Pleading?—to whatever gods listened to vampires for clarity. He wanted a bright future for his fledgling and all his thoughts led to nefarious choices. Drinking Ruby dry was wrong. He had spent weeks in the castle dungeon, fighting for his sanity. He had thought he was under control, then he'd bound himself to a starving baby vampire. He took a deep breath and dove into old memories, those of when he was human, a leader among his people. In those days, he knew right from wrong. Something should still remain to help guide him.

Ruby backed away into the kitchen, hands clasped to her throat. The concern on her face was honest and pure. She loved her sister. That much was obvious. Maybe there was hope for Trixie. If he failed, she had Ruby to lean on.

"There are other ways to feed." The red fog of need faded enough for his thoughts to clear. "I need a phone."

"Mine's broken." Trixie's big blue eyes met his. He could spend eternity swimming in her gaze.

The jingle of keys and change pulled his attention away from her beauty. Ruby was emptying her purse on the counter top. She grabbed her phone and tossed it toward him. "Use mine."

He dialed, knowing the number by heart. Once it rang, he returned it to Ruby. "Tell them your address and that the delivery is for Viktor. It is all they need to know."

Ruby did as ordered.

"Now that food is ordered, bedroom?" He guided Trixie toward the closed doors.

Ruby set her hands on her hips. "What are you planning to do? Fair warning, Trix. I think your *master* is into BDSM."

"*Ruby*." Trixie pressed her hand to her forehead.

"Give me a break, I'm not an idiot. I know the culture. You don't. Mr. Control Freak keeps talking about being chained in a dungeon. Duh." Her sister, though standing across the room, looked ready to tackle him.

His charge dropped her face into her hands, ears flushed.

He tucked her hair behind it and traced the lobe. "I too know this culture, but I refer to the dragon's actual prison hold in his castle and he is *not* my lover." He shuddered.

"Thank you for that horrid image, Ruby. It will take weeks for me to forget it." He leaned closer to Trixie and whispered, "Show me your room."

CHAPTER TEN

Trixie pried her hands off her face. The heat on her cheeks felt like sunshine and she was amazed that she didn't turn to ash. BDSM? Ruby *had* to make this about sex. She couldn't really blame her with Viktor parading around half-naked, arriving with a collar and chain, but to blurt it out was not cool.

Viktor nudged her.

"This one." She opened the closest door a crack. She assumed he wanted to place a wall between her and Ruby. That did seem best, but they should put a whole city and a castle wall, guarded by dragons, between them. "Why didn't we go with Eoin?"

"Because your sister is afraid of you."

"Shouldn't she be?"

"Not forever. You both need to understand that with a little planning, you can still be a family."

Something fluttered in her chest that had nothing to do with her heart. She concentrated on it for a second and decided to name it hope. Since leaving the castle in Nick's arms, she'd been lost in despair, unable to believe she could return to her prior life. She smiled. It was weak and shaky. "Thank you." He understood that hurting Ruby would destroy her. Maybe he wasn't as unstable as she had thought.

Viktor gently pushed her inside the bedroom. He glanced at Ruby. "Tell me when they arrive." He followed Trixie inside and halted over the threshold, mouth hanging open.

She pressed her lips together and waited for the comments. Everybody had an opinion on her hobby once they discovered she had one. Even when she didn't ask for one, they told her what they thought. She waited some more.

Viktor strode inside, examining the drawings taped to her walls. His movements were deliberate, quiet, watchful. He communicated tightly controlled aggression yet he touched some of her work with such care it was at odds with his nature. Their nature. "You drew these?"

She nodded then realized he had his back to her and couldn't see. "Yes." Her voice cracked and she cleared her throat. Being an artist was tough. People weren't standing on the street corner shelling out money, no matter how talented. An artist needed connection, drive, and people skills. A breakthrough moment that came as often as winning the lottery. She had none of those. She just wanted to draw.

"You are very precise." He stepped back, assessing the whole wall. "I assume this is not all your work."

"Just my favorite pieces." Under her bed, she had boxes and folders full.

He crossed his arms, the muscles in his chest flexing in a distracting way. "Eoin paints and sculpts."

"Oh." She wasn't sure how to respond. Great for him?

Viktor closed the bedroom door with his foot.

The space was small. She had enough area for a twin bed and one bureau. It was more of a large closet than a bedroom. Ruby's was bigger since she had so much more maintenance needs. Viktor's presence seemed to suck all the air out of the room. The vacuum he left in his wake pulled at her.

"If you want to fix my relationship with Ruby, maybe we should wait on the couch." Not alone, with a bed, and her with an increasing fascination.

"It will be dawn soon. We must secure a safe place to rest."

"Oh." She tried not to sound disappointed and failed miserably. The small mirror over her dresser reflected a prettier version of herself. Blood stained the front of her shirt and dirt caked her back. "Holy crap, I'm a messy eater." She gestured to her back. "And where did I get all this?"

Viktor threw back his head, mouth open so she could glimpse his saber tooth fangs as he let out a deep, rolling laugh. "The dungeon floor is never swept. I will log a complaint with Eoin next time we meet." He tapped her under the chin with his knuckle. "You *are* adorable."

"Yeah, thanks. That's what I strive for." Not for him though. She wanted to see something else in his eyes besides amusement when he looked at her. "I need to change. Could you step out?"

His smile vanished. "Last time you were left alone, you ran."

"I ran here. I've got nowhere else to go."

He trailed his gaze over her. There it was. The hunger she desired and her heart hiccupped. Okay, she wasn't ready for more, like she had thought. Viktor was out of her league in every aspect of the word and he'd be appalled at her attempt of seduction.

"No," he said as he turned his back and looked at her art work. "You have ten seconds before I turn to watch." He counted down.

"You're such a jerk." She dragged open drawers, grabbed the most available items, and changed off clothes with swift tugs.

"Eight." Viktor spun around as she zipped her jeans shut. He frowned, eyes narrowing. "Next time you only get five seconds."

"There won't be a next time." But then she recalled he was her sire. That meant they were bound forever. That was a long time and this stranger would be part of her future, like it or not. She sat on the edge of her bed. The empty pit of her stomach howled in protest again. Viktor was a good distraction—he had turned her thoughts away from Ruby until her body reminded her again. Had he done that on purpose? She didn't know how to read him. Part of him seemed playboy and the other part dictator warrior.

He seemed engrossed in her Mandela experiments. "These are so intricate. Freehand or traced?"

"Freehand." She stared daggers at his back. Like she would bother with tracing. Those designs were hard to draw. She had even mathed to get them right. Her geometry teacher would die of shock if he ever heard.

The doorbell rang. It was the sweetest sound. She didn't need her super hearing to know Ruby answered the door. The walls were paper thin. A second heartbeat joined Ruby's. Trixie pressed her hands to her ears, not having realized she'd been focused on her sister's pulse all that time. The heart sounds called to her to join them, make them quiet.

Viktor cracked the bedroom door open, placing his big body between her and escape. "Let him approach." She could hear him even with her hands over her ears. Stupid vampire hearing.

90

She dropped her hands since they were useless in silencing the siren call of pulsing blood.

A man in a three piece, navy blue suit stood outside her room holding a small cooler.

"Who's that?" She rose to her feet, unable to resist the scent of what he was carrying.

"HDBP, ma'am." The stranger handed her a card. Home Delivery Blood Professionals.

"Oh honey, you ordered take out?" She pocketed the card. This couldn't be real.

The delivery man opened the cooler. Five bags filled the case. "Tonight, I'm carrying blood from a vegetarian, some with high cholesterol for a richer bouquet, a competitive runner for a pick me up. This one —" He fingered a bag. "Drank three espressos before donating and this one drank five ounces of fifty-year-old scotch."

Her eyebrows rose higher with each description. Choices? "Do they taste different?"

"Yes," answered Viktor.

She didn't know what she'd like.

"Were they tested?" Viktor asked.

"None of them are anemic. All iron levels are within normal limits." The HDBP representative handed Viktor some paperwork, which he flipped through. She had been thinking diseases when he'd brought up tests, not lab work.

"We will take them all. Charge my account, George." Viktor closed the lid and took the cooler.

"It's always good doing business with you, sir." He paused to offer Ruby a card. "In case you're looking for a side job. I can always use pretty girls."

Ruby didn't need any encouragement to be bad.

"Stay away from my sister." Trixie tried to exit, however Viktor's iron grip prevented her from moving.

She walked George out and Viktor closed them back in her bedroom before Trixie could listen to their whispered conversation.

"Wait a minute…" Her nostrils flared as he opened the cooler. "Are they all for me?" She clapped her hand over her mouth, ashamed at how greedy she sounded. "Sorry."

"No apology needed. I was half-expecting you to tear the cooler from George's hands. You are quite well-behaved for a young vampire." He tapped her nose. "You get two tonight and one in the morning."

He sorted through the bags and handed over her share.

That was the last thing she recalled until she blinked and discovered she hunched in the corner of her bedroom, empty bags in her hands. She dropped them as if they were made of fire.

Viktor peered over her shoulder. "You didn't spill a drop this time." He sat on her bed. An empty red tinged wine glass sat on the floor next to his feet. Ruby had given him their one good glass? She noted the cooler wasn't around.

"Where's the rest?" Her head spun as she jumped to her feet.

"Your sister was kind enough to store the other bags in the fridge."

Trixie rested her hand on the wall for support since the room tilted dangerously to the left. "Why do I feel so weird?"

His lips quirked as if he fought not to laugh.

"You gave me the one filled with whiskey?" She slurred her words. "Why?" She already felt out of control. Adding alcohol to her system seemed dangerous.

He patted the mattress. "Sit."

"Oh no, Mister. I'm not that kind of girl."

"I think you meant *Master*." His eyes sparkled, even though he kept a stern face. "And are you implying I would take advantage of you in your inebriated state?"

She wished, because even drunk she didn't have the nerve to make a pass or accept one. Instead of sitting on his lap and pressing her lips to his, she rubbed her fuzzy head and struggled to remain vertical. "Even if you tried, I'd probably throw up on you."

Viktor slid off her mattress and stalked the short distance between them. "I had intended for us to share the bag. I miscalculated your…"

"Selfishness?"

"Drive to survive." He caressed her face tenderly. "You were hungry. There is nothing wrong in taking care of your needs." With that, he scooped her into his arms. "But it does mean I have been a poor sire so far." He set her on the bed and tucked her under the blankets.

"Why get me drunk if you won't even try to kiss me?"

He pushed her hair from her forehead and pressed a kiss there.

CHAPTER ELEVEN

Trixie woke the second a breath whispered over her exposed neck. Her beating heart ached. She recognized that masculine scent, but it was so close. There wasn't any reason for it to be coating her every breath. She opened her eyes and found herself considering the face of a vampire. He was lying alongside her, head pillowed on one hand.

"What are you doing in my bed?" she asked, too shocked to filter her question.

"There's only one in the room." His hair flowed over his bare shoulder in a wave of midnight liquid, though the only light came from under the bedroom door. "I do not mind sharing. Do you?"

Raising a hand, she touched his hair. Cool strands slid through her fingers and she groaned. "Yes."

His eyebrows shot up. "Am I so grotesque?"

She rolled onto her back and flung her arm over her eyes. The opposite was true. Viktor made all her girly parts tingle and her rethink her resolve to wait for her true love for sex. Lucky for her willpower, she had a jack hammer pounding her brains. This was worse than last week's tequila Tuesday, except she had awoken to feeling sick and had to ride the porcelain bus all day. "I have a headache."

Viktor's weight crushed her into the mattress and the springs poked painfully into her back. He dragged his hard-muscled body over hers as he crawled off the bed.

"You're heavier than you think." She gasped for air and sat up.

He pulled open the thick curtains covering her tiny window. Darkness bled into her room and her heart grew heavy. She would never feel sunshine on her face or see a bright, blue sky again.

She slowed her breathing. No more tears. She had to deal with her new reality. She ground her teeth and winced. Her fangs were sharp. She tongued the little daggers in her mouth. They weren't as big as his. How was she supposed to puncture a person's jugular with these? The idea of biting into flesh made her shudder.

Viktor turned his hooded gaze on her. "Are you hungry?"

She closed her eyes as the hunger swept over her body in agonizing acuity.

The bed dipped next to her and Viktor brushed his fingers over her eyelashes. "Of course, you are. Silly of me to ask. I am old and do not remember what it was like to be newly turned."

Ugh, compassion was the last thing she wanted to hear. She jerked her face away from his touch. She'd known him for less than twenty-four hours and they were sharing a bed. Ten years of stoically saving herself against his centuries of experience. She was doomed. "Stop touching me." She yanked off the blanket and quickly scanned her body. Thank goodness she still had her clothes on. "You got me drunk." Via blood. Who knew that was a thing?

He pulled her onto his lap. "You needed to rest. You were very anxious. I did not think you could achieve sleep without help. In my defense, it did not take much."

"It never does." She went clubbing with her sister and Betty and their friends every weekend, but she went to dance. She usually sipped gin and ginger ale on ice straight-up with a twist of lime and it took her all night to finish. Though, there had been a few times where she had indulged in more. Her head pounded. "I can still get hungover. Nice. I thought being a vampire would give me super healing. If I start puking, I'm aiming for your hair."

He scooted her off his lap with magical speed. "You will feel better after some blood."

She couldn't deny that sounded like an excellent idea. Her head hurt, her stomach ached with hunger pains, and her body felt overly sensitive to Viktor's presence. Being a vampire sucked so far. "I get the one with the espresso."

He bowed. "Anything my lady desires." Then he exited the bedroom.

She glimpsed Ruby hovering by the door.

"How is she?" she asked Viktor.

"Better than I expected. Young vampires can go feral if left hungry too long."

Trixie hung her head, trying not to go feral and ravage New Port's human population.

"The blood?" he asked.

"Let me get it." She heard Ruby hurry across the apartment and return.

Viktor carried two bags and handed her one labeled *three espressos*. This would so hit the spot.

Ruby had followed him inside. Behind her, it looked like she had turned on every light they owned. "Hi." She shifted her weight from one foot to the other.

"Hi." Trixie couldn't meet her sister's gaze. Would Ruby want her to move out after she'd tried to eat her last night? Would Ruby ever feel safe alone with her?

Her breath caught in her throat. Would *she*?

"Can I do anything for you?" Ruby still stayed close to the exit with Viktor between them.

He bit into his high cholesterol bag and poured the contents into a tall glass with an expert's ease.

She watched, fascinated. "No." She wanted her life back, but Ruby couldn't save her. The beat of a drum called to her like an ancient warrior's song. It stirred strange urges. Trixie wanted to track and hunt. To run in the night and chase her prey. She glanced around, searching for the source. Her gaze landed on Ruby.

Well, shit. It was her heartbeat. "I think the best thing you can do for me is to stay away." Her voice shook. It was the hardest thing she'd ever said, but the easiest decision. They had never been apart for longer than a weekend.

But Ruby would be safer far from Trixie.

Her sister shook her head. "No, we'll figure this out together. I will not—"

Viktor gently guided Ruby from the room. "Let her learn control. Then I will return her to you."

"How long does that take?" Ruby pushed against the closing bedroom door.

"Everyone is different. It takes as long as it takes." He leaned against the door as her sister knocked. "Go away, Ruby." He glared at Trixie. "Is she always this stubborn?"

"You have no idea." She stared at her breakfast, restraining the urge to bite it and drink straight from the bag.

Viktor joined her on the edge of her bed. He tore open the container and poured it into another glass. "Drink slowly this time."

She gulped it down.

He grunted and clinked his full glass against her empty one. "*Za zda-ró-vye.*"

Viktor sipped at his meal. Being older, he did not require as much blood as Trixie.

"What did you say?" she asked.

"A toast." He paused in thought, consciously switching languages in his head. "Means *to your health.*" The familiar beat of wings reached his ears. The sun had barely set and the fucking dragon was back to drag him to his dungeon. Eoin had never been so persistent. Maybe their past failures weighed on the dragon as much as him.

"What the fuck?" Ruby pounded on the door again, this time with more insistence. "Trixie. Viktor. There's a naked man on our fire escape and he looks pissed off."

The two sisters were polar opposites. Trixie was sweet and kind and thoughtful. She made him want to be a better person. To protect her, to teach her to be a better vampire than him. Ruby only made him want to block his ears.

His fledgling sprinted out of the bedroom. She set herself between Eoin and her sister.

Viktor retrieved a towel from the bathroom and tossed it to the dragon. "Cover up," he ordered, speaking past a sudden possessive edge that honed his protectiveness to a jagged gleam. That was a surprise. He was a predator at heart, a facet of his personality he had learned to live with. He had never been possessive.

Or maybe, a long silent part of him whispered, he had never met anyone he had wanted to possess.

"You don't have to for my sake." Ruby seemed recovered from yesterday's fiasco.

Trixie's cheeks matched her hair color, only endearing her more to him.

The dragon climbed through the open window, towel wrapped around his hips. "Time for both of you to return home with me."

Viktor scratched his chin. "About that…I think we should give the Riverbend situation more consideration—"

"Not that again." The walls rattled with the force of Eoin's shout.

"Shh." Trixie hissed. "My neighbors are quick to call the cops ever since…" Her gaze darted to her sister's red face. "Never mind that. Just keep it down."

The dragon gave Trixie a slow blink, not used to being hushed.

Viktor fought a laugh. He slung his arm over Trixie's shoulder, pulling her closer and making it clear that she was under his protection. She was a vampire, which meant she was more resilient than a human. It didn't mean she was indestructible.

"Pack light." Eoin addressed her. "You'll need to carry your own luggage during the flight." Eoin whirled back out to the fire escape. Quick as a flash, he changed shape and clung to the side of the building as the towel fluttered to the living room floor.

Trixie shrugged out of Viktor's hold. "Stop grabbing me." She strode to her bedroom, mumbling things like *possessive jerk* and *over-bearing ass* under her breath. His sensitive ears had no trouble hearing her.

Ruby leaned in to whisper, "Just in case you are misunderstanding my sister's cues. That means she likes you."

"She has a strange way of expressing herself."

"Oh, if she didn't like you then you'd probably be clutching a wooden stake stabbed in your heart by now."

He fingered the stake in his pocket. The one Trixie had been found carrying when she'd died.

Ruby grinned but the smile didn't reach her eyes. "I'm still on the fence about you so watch your back."

"Are you threatening me?" Now, he laughed. "You are almost as crazy as I am."

"Might be why she likes you," muttered Ruby.

His laugh faded. He did not like this idea. If she truly thought him crazy then any relationship they developed could be based on pity or an obligation since he'd saved her life. Neither was something he wanted, especially in the long term. Trixie would be tied to him forever in some capacity. His friendship with Eoin worked because of mutual respect. They were both predators, top of the food chain that chose not to kill.

He winced. The dragon was doing better at this pact. He and Trixie needed a similar connection, something closer maybe.

Ruby stared out at Eoin's dragon form, but addressed Viktor. "You'll take care of her."

"I did not go through the pain of saving your sister only to allow harm to befall her." He still saw doubt in her eyes. "Do you know how many vampires I have created?"

She shook her head.

"One." He pointed in Trixie's direction. "I take that responsibility seriously."

Ruby's eyebrows drew down together.

"I'm ready." Trixie returned with a backpack slung over her shoulder. She pointed at Viktor. "I'm not sleeping in a dungeon so don't piss off the dragon anymore."

Eon's great eye peeked through the door. "The deal is Viktor remains at the castle for one week without incident."

Trixie paused mid-step. "Incident?"

Ruby shoved a cell phone in Trixie's hands. "It's mine. I'll get you another one and use it until you come home. I'll text you the new number, okay?"

She gripped the gift tightly and gave one sharp nod before placing it in her back pocket.

Viktor took her pack and guided her through the window. "Watch your head. You have flown via gargoyle. Now it is time for a real treat via dragon." He settled her safely in Eoin's waiting hand and glared at his friend. He would take care not to drop her, he was sure.

Eoin's claws encased her torso.

Her eyes went big. "What about you?" She reached for him as Eoin lifted her so he could grab Viktor with less finesse.

The dragon rumbled. "He's lucky if I don't drop him a few times on the way home."

Eoin spoke the truth. The dragon had dropped him a few times in the past, and looking back, Viktor had deserved it.

Their trip was short due to Eoin's powerful wings. Trixie stared over the bright city lights, arms extended and hair whipping in the wind. Viktor fell for her all over again. He saw New Port through her eyes and shared in her wonder.

They landed in front of the castle with Eoin depositing them on the ground then shifting midair. The dragon landed next to Viktor.

Angie strolled out, carrying her mate's clothing. She rounded on Trixie. "Why did you run away? I was worried sick." There was no anger in her voice, only concern. "And you." She slapped Viktor's shoulder. "What the fuck?"

"I needed to see my sister." Trixie glanced in his direction. "I know now that was a mistake and Viktor kept me from hurting her."

Angie narrowed her gaze in Viktor's direction. "Color me surprised. I thought you were just focused on escaping."

He bowed, letting her stinging words roll off him. "I have not *always* been chained in your dungeon. There is a man behind the monster."

Trixie stepped closer and tangled her fingers with his.

He straightened. The heat of her touch sizzled through his flesh like sunlight. Their gazes locked and there it was — that innocent trust. He wanted to deserve it. To be the man she wanted, but he was a ticking time bomb of violence. He brushed the back of his fingers over her cheek. So lovely. Maybe if he ever found control...

Eoin stepped behind her, coming into Viktor's view.

He sighed. "Before you lock me away, I need to speak with you in private, Eoin."

"No." Trixie shook her head. "No more dungeon. He said you needed to be at the castle for a week. There was no mention of a dungeon."

Viktor pushed her hair behind her ear. "I don't mind. It is like a second home."

"What if I need you?" she whispered. She tossed a pleading look at Angie.

The female dragon crossed her arms. "No more vampires in the dungeon. New house rules." She gestured to Trixie. "Let me show you your rooms while the boys talk. I had time to dust and clean it properly."

CHAPTER TWELVE

Spine held straight and shoulders back, Trixie glanced at Viktor over her shoulder as she followed Angie into the castle. Confidence in her every move, yet she chewed her bottom lip when she thought the dragons weren't looking. Did she think he would abandon her to the dragons?

Eoin stood next to him watching the woman as well. "What a cluster fuck." He ran his hand over the stubble on his head. Peach fuzz, Viktor had once referred to it, then Eoin had cracked his skull. Dragons were such sensitive creatures.

"Maybe." He shrugged. "Maybe it was fate."

Eon blew smoke in his face. "I don't want to hear your ideas on fate again. And it wasn't karma or bad luck either. It was an accident and we tried our best to fix it."

"That sounded scripted. Have you been practicing it all night?"

"On Angie. She feels awful." Eoin snorted and abandoned Viktor on the front grounds as he stormed the castle.

Viktor shadowed at a more leisurely pace, absorbing the age of the stone and the thickness of the dust as he climbed the staircase—not the one Trixie had fallen on. They were in a different tower, which led to Eoin's workroom at the top. Discarded paintings lined the wall, some singed. Viktor flinched at the sight. For some reason, Eoin was convinced he had no talent when the opposite was true. "Trixie draws."

"Hmm…" The dragon cleaned his favorite chair of discarded rags. "It wouldn't be Trixie's karma that caused this disaster. It would be yours." Absentminded words but they struck Viktor like daggers.

"My karma?" He did not like this turn of conversation. "I have done terrible things, yet I see no punishment in having made Trixie vampire." Temptation? Yes.

Eoin sat in his usual tattered chair and pulled out a jar of special ink Viktor had mixed. Vampire skin did not hold tattoos for long. They metabolized the ink. Also, the older the vampire, the harder their flesh was to pierce.

Viktor was very old.

Regular needles bent, even diamond coated ones. He could carve his flesh with knives but it was time consuming to keep them sharp. Then he discovered dragon claws did not lose their edge. How he had made this discovery was a long story. He did not ask anything fancy from Eoin, just the names of his victims. Time made all things fade and they deserved to be remembered. This was his burden. "How did you know what I wanted?"

Eoin rested his chin in his hand. "I know you. I also know that Trixie's name doesn't deserve to be added to your list. You didn't kill her."

"My bite was what stopped her heart."

"My point is that you saved her. She was dead otherwise. You gave her a second chance and she seems happy with it."

Viktor scanned his torso for an empty spot. He wanted to see her name without the use of a mirror. She was the only one he had turned into a vampire so she should have a place of honor.

Eoin thought he'd saved Trixie. He cocked his head and met his friend's falsely innocent stare. "You have not explained how saving Trixie is karma, in your opinion."

"I don't believe in karma, but for your sake… She's your chance at redemption."

Was that possible? He did not dare move as he considered Eoin's suggestion. Could he be redeemed? He knew the names on his body would not agree.

"You're over thinking things, Viktor." Eoin held up the ink. "Where do you want her name?"

There wasn't much space left. He offered Eoin the inside of his bare right wrist. "Here." No names adorned his limbs.

Eoin bent over his flesh. "Don't move." And he carved out her name in clear letters. The spot was sensitive and Viktor clenched his teeth, fighting a groan of pain. The dragon cut extra deep this time. "Maybe by teaching Trixie to be a model, law abiding vampire, you will be teaching yourself."

"I am more apt to turn her into a mass murderer."

"If you leave her alone, she will become one for sure." Eoin knew the details of his past yet remained his friend. More proof that dragons had poor judgment.

"The New Port nest will look after her training." The best thing he could offer Trixie was his absence, though their short time apart at present was already making his skin itch for her touch. "My lieutenants are very loyal and have dealt with many fledglings over the years. She would be much better off."

The dragon stopped carving into his flesh.

"You do realize I am made of skin and bone, not scales and hide?" He stared at dark blood forming a puddle at

Eoin's feet. "I do not think you went deep enough. Her name is not etched on my bones."

Eoin applied the ink and the tissues sizzled.

Viktor hissed.

"Sissy." Eoin turned his wrist into the light as he wiped it clean.

His healing abilities sealed her name into his skin. He examined Eoin's penmanship. "Well done. I half-expected you to place hearts over the *i*." Instead, the dragon had done scroll work. A piece of original dragon art. No matter what, Viktor would be reminded of her every night.

"What else do you have to occupy your time if not teaching her while you are my guests?" Eoin leaned back in his chair.

"There is that pesky problem of a spell book in the hands of an idiot." Viktor flexed his wrist as the pain vanished.

"Consider it a done deal." Eoin grinned. "I called Riverbend's wolf pack alpha and explained the situation. He'll take care of it."

Viktor slapped his forehead. "He is a puppy." The last thing they needed was a shifter/vampire incident in Riverbend. As senior vampire in the territory, he would eventually be dragged into this. Better to nip it in the bud.

"Chris has an interest in this."

"Is that his name?" The young alpha's name would not be on his radar unless he retained pack control for more than a few years. Werewolf packs changed alphas often, keeping them too unstable to obtain any real power. Ryota had had control of New Port's pack for decades. For this, Viktor bothered remembering Ryota's name.

"Did you know Betty and Chris were a couple before she moved to New Port?" Eoin cleaned his hand with one of the discarded rags.

Viktor recalled the little shifter girl. She had a rare tattoo spell inked on her arm. He eyed the dragon, who was not prone to gossip. "What is your point?"

"Let's just say the tattoo artist destroyed the alpha's future with Betty. He'll find her, is my point."

"Fantastic." Viktor tossed his hands in the air.

"I thought so until now. Why are you so angry?"

"This is why you should leave vampire matters to the vampire master." He paced the room, fisting his hair. "The puppy will kill the dumbass dhampir tattoo artist. Then the dumbass' nest will hunt the puppy. Then his pack will cry foul play and attack the vampires." Viktor slapped his chest with both hands. "Then I will be called in to kill them all." He paced the room that suddenly seemed too restricted. "Stupid," he shouted at the wall.

Eoin's eyes narrowed. "What did you call me?"

"Shifters." He turned to face the fire breathing dragon whose eyes had changed to slits. "You all think with this." He tapped Eoin over the heart. Not intimidated. He was not fire proof but neither did he care if he burned. *Except, who would care for Trixie?* whispered a distant voice in the back of his mind. He retreated and gave Eoin space to breathe. "I ask that you let me take care of this discreetly." He pushed that small urge back inside the box it had escaped. He would not be tempted.

Not until she was trained…

No. He shook his head.

"You didn't explain why. If you had, then I would have…" Eoin scratched his head.

"I was not aware that Betty and the puppy had a past. That is what changes everything. The alpha would not have cared enough to kill the dhampir otherwise."

"I still can't set you loose. Not in your…" He grinned showing sharp teeth. "Delicate state."

"Fuck you, Eoin. Vampire territories are much larger than shifters. I let the nests run themselves but I won't let a war start."

Eoin slapped him on the shoulder, harder than necessary. "Old friend, I wouldn't let that happen. Let me talk to Riverbend's alpha again. I'll make sure he doesn't kill the dhampir."

Viktor was sure that conversation would go over well. Heartbroken with everything to prove to his pack? There was no chance at all the young alpha would listen to Eoin.

He sighed. Dragons. "I am sure all will be well." He held up his new tattoo. "Nicely done. I will go check on Trixie."

The night was young, after all.

Trixie stared out of the bedroom window. Dark forest her only view in any direction. Her tower room faced the opposite direction of New Port. As a child, she'd always dreamed of being a princess who lived in a castle. Now all she wanted was to escape.

Not to see Ruby. She'd learned her lesson. She wouldn't endanger her sister again. She needed to learn control before she returned home. Trapped in this tower, she wouldn't learn anything.

She turned her back to the view and her old life. The clock on the wall showed that her shift with New Port's animal control would have started if she hadn't been suspended. She hung her head.

Angie had left her in a similar bedroom as before. The furniture had seen better days, however it was in better condition than anything she owned. Antique wood edged the floral material of the chairs and loveseat. Everything *matched*, like it was a *set*. Not scraped together in thrift store chic. The bed took half the space of the room. It was monstrous with thick tapestry curtains that hung from a canopy. Very Bram Stoker. It never would have fit in her bedroom.

Viktor strode in without knocking and closed the door behind him. "We have to leave."

Heart in throat, she'd spun around. "Can you read minds?" In vampire movies, they had mind control powers and could turn into bats and other cool shit. She'd rather he not poke in hers.

"This is not a joking matter." He crossed the room to the window and scanned outside.

"I wasn't joking. You said the exact thing I was thinking."

He tossed her a surprised glance. "I thought I had made it clear how returning to your sister was dangerous."

"I don't want to go home. I want to learn how to control my hunger so I *can* return to her safely. I don't think I'll learn that inside this castle with bag blood room service."

The corner of his lips curled, turning her into honey. Now, that was a super power she wanted.

Viktor could have deserted her with the dragons to babysit. "Why the sudden change of heart?" Trixie asked. "You gave Eoin your word you would stay here." He was including her in his plans though and acting saner. Maybe he was ready to go out into the world, or she was hanging her hopes on her sire so she could try her vampire training wheels.

He wagged his finger. "I gave my word that I would return here. I never agreed to stay." He shrugged. "I had to promise him something last night or he would have dragged both of us to the dungeon. By the time the dragons discover we are gone, we will have a head start. First, we need a vehicle."

Trixie's teeth clicked shut. "You bluffed the dragon?"

"No, I lied to him." He frowned. "I do not like males in that way so I certainly would not bluff one."

She jerked her head back and frowned. *Bluff*? Maybe he thought she'd said blew? English wasn't Viktor's first language, obviously, so she let the misunderstanding slide. She shook her head. It would take too much time to explain and they had an escape to plan. "How will we get out of the castle without the dragons knowing? I doubt they'll let us walk out the front door."

"Impossible. Eoin will have spelled the doors by now. It will chime if a vampire crosses the threshold."

"You know this how?"

"I have attempted to escape during my other stays."

"Did any of your escapes ever work?"

"No." Viktor opened the window.

They needed to chat about these imprisonments. Normal friends didn't lock each other up routinely. It sounded like they'd been doing this for decades and maybe her sire needed an intervention on abusive relationships. Did Eoin hurt Viktor during these stays?

She drew closer to her sire as he scanned the castle walls below them. "What did you speak to Eoin about that you needed to be alone?"

He glanced at his wrist but didn't show it to her. "Nothing. Well…that is not the truth. I want to find the tattoo artist who spelled your friend, Betty. The one who prevented her from ever shifting to her wolf form. Eoin has a lead on her."

She gasped. Betty had suffered so much for such a simple mistake, all because some artist used a spell book as art examples for tattoos. Betty had picked one, not knowing the symbol was black magic. The person who had done this needed to be stopped before she wrecked anyone else's life. Betty was her best friend. Not once had she ever let Trixie down. Even when she'd turned up at Betty's dog rescue in the middle of the night with an unconscious werewolf in her animal control truck. Betty had just rolled up her sleeves and helped carry his heavy ass inside.

Friends like that were for life and someone had hurt Betty. Possibly others too. Trixie rubbed her temples. "I'm in." She wasn't a vigilante, but she couldn't ignore this opportunity. "Let's blow this joint."

"Bluff," responded Viktor as he tested the windowsill with his weight.

"No, blow." She pressed her lips together. "How long have you been living in this country?"

He stopped what he was doing. "Why?"

"Because someone your age should be able to speak the language properly without an accent."

Viktor slid back into the room with liquid grace. He slowly stalked her. "You do not find my accent alluring?"

Her eyes followed the shift of lean muscle and male strength. He was built perfectly in proportion. His body well defined and his skin glowed with the moonlight — smooth and lineless — *that* she found mesmerizing.

"Do I meet your liking?" He loomed over her and her eyes met ones that glowed with a predator's light in the dark.

Her mouth was bone dry and her skull full of liquid intelligence. "It's not the accent, but your vocabulary I'm annoyed with." *So* smooth. Her flirting skills killed. Literally, they were killing her. His presence pushed against her — stroking, electrifying, persistent. He had tied his long hair at the nape of his neck with a leather strip, exposing the strong line of his jaw.

"Maybe I annoy you on purpose to see you inflamed and hot." He trailed his fingers over her heated skin. His touch made every nerve ending ignite, but she held strong against the urge to lean into his hand. She could handle him. She'd turn down men just as sexy.

Wow, her self-denial was good.

Viktor let his hand drop and leaned back against the windowsill, gesturing for her to approach. "Come."

Without hesitation, she moved toward the most dangerous predator she could imagine.

CHAPTER THIRTEEN

Viktor jerked Trixie against him, arm wrapped around her waist in a vise-like grip.

She let out a surprised noise.

He leaned her over the windowsill and pointed to the rough surface of the wall. "We will climb down along this route to the ground."

"You *are* nuts." She tried to push free but he held her fast.

"No, not anymore. Your birth pulled me out of my blood delirium. You are stronger than you know, Trixie." He leaned them forward. "What will happen if you fall?"

She breathed heavily, gripping the edges of the window. "I'll die."

"No, you might break a few bones, but they will heal quickly."

"Oh, is that all?" She gave him a watery smile. "Just a few broken bones? Won't that *hurt*?" That was a far fall, and she was pretty sure she'd die, no matter what he said.

He raised an eyebrow. "Did I mislead you by saying that?"

"You said I wouldn't die."

"You would not, but your bones are still fragile and breaking them does cause considerable amount of pain."

"And screaming. Don't forget the screaming."

He frowned, staring at the ground. "I am not used to dealing with fledglings."

"From this height, I'll break every bone in my body and live to feel it."

"Yes."

"How is this supposed to convince me to climb out this window? You're really not selling me this idea."

Viktor pulled them back inside and stripped the sheet off the bed. Twisting the material and tying them together, he made a poor excuse of a rope.

"That won't reach the ground." She inched away.

He snapped it like a whip. "It doesn't need to reach the ground. I will tie one end to your waist and the other to mine. If you fall, I will anchor you to the wall."

She wanted to smack him upside his pretty head and make sure it didn't ring empty. "And what if you fall? I get to land on top of you?" Shaking her head, she stormed to the door. "You climb. I'll take my chances with the stairs."

He snapped the sheet and it twisted around her arms and torso. Slowly, he reeled her in. This time she saw no amusement in his glare. "I don't fall. Even if I did, I would not allow you any harm. I would catch you."

"With your shattered arms?" she whispered, unable to stop arguing. This was unlife they were discussing and how climbing down a freaking tower would be good for her. He had admitted to not being used to new vampires. He'd also been a prisoner because he was coocoo in the head. Was she supposed to toss caution to the wind every time he batted those thick eyelashes in her direction?

Nay, nay.

"My dear, my bones don't break." He unwound the sheet, freeing her arms then tied it tight with an intricate knot around her waist.

"Do I have a choice?" She wasn't silly enough to think she could fight him. The best she could do was survive this ordeal. Think like a cat, climb like a cat, land like a cat.

Except cats didn't climb castle walls.

"This is important, Trixie." He said her name carefully as if listening to the syllables tumble off this tongue. The crazy vampire she'd met in the dungeon was no longer present. He'd been replaced by a confident man who captured her attention. "I need you to know that I would not endanger your life, and I am trying to prevent needless deaths." He tied the sheet around his narrow waist, connecting them with a life line of very old cotton.

Yeah, she felt safe.

"The spells kill?" Then Betty was lucky to only have been cursed.

"It's a complicated situation made worse by a helpful dragon." He lifted her onto the windowsill as if she weighed nothing. His eyes brightened. "I could just carry you as I climb."

"No way." She frowned and swung her leg over the side. "How could you think that is better?" Totally dependent on his skill while her body unbalanced him more. She clung to the edge of the sill, her legs dangling. "I just want you to know that so far being a vampire sucks." She'd flown over the city twice in one day via either gargoyle or dragon, been drunk on alcohol-infused blood, now she was scaling a castle wall. What next? Storm the citadel? Juggle grenades?

She could her Viktor in her head. *Do not worry, Trixie. They might blow your hands off but they will eventually grow back.*

Heart pounding so hard. "Why do I feel short of breath? Can't we live without air?" She felt the wall with her shoes and couldn't get a sense of purchase. Kicking them off, she tried barefoot. Spread toes worked better and she managed to hold her weight.

"You are not dead. That's just a myth," he whispered. "Silently now. We do not want to alert the dragons."

Think jail break. Think Alcatraz. "Sorry, I babble when my life is in danger." She forced her hands to move, struggling not to close her eyes.

"Shh…" Viktor fed the rope out the window as he followed her out.

"Don't shush me," she mumbled under her breath. "Flipping vampire thinks I'm a spider. Do I look like I have eight legs?" She continued at a snail's pace, a litany of whispered verbal trash flowed like an unconscious stream of thought. "Chipped my nail. Owie. I'll have to redo my nail polish."

Viktor patiently followed. As long as she kept her voice low, he didn't seem to mind her nervous talk.

Halfway, she hit a ledge and clung to the wall for a rest. She flexed her cramping digits. *Don't look down. Don't look down. Don't look down.* She turned her head so her sweaty face pressed to the cool stone.

A gargoyle met her gaze. His head bent to the side as if confused by her appearance. "Trixie? Is this some sort of vampire initiation thing?"

Her mouth dropped open, but she *had* to stay quiet. The scream went inside and her ears popped. The only sound she made was so high pitched she was sure only dogs and werewolves heard it.

Nick steadied her with a hand to her elbow. "Easy, darling."

"Will you stop startling me? I can't afford to die again. I'm not a cat shifter with nine lives to spare."

Nick dropped his chin to his chest. "Sorry about that." He tossed her a furtive glance. "Why are we whispering?"

"Never mind that." The gargoyle was her deliverance. "Can you fly me to the ground?" She tried to untie Viktor's complicated knot with no result. She glanced up.

The vampire smoothly crept over the stone as if his palms and soles were made of glue.

A rattle caught her attention. "I can't. I'm castle locked." Nick held a familiar chain. Eoin had a weird prisoner fetish. She and Angie would have a talk about this if Trixie ever saw her again.

Viktor dropped behind her. His body a velvet heat to her back. "How long did he say you had to remain?"

The gargoyle shrugged. "He hasn't spoken to me yet. Just locked me to the wall and blew flame."

Viktor nodded. "He's probably trying to let his anger cool so he doesn't smash you into gravel."

She noted the scorched stone skin on Nick's wings. "We can't leave him here."

The vampire sighed. "Trix—"

"I'm climbing down a wall for you. The least you could do is help me free Nick."

"May I remind you, he's the reason you're a vampire." Viktor's breath caressed the back of her neck, sending a shiver down her spine.

"It was an accident." She lasered the gargoyle with a warning look. "He'll stop startling people."

Nick pressed his hand over his heart. "*You* climbed down to *me*. I didn't follow you. It's not my fault this time."

They both stared at the gargoyle in silence.

"Fine, I promise to behave. No more scaring vampires."

She pressed her back to the wall as Viktor reached for Nick's collar.

"This isn't made of the same material as my collar. This is just plain steel." His thick arm brushed over her chest. Desire shot through her nerve endings. He was so close she could breathe him in. The muscles in his forearms bulged as he struggled with the metal.

"Steel trumps stone," responded Nick.

The collar groaned and warped until, with a loud cling, it snapped open.

Nick threw his meaty arms in the air, his mouth open and a cry of victory apparent in his features.

Viktor slapped his hands over Nick's mouth. "I am surrounded by amateurs. Silently." He withdrew from crushing her against the castle and her body ached from the sudden loss of support. "Fly Trixie to the ground. Right below me where I can see." He pointed to the spot. "Attempt any trickery and anything the dragon has done will seem like a mercy once I am finished with you."

Ice flowed in her veins at Viktor's tone.

Nick scowled and waited as Viktor untied the sheet from both their waists. The material fluttered on the wind like a deranged angel on a binge.

She watched it glide and a coat of sweat covered her skin as she did the one thing she told herself not to do. She looked down. The sweat trickled along her legs to her bare feet. Her knees turned into Jell-O and she struggled to stay standing. Her jaw moved but she couldn't ask for help, her tongue had packed its bag and abandoned her. Her feet slid on the sweat. The ledge was narrow. Like a rag doll, she slid off the castle wall.

"Trixie!" Viktor cried out, his demand for silence broken. He dove after her, caught her in his arms, and then cradled her body to his.

She squeezed her eyes shut, clenching her teeth in preparation for the worst pain ever. She waited, nails digging into Viktor's arms.

And waited.

Their momentum jerked to a stop.

She opened her eyes. They hovered a foot off the ground.

Viktor grinned down at her and straightened his legs to stand. She could see Nick above them. He gripped Viktor by the shoulders, wings extended like a parachute.

Viktor set her on her feet. "Why did you jump? I just do not understand you."

She poked him in the chest. "We will not speak of this again." Like she would explain she'd slipped on her own damn sweat.

Viktor eyed Nick. "Go before I regret helping you."

"Trixie, I need to ask you one thing before I go." Nick still hovered above them. "How does your sister feel about cross species dating?"

She slapped her forehead, but this night could get weirder, so why not? "Honey, you don't want to date my sister. She'd eat a nice gargoyle like you alive." The trail of broken hearts that led to their apartment was miles long. "You should find a nice girl." She loved Ruby. She was Trixie's rock, but she used men like toilet paper. Nick, well, under all that stone, he seemed vulnerable. Ruby really would eat him alive.

"Is that a yes?" He scratched his head.

"It is a yes." Viktor spoke before she could. "Go buy her flowers or pineapples or whatever your kind does. Go now." He waved his arms at Nick, shooing him away.

"Viktor…" She glared. He'd just set a gargoyle after her sister, and she was more worried about the monster.

The vampire searched the night sky. "I cannot believe the dragons did not hear our commotion."

In the distance, she could faintly hear a woman crying out Eoin's name over and over. "Is she in trouble?"

Viktor stared at her as if she'd grown a second head.

Oh, were they... "I was joking. Don't be so serious all the time." She turned her back to him so he wouldn't see the blazing blush scorch her cheeks all the way to the tips of her ears.

"We are lucky they are occupied." Viktor's long strides made it easy for him to outpace her. "They will not notice our absence for a few hours." He scooped up her shoes and handed them over. "Watch your step. There are shards of glass from years of castle abuse." He waited as she slipped her feet back in her sneakers before marching on.

They turned the corner of the castle and he led her to an old stable. Viktor slid the door open and the stable turned out to be a garage. "Now this is more like it."

A spread of cars lined the long, narrow space. The building seemed in better condition than the castle.

"I remember when Eoin stored horse carriages in here." Viktor strolled between the vehicles, trailing his fingers over the hood of a red sports car. He then broke open a metal cabinet that vaguely looked like a safe. It was empty. "Fuck, Eoin removed all the car keys."

"He what?" She spun around, expecting the dragon to land. "He knew you would try to escape."

"Bastard. He is always one step ahead of me."

"Why can't you run to the city?" she asked. It seemed strange for a vampire to be car dependent.

"I can, but then I would have to leave you behind."

She sighed. "Because I'm too young to keep pace with you."

"There are many dangers to traveling in the open. You will learn this in time. The number one problem is sunlight. You must always think ahead about shelter." He scanned the sky. "We have time to walk to New Port, then we would have to hide before leaving for Riverbend."

"Giving Eoin time to find us." Her respect for the dragon leveled-up with every encounter, but so did her admiration for Viktor. He didn't know how to surrender. "I can hotwire that black sedan." It was an older model that wouldn't have any of the computer systems the modern ones had. "Think it still runs?"

Viktor's smile turned salacious. "Trixie, Trixie, you make me curious to find out what other secrets you hide."

She went to the toolbox against the far wall and pulled out what she would need.

Viktor crouched outside the car, watching her work under the steering wheel. "Why did you learn this?"

"To survive." The car started with a smooth purr.

CHAPTER FOURTEEN

Trixie triggered Viktor's protective instincts. It had been a kindness to set Nick free. He understood this in a cerebral manner, but in their world such weakness would be preyed upon. She needed a predator's skillset to survive as a vampire and he wanted to be the one to provide it, but he had an interspecies incident to prevent. She deserved a better environment to learn in than running into the heart of dangerous shifter territory blind. What kind of sire was he to place her in that situation?

A selfish one.

The largest vampire nest was in the center of New Port. All nests in the tri-city area called him Master, but he was not attached to any of them so as not to show favoritism. Being old and powerful also meant being alone. Trixie needed teachers and a safe place to stay until his return. She could not afford for him to be possessive. Time among her people would allow her to grow strong. Staying at his side? Well, he had never been known for his self-control.

He sped down the road winding down the dragon's mountain, glancing in the review mirror repeatedly for a glimpse of wings. So far, their escape was undetected.

In the passenger seat, Trixie clung to the bar overhead, knuckles white. The tires screeched when he took the corners at high velocity. Her chest heaved and the scent of fear tinged the air.

"I have not crashed in years."

The lines around her mouth deepened. "Not helping."

"You are safe with me."

"You know what? I've never crashed. Not once. That's what safety means." She pointed to the curvy road that descended at a steep angle. "At this speed, this is not what I'd call *safe*."

"When Eoin discovers we are missing, he will hunt for us. Ever been hunted by an angry dragon?" Unfortunately, he had. Not always Eoin. Over the centuries, he had had the pleasure of angering a few others of the dragon race. Those memories occasionally plagued him in nightmares.

She shook her head, eyes growing darker. She glanced back at the castle. "He wouldn't kill us."

"No, but that would be a mercy in some cases." He took another sharp corner. "I need to be in Riverbend before dawn otherwise I will be trapped on the road until he finds me."

"Wait a minute. You said *I*. Shouldn't it be *we*. I thought I was going with you." Her glare was sharp, filled with determination. He kept thinking of her as weak, but she proved him wrong. There were not many people who argued with him. Maybe that was one of the things that had lured him to her?

"I am leaving you with a local nest."

"Why make me leave the castle?"

"Because the dragons cannot teach you anything about being vampire." He wanted her to have all the things he had not had as a new born creature of the night.

"Eoin is going to find me." She gasped. "Are you using me as bait to draw him away from you?"

He grabbed her hand and pressed his lips to her fingers, her words shards of glass. "Is that truly your opinion of me?" Every action he had taken since her birth had been to protect her.

The steel in her gaze softened. "No." She paused as if in thought, then he saw her conclusion dawn on her face. "You're drawing Eoin away from me. You're hiding me." She yanked her hand free. "No, no, no. That wasn't the deal. We escaped the castle together and go after this crazy witch in Riverbend. I want a piece of her. She almost wrecked Betty's life and may be doing it to others. I'm going to stop her." She crossed her arms, chin held high as she glared ahead.

He admired her loyalty and envied her friend. Trixie sought vengeance and retribution for the wrong doing. She would also get them both killed. "You need to learn control over your hunger first, among other things, before you can become a warrior." He merged into traffic on the highway that led into the heart of the city. "You must listen to me."

"Must?" She quirked an eyebrow.

He recalled how she'd laughed at the thought of calling him *Master*. "*Should* listen to me. Remember what happened when you ran to your sister?"

She flinched.

He hated to use that as a weapon, but she had to understand that he was not rejecting her. Not abandoning her. He needed her *safe*. He also realized she had to agree to stay of her own freewill, otherwise she would run. Viktor would use whatever means necessary to ensure her cooperation.

Trixie's shoulders sagged, her gaze dulled. "Fine." He knew she did not want to cause harm to an innocent. Nor did he want her to.

Silence blanketed the vehicle until they parked behind the most exclusive club in the city, Onyx. He exited the stolen car and opened her door before she had unbuckled

124

her belt. He offered his hand; her long fingers hesitated before placing her hand in his palm. He helped her out.

"That was…different." She tugged the hem of her T-shirt over her jeans.

"My speed? That comes with time as well."

"Not that." She laughed quietly. "I don't know any guy who would open a door for a girl."

"That does not say much for the men in your life."

"No, it doesn't. That's why I don't have any in my life." She looked at the club's entrance, the obnoxious neon lighting painted her hair in shades of purple and reds.

He grinned at her declaration of being unattached. He hadn't the chance to ask directly, but had not seen or smelled evidence of a man in her bedroom.

A red carpet led under a canopy, where one of his soldiers guarded the nest door in guise of a bouncer.

"Onyx is a vampire nest?" She stared at the guard with wide eyes. "I've always wanted to go inside."

"What has stopped you?"

She snorted. "The cover charge is more than I make in a day."

"Master." The bouncer's gaze took in Trixie, lingering on her long legs.

"Bruce, nice to see you again." He moved into Bruce's line of sight, blocking the view. "Where would I find Paulo?"

"He's below, attending business."

"Hello, Bruce." She held out her hand. "I'm Trixie."

The guard gently shook it. "Miss." Bruce opened the door.

She leaned close and whispered, "Who's Paulo?"

"Paulo is one of my lieutenants. He takes care of the nest's daily problems, and technically, the nest is below the club."

Viktor set Trixie's hand on his arm and led her inside her new home. "Night life, income, and a hunting ground all in one place." Compared to the old days, this was a paradise. Trixie would want for nothing.

He led her farther inside. Laser lights flashed over the crowded dance floor while the music pounded in his bones.

Trixie glanced down at her attire then at his. "We need to get you a shirt." She rose on tiptoe to search the crowd. "Everyone looks so posh. There's no way Ruby and I would have gotten in."

He would not apologize for that. If anything, it gave him relief that she had not been one of the nest's victims.

"Do any of these people know vampires live here?"

He chuckled. "Did you?"

She shook her head. "Hiding in plain sight. Living in the shadows. You know, most people suspect you exist. I mean, if shifters and magical creatures do, why not vampires?"

"I will not be in any hurry to *ever* give television interviews like the wolf pack's alpha." He could not imagine a faster way to get staked. "We prey on humans. It's only natural that they would fight back eventually." As a race, they had seen it happen time and again. As soon as a nest grew too confident in their relationships with humans, they were wiped out. It only took a small percentage of the humans to lead a mob. "No one likes being food."

Her gaze followed a young woman gliding to the bar. "Then these people don't know they're on the menu?" Her grip on his arm tightened. "That seems wrong. The nest doesn't kill any of them, do they?"

"Who said anything about killing?" Her reaction eased some of his worry. Her soul was still mostly human. "I have not heard of any massacres on the news." He winked. "If we feed every night, then we don't require much. The humans are not even aware." He pulled her toward the elevators, her eyes still full of wonder.

"How can they not know?"

"Shh, not so loud," he whispered, amused by her conspiratorial glance. "Our bite contains a toxin. Once bitten, their memory is malleable. A bite becomes a kiss or a nip on the throat." They entered the open elevator and road it to the lower levels. "It also helps the bites heal quickly."

"We have roofie venom?" Her lips curled with a sinister smile. "That's terrible."

"Well, not so powerful that the human loses consciousness. The effects are short term and are to detract from attention, not draw it." He ran his hand over his face. Once Trixie's hunger returned, her charming morals would vanish and the dancers would be dinner. He wouldn't let that happen.

The elevator dinged open and they crossed into a cavern. The walls were left as natural stone but modern comforts, such as indoor plumbing, were readily available. Thick carpets absorbed the sounds of their footsteps and electric lighting lit their way.

Paulo stood in the center of the large gathering room, dressed in pale gray slacks and a white shirt, button undone at his throat. He set aside the file in his hand. "Master Viktor." His gaze traveled slowly over Trixie from head to toe, absorbing every little detail. "Hello." He dragged out his greeting and cupped her hand to kiss her knuckles. "I

127

am Count Paulo Luis de Corcoles, lieutenant of this nest. Who may you be?"

"Patricia Russell." Breathy voice. "Everyone calls me Trixie."

Viktor moved, forcing Paulo back and breaking his hold on Trixie. She had never told *him* her full name. "Introductions are over."

Paulo bowed. "Patricia of the pink hair, a pleasure to meet you." He gave Viktor a knowing smile. As soon as he had a moment alone with the Count, Viktor would remind him again who was master in this city. But in all honesty, that would not matter to Paulo when it came to a woman. The little bastard would wait until Viktor turned his back to seduce her from him now that he had had a taste.

"Where is Callencia?" Viktor smiled back, with fang. He would hand Trixie's training over to Paulo's second in command. She would guard his innocent fledgling from the likes of Paulo or other males in the nest.

"Alas, she left."

A muscle in his eye twitched. "Again?" Who else could he leave Trixie with? He rushed through a list of names in his head.

Paulo's smile turned sharp enough to cut. "Yes, again."

"What did you do?" Viktor knew Paulo well enough that he was most likely at fault. Especially when it came to Callencia.

"Her pet liked me better."

"That is bad manners even for you. No wonder she left." Vampire pets were cherished humans that could be trusted to keep the nest secret. Viktor kept a tight leash on his vampires having pets. Too many humans knowing about them was risky.

"She was growing too attached to him." Paulo examined his fingernails.

Viktor resisted the urge to roll his eyes. "What of Jaya?" She was not a lieutenant but a respected business woman. She could be a good influence on Trixie.

"Business conference in Japan."

"I have been away." Viktor blinked, trying to relieve the discomfort.

"I noticed. How *is* the dragon?" Paulo's grin widened. "Would you like an updated roster of the vampires in the city?" He opened a file on his phone.

Viktor ran over the names. So many were too young. Or too male. He watched Trixie as she soaked in all the details around her with wide eyes.

Paulo maneuvered around Viktor, his gaze carried a predatory gleam. "Can I offer you a drink, Patricia?" He waved for her to come closer. "Please, come in. Sit beside me." He gestured to the loveseat made for two.

"No." Viktor blocked Trixie's way. Why had he expected Paulo to resist Trixie when he could not? His lieutenant was a brilliant with finances, but terrible with women. If Callencia or Jaya were here, he would feel safer leaving Trixie in their care. With Paulo, Viktor suspected Trixie would end up in his bed. He could not leave her here. Not with his lieutenant taking Trixie's lingerie measurements in his head. "Our visit is brief."

"And?" Paulo prodded.

Viktor pressed his lips together. Well, he was not going to admit his true intentions had been to leave Trixie here. "I am going to Riverbend for a few days. Watch over the city for me in my continued absence."

Paulo raised an eyebrow. "Don't I always?"

Inside his head, Viktor silently stabbed him in the heart repeatedly until his imagination was soaked in blood. "Keep up the good work."

Trixie turned her questioning gaze in Viktor's direction. The only betrayal of her emotions was how she bounced a couple of times on her toes. "And to borrow a shirt," she added.

Viktor nodded. Once in Riverbend, he doubted they would have time for him to shop.

Paulo stripped off his and held it out, displaying himself to Trixie. "Will this do?"

He snatched it out of his lieutenant's hand. "Yes." Then swept Trixie ahead of him back into the elevator. Instead of leaving her in the safety of the nest, he would keep her with him as she'd requested, because he was a selfish bastard.

He pulled on the shirt, busying himself with the buttons.

Once the elevator doors closed behind them, she slowly turned, crossing her arms, a huge grin on her face. "You like me." It was more of an accusation than a declaration.

"Of course, I like you." The doors opened on the main floor and blaring music stopped him from describing how much and what he planned to do about it.

Who was this woman who blurted that out? It couldn't have been *her*.

But Trixie had seen the sharp edge of jealousy in Viktor's eyes when Paulo had kissed her hand. Paulo's carnal interest was palpable. She wasn't a stranger to those looks. She was a full-blooded relative of Ruby's, after all, but whenever she went out with her sister, Ruby outshone her.

The looks other men gave Trixie changed once they met Ruby.

Except Viktor. He had barely noticed Ruby half-naked.

If Viktor had left her behind, she wasn't sure what would have happened, except Paulo would have been the proud owner of a brand new black eye.

Even after Viktor's mini rant about her learning to control her hunger, he had changed his mind the moment Paulo had come into the picture. The only factor in this situation that made any sense was Paulo's flirtation. She was right. Viktor like *liked* her. Her heart fluttered.

The club music thumped against her eardrums with a primal beat that stirred other pounding needs. Viktor's answer had sounded nonchalant but his predator's glare had daggered her to the spot. She had met werewolves and dragons and gargoyles. None of them flamed her hidden desires like Viktor. None of them tempted her.

Like a lot of kids in the city, she and Ruby didn't have it easy. The neighborhood was rough. The people rougher. There were a lot of good times, and some not so good ones. Ruby had learned early to use her beauty as a weapon to get what she wanted, what they needed. Trixie had learned to hide hers, not draw any attention to her body, to disappear behind Ruby's dazzle. She'd seen what her sister did to survive and the pieces of Ruby's soul it cost. Trixie wasn't as strong as Ruby. She'd chosen a different path and learned different skills to help with money. Trixie's body belonged to her and she would give it to someone who deserved it.

The elevator suddenly seemed very small and the air too thin. Viktor closed in, his arms trapped her, each hand by her head as he leaned his solid body forward until their lips almost touched. "What will you do about my liking you?"

Her brain overloaded. She blinked. "What?"

His lips were so invitingly near. Full and sultry, the kind of mouth a woman wanted to kiss all night long. He raised an eyebrow. "Are you teasing me, Patricia? That is a dangerous game to play."

Pure male heat. That was what she saw in those vampire eyes, raw and hungry and dominant. She pressed her thighs together. Viktor would take over in bed. She had no doubts. The vampire liked control.

He licked her bottom lip. A delicate touch that sent a shiver straight to her core.

She sucked in a breath, breasts rising. She was buried so over her head that when Viktor was done playing with her, nobody would find her corpse. Her teasing him? More like she hadn't a clue what she was doing. No, she'd seen her sister flirt enough times. Trixie knew how it was done. She just didn't know where to start or stop. What she *wanted* was to run her fingernails over the hard edges of his muscles. She groaned at the image in her head.

Yeah, he liked her. Now what the fuck was she going to do about it?

She pressed her hand to his chest and pushed. It was the single most difficult thing she'd ever decided to do. "I'm not teasing. I wouldn't do that. But I'm not the kind of girl you want." No-bed-skills-Trixie. Viktor needed a woman who could fulfill his every desire. Do things that she couldn't even imagine. Not flounder in the sheets like a fish out of water. Maybe this whole virgin thing wasn't such a great idea after all. She'd finally met someone who spun her head and she feared her lack of experience would bore him.

She tried to take deep, calming breaths before she hyperventilated.

He leaned his weight on one elbow giving her room to escape. Before she could move, he whispered loud enough for her to hear over the music, "I like women, not girls. You do not think you are woman enough for me?"

She cleared her throat since her mouth had gone so dry her tongue stuck to the roof. "Nope. You're definitely out of my league."

A smug smile. "Fair enough." He pressed a chaste kiss to her forehead. "But I do like you."

Oh no, what had she done? She'd gone from sizzle-her-panties-off to little-sister chaste kiss. She pushed away from the wall and headed for the nearest exit, blind and deaf to her surroundings. She didn't want to be shoved into the friend zone.

They left the club.

Viktor opened the passenger side door for her. So lean and tall, he hadn't enough extra flesh for her to bite. The ends of his fabulous black hair fluttered in the breeze. He looked like a dark angel.

Yeah, she cared. She didn't want to be just friends. She wanted it all and she'd screwed it up. Backing off now would only confirm to Viktor that she was off limits. She had to act though all her gut instincts told her to run.

She rose on tiptoe and looked him in the eye. "I really like you too."

ℭHAPTER ℱIFTEEN

She clung to the chick bar as Viktor broke all the laws of physics as they sped out of town. He drove like an immortal. Technically, she was one too, but her brain registered itself as still human. She might survive a crash, but she'd feel every broken bone and ruptured organ. "Viktor, I understand the urgent need to leave New Port." The dragon could do more damage than a car crash, she was sure. "I don't want Eoin catching us either." He would toss us both in the dungeon this time, complete with matching chain work. She hadn't come from medieval times and hadn't developed Viktor's amazing coping skills to deal with dark, dank dungeons. "But I don't want to go to human jail either. I doubt they have sunlight proof cells. *Slow down.*"

He gave her the side-eye. "Like a human jail cell could hold us." He chuckled.

"I'm glad I amuse you, but I'm serious. Slow the fuck down before you cause a sonic boom."

This time he tossed his head back with a laugh. It was a musical sound. Deep and hearty and very masculine. "Nothing would please me more than to comply, but we are on a tight schedule." He tapped the clock on the dashboard.

She stared at it, waiting for her mind to comprehend the cryptic reference. Nope, not happening. "I give up. Why am I staring at the time?"

"Sunrise. Your existence will revolve around when the sun sets and rises. We have just enough time to reach

Riverbend and find shelter. If I hurry, we will have a better cushion to find shelter for the day."

"Oh…" She glanced at the starry sky. They had had a busy night. Flying to the castle from her apartment, escaping said castle, and a pit stop at the club. The last one, she could consider a waste of their time, but Paulo had helped her realize Viktor had a real thing for this pink haired woman. A flame she needed to stoke. Somehow. She wished she could reach out to Ruby, but her sister hadn't texted her with her new number. Trixie had never needed to text Ruby so bad. Her sister would know how to get Viktor naked in thirty seconds flat. Her, she would probably scar him for life with her ideas of seduction.

"Have you ever seen what happens to a vampire caught in sunlight?" Morbid, she knew this, but if she was going to make it as a vamp she required some basic knowledge. All she had to go on were bad movies.

"No, or I would be dead myself, but it is not pretty."

"How do you know?"

"I know."

She ground her teeth. He wanted her to blindly follow his orders, but that's not how she had been raised. She questioned everything, otherwise she'd be dead by now.

Uh, well, shit, she had died. So maybe she wasn't so smart after all.

"The screams," he spoke softly.

She jerked in her seat. "Did you say screams?"

"I heard them. My companions." The glassy, black stare of a shark turned toward her. "This is one rule you cannot bend or break. No matter how old you are, the sun will destroy you." He sighed, returning his attention to the late night deserted road. "It turns us to ash. This is a fate I would not wish on my worst enemies."

"Sorry." She placed her hand on his thigh, resisting the urge to pry for more details. She wanted to know everything about Viktor, but she had forever to figure him out. "I didn't mean to bring up bad memories." Silence rubbed her raw. He looked lost in thought, not good ones, and she had caused it. "So, we're racing against the sun?" She did her best to fill the void.

"Always."

She left her hand where it was, enjoying the tense muscle under her palm. An electric charge ran between them, resulting in an attracting force, and this time she didn't pull away. "How did you travel between cities before cars?"

"What makes you think I'm that old?" Dark memories swept away, he turned his full focus on her.

She hid her smile. "You've *hinted* at your magnificent old bones being so indestructible."

He snorted.

"You say things like *word of honor* and do things like open my door like a gentleman. Makes me think you're old." She caught his scowl. "Uh, older. Not that you look old." Hell, he looked barely legal. It was his confidence and expectation that everyone do his bidding that aged him. He was so beautiful it made her brain cells die. She hoped she'd grow immune soon because she'd be a vegetable within a week.

There was that smug smile again. Almost as if he could read her mind. "No offense taken. I am old. The oldest vampire in New Port, Riverbend, and South Harbor Beach. These are all my territories."

She regretfully pulled her hand off his leg so she could turn and see him better. The moonlit shadows clung to his hair, veiling his body. "Vampires claim land like shifters?" She felt no urge to lay claim on anything but Viktor, but she was still new to this lifestyle and not being human.

He scrunched his nose. "Not land, but people. Think of it as a hunting ground. The more populated the area, the more vampires it can support."

"That's disturbing on so many levels." Hunting sounded like something other people did. Those who lived in rural areas with pickup trucks. She'd always been more of a salad person. "You need three cities to hunt?" Damn, that was some appetite.

That grin again, the amused one with a sharp edge. "Why not? I like variety."

She stared at him. Not sure what to say without being insulting.

He winked.

"You're pulling my leg."

"I am not touching your leg. You were touching mine." He nudged his thigh against hers. "You can again if you want."

"Only when you behave." She fisted her hand. She wanted to, but she wasn't sure she'd stop at his leg and they were driving at the speed of light.

"I have three cities because I am strong enough to control them. I police the population. I think that describes my role best. Keep the vampire/human ratios at a manageable level. Make sure there are no unnecessary killings…" The dead look returned to his eyes.

"It can't be an easy job."

He leaned forward, his attention taken by something ahead.

She followed the direction of his glare. "Oh-oh, looks like a speed trap. We'll be pulled over for sure." She raised her eyebrow and smirked.

Viktor shook his head. "I blurred the officer's mind. He did not notice us."

Now, she leaned forward. "We can do the Jedi mind trick? When will you teach me to use mine?"

"In a few decades. Power comes with age."

She flung herself back. "That's not fair. You get mind blurring and I get to suffer with broken bones. Only the old get all the cool tricks." She enjoyed his tight-lipped response. "But you don't look old."

"Can you imagine young vampires with such powers? I would have to kill them all to keep our existence secret. Age and experience is needed with such responsibility."

"You told me you couldn't read minds."

"I did not lie. I can influence people. Make a human inattentive or a shifter jumpy. It is more of a suggestion — the strong willed can fight me." He visibly relaxed in his seat and ran his hand over her knee. "But I am disappointed that I cannot turn into a bat or fly."

"I guessed that when I fell from the castle wall." Instead, Viktor had curled his body around hers, preparing to take the brunt of the fall. She was so glad they had set Nick free so he could stop their fall. That impact, according to Viktor, would not have broken him, but she was sure it would have hurt. She leaned across the seats and kissed his cheek. "Thank you for not leaving me behind."

A loud pop startled her enough to cry out.

The car swerved out of control. Viktor slammed his arm across her chest, pinning her to the passenger seat. "Hold on." With one hand, he steered the spinning car, regaining some control. Back and forth, he guided it across the lonely road. Gas, brake, then gas again until they rolled to a bumpy stop on the dirt shoulder.

He continued to pin her to the seat and glared out of the windshield. "That was close."

She clutched his arm with as much fierceness. "I thought we were going to eat asphalt." She rubbed his limb. "I'm good. You can let me go."

His gaze narrowed as he faced her. "I meant, we were close to making it to Riverbend."

"Good." She glanced at the time. "Because sunrise is soon." She didn't want to experience being a marshmallow over the campfire.

He crossed his arms and shifted in the seat, silent in thought.

"What was that popping noise?" They were stopped in a rural stretch of land between cities, surrounded by forest. No other traffic passed them. Probably due to the hour. The car appeared intact from where she sat.

Viktor charged out of the vehicle and she followed. He stood by the passenger side front tire. "A flat." Thick shredded rubber surrounded the rim.

"Wow." He regained control of the car driving on that? If it were her, they'd have been accordioned against one of the many trees lining the road.

Viktor squinted at the sky. "If we work fast, we might reach Riverbend in time."

She swallowed. Sunbathing no longer sounded appealing. "Point me to the jack. You get the spare out."

"You know how to change a tire?"

"My skills aren't limited to hotwiring cars and catching stray dogs." Steeling rims had paid the rent a few times. "It's disengaging car alarms that I have trouble with." And that was how her short profession as a thief had ended and she learned that jail food tasted worse than Ruby's cooking. Thank goodness for a tolerant judge and a stern probation officer.

Viktor popped open the trunk and handed her the jack kit. "Looks like the spare is underneath. Can you loosen the bolt to lower it?" He pointed at the floor of the trunk before kneeling to look under the vehicle. "Fuck that dragon."

She paused as she fitted the tool to the bolt. "What now?" She did her best to ignore the dark forest on both sides of the road. She had seen a horror movie with this exact scene and she could swear she saw movement in the underbrush.

Viktor scooted out from under the car. "There is *no* spare."

She dropped to her knees and scanned the undercarriage. "That's impossible. Who does that?"

"A shifter who has wings and can carry a car." Her sire leaned against the vehicle's side and slid to sit next to her.

"*Viktor*." Panic pitched her voice higher. She crept closer to him. "We won't reach Riverbend now." Her heart was a tattoo in her chest.

"Come here." He held out his arms and guided her into a hug. "We will find shelter. I did not reach this age because I lack the intelligence to problem solve."

His arms were strong and gave her an anchor to cling to as she scanned the forest for a cave or cabin or a trash can with a lid. "You never answered my question about how

140

Annie Nicholas

you traveled between cities before cars." She twisted to face him.

"Like everyone else. By horseback or carriage or my own two feet." He tucked her hair behind her ears, his gaze steady as if admiring her face. "When there was no shelter available, we would bury ourselves in the ground."

"Say—" Her voice cracked and she cleared her throat. "Say what?"

"That is where the myth of us being dead came from. Someone must have witnessed a vampire digging their way out of the ground."

Oh, it was fun fact time. Not. "You want to bury me in the ground." She paused. "With bugs. I mean, what do you do if one crawls in your ear. Is there wiggle room? Are we going to hide in the same hole? What if it rains? We can't dro—"

He pressed his finger across her lips for silence. "Have I not taken care of you so far?"

"Yes." He'd done nothing but take care of her since she'd awakened as a vampire.

He rose to his feet in a fluid motion, a grace that spoke of deadly stealth and agility. It stole her breath. With less poise, she scrambled to her feet as he bent to assist her. They collided midway, his hands supporting her elbows and his hair a veil around their faces. She couldn't move, caught in his dark gaze, she had no desire to retreat from his hold.

An amused smile tugged at his lips as if he knew exactly what kind of effect he had on her.

She licked her dry lips.

His gaze darted to the movement, riveted by the small gesture.

She deliberately took a step back. This wasn't the time or place and she didn't want to distract Viktor from saving their collective bacon before it was sizzled. "What do we do?"

"Place the vehicle into neutral gear." He closed the trunk and rolled up his sleeves, resting his hands on the car. "When I push, steer toward the tree line."

"Why?" She didn't see any path or dirt road.

He scowled. "Do it."

Trust. She was supposed to blindly trust this person she just met yesterday.

He pushed the sedan, flat tire and all, onto the wild growing grass strip separating forest from road.

She did as ordered. What could she say? He'd survived centuries. She hadn't lived thirty years yet.

He kept the momentum until they were well into the forest, packed between the trees, under the canopy.

She scanned the tree tops. "I don't think the foliage is thick enough to block out the sun." She didn't think such a forest existed.

"No, but they will provide shade so the trunk stays cool."

She spun to face him. "Did you say trunk?"

He popped it open again and tossed the contents on the forest floor. He paused when he came out with a bugle. "The dragon has this but not a spare tire." He shook his head, muttering under his breath in what sounded like Russian. Once done, he gestured to the empty space. "Climb inside."

The bottom went out of her stomach. "You're going to close me inside?"

"I can dig you a hole." His grin could have cut glass. "I am sure the bugs will not mind."

She sat on the edge of the trunk. "This is fine, but I hate enclosed spaces." She crawled inside and lay on her back.

Viktor followed. "I will keep you distracted."

"There's not enough room for both of us." She was tall and had to bend her knees to fit. Viktor was even taller. Not to mention the width of his shoulders.

"Nonsense." He wedged himself inside, shoving her against the inner wall. "See, like sardines." With that, he closed the trunk lid.

"How are they supposed to get out?" She peered in the dark, allowing her eyesight to adjust.

The iris of Viktor's eyes glowed with an inner light. A predator's gaze. "I will break the lock from within." He said it as if they should do these things, like break locks, every day. Silly her.

"Can you see in the dark?"

"Yes." He groaned and adjusted his legs.

"Is this another talent that comes with age?" Her vision had improved a lot but she wouldn't say she could see well in the trunk.

Viktor squirmed again. "Trixie, your knee." He tapped her leg. "It is crushing my family jewels."

"Your what?"

"My balls."

She gasped and hit her head on the lid. "Sorry." With a little contortion, she managed to shift her position. Now, she was on top of Viktor.

He rested his hands on her ass. "Much better."

CHAPTER SIXTEEN

Viktor bit back a moan as Trixie wiggled and did little female movements as if trying to give him more space. She succeeded only in getting closer and him more aroused. He listened to her racing heartbeat, smelled the sweat beading on her skin. The hunger gained strength, but instead of blood, it unfurled into a fiercely sexual desire.

Her luxurious hair — a gift from vampirism — poured over his chest and shoulders. He could not resist stroking it. Petting her.

"Viktor?" She clutched his biceps. "I can't breathe."

He stopped what he was doing and reassessed Trixie's scent. He had mistaken her stress for arousal.

She pushed against the trunk's lid. "Open it."

"We will both die if I do. The sun has risen." He pulled her hands into his, pressing kisses to her palms.

"We'll die if we stay in here." She panted.

"We will not." He stroked her cheek unable to stop touching her. Skin so soft and unblemished under his fingertips.

Vampires by nature were beautiful. He would even dare say they evolved this way to hunt, so much easier when the prey came to you. His growing attraction to Trixie had less to do with her exterior. Her kindness disarmed him. Her soul pulled him in. She was the flame to his moth and the burn of her touch was excruciating pleasure.

Her breathing slowed.

He kissed her forehead, taking his time. They had all day to explore each other.

"How can you tell the sun has risen?"

"I can sense it." He guided her head to rest over his heart. "Close your eyes and clear your thoughts. You should sense it too. This is a basic survival instinct in our race."

She grew quiet and still. "I—" She hesitated and squirmed some more.

Have mercy.

"I think I'm hearing it." She shook her head in the tight confines. "Hearing is the wrong word." She tapped the inside of the trunk. "It's that way. The sun pulls at me."

"Correct. Some of our scientists think we sense the sun's gravity.

"We have scientists?" Her tone flat.

He chuckled. "Of course, we do. Not all of us live under nightclubs." She had the whole world to explore and learn. He envied her this. She would grow into her vampire senses, but until then he would not leave her side and maybe, experience some of her wonder.

Her weight was slight, her whole body built lean and lithe. He felt the goodness in her heart when her eyes looked into his, felt her strength of will inside those fragile bones. She was strong and she would need that strength to control her predatory nature.

She shifted her legs and straddled his hips. "That's better. I don't feel so squished, but something's poking…" Her breath hitched and he knew she was blushing fiercely. He could almost taste it in the air.

He was used to his sexuality, but what he wasn't accustomed to was it reacting so intensely to a woman he'd barely met. His body betrayed how much he enjoyed her proximity. Hundreds of years old and suddenly his dick thought it was seventeen again. He relaxed his arms, resting them at his sides.

She did not push him away or roll off. The cramped space did not give them room to maneuver, but remaining in this position was not required.

"Sorry," she whispered and surprised a chuckle out of him.

"For what? Being so charming." He exhaled close to her ear. "I thought we had agreed that we liked each other."

She pressed her hands flat against his chest. Her touch was pure fire. The burn sealed his decision. He would have her. Vigorously. In this car. Repeatedly. Until she begged for mercy. Then he would have her again.

She undid the top buttons of his shirt. Her hands trembled as her fingers slipped inside, branding his skin. "Is this okay?"

His eyebrows shot up. "Of course." Why would it not be?

Viktor's hard body lay very still under Trixie's. He'd gone from caressing and kissing her to his hands at his side.

Was she doing it wrong? His erection still pressed against her. That was a good sign.

Dangerous and powerful, Viktor was the most exotic man she'd ever met. The urge to run her fingers through his hair was impossible to resist. She breathed a soft sigh of frustration. He was too big, too intimidating. She withdrew her hand. What was she thinking? She wasn't worldly. Seducing someone like Viktor needed know how and she was all virgin thumbs.

"Do not stop." His voice had gone rough. There was nothing threatening about his tone, but it was full of demand.

She undid the remainder of his buttons. Smooth skin covered granite muscles. Fascinated, she couldn't resist stroking him.

His fingers tunneled in her hair and he pulled her closer, brushing a kiss over her lips.

She played with fire. Viktor wouldn't stop if she told him to because he wasn't some human boy she'd met at a dance club—he wasn't someone who followed anyone's commands. Not even a fire breathing dragon with anger management issues. And still she ran her hands under his shirt, caressing his flanks, as if willing to do anything he desired. Subconsciously, she didn't want him to stop.

He retreated.

Her mouth tingled with sensory memory of his lips. She ran the tip of her tongue where they'd been, soothing the empty ache. He wasn't her first kiss, but damn, in comparison to her previous experience he might as well have been.

Viktor threatened it all. Her mind, her heart, her vow. She was willing to hand it all over. Her hands moved to grip his shoulders, pulling her closer for another kiss that was so luscious, she melted. He was all slow heat and seduction against her mouth while his hands moved under the hem of her T-shirt.

The lightning in her bloodstream was a heated caress, the pulse between her legs an unsettling but exquisite pleasure.

He was driving her mad. His hands cupped her lace covered breasts.

It didn't matter. She was already insanely crazy about him.

He kissed a line down her throat, speaking between each caress. "I want to be inside you." He thrust his hips, sandwiching her hips between the trunk lid and his hard package.

In the dark, stars still flashed in her vision at the unexpected onslaught of carnal sensation. A whimper escaped her throat, her hands spasmed on his shoulders. He was magnificent. "Oh my god," she gasped. "I thought I was doing this all wrong."

The grinding slowed. "Why would you think that?" His hands slid from her breasts to her hips.

She petted her hands over his bare torso like before and leaned in for another kiss. "No reason."

Instead of accepting her invitation for more, he gripped her wrists. "You are a terrible liar."

Her heart thudded violently enough to hurt. She'd never been so thankful for the dark. Yet she hid her face against his chest.

"Trixie, what are you not telling me?" He stroked her hair. Soothing. Caring. Then he gasped. "I remember, in my cell tasting your human blood."

The earlier inferno of passion extinguished. She should have been relieved but she was surprised to feel disappointed.

"Virgin," he whispered.

She kept her flaming cheek pressed to his chest. It wasn't shame that made her feel so awkward. It was fear of rejection. "I don't know what I'm doing."

He let out a long, slow breath and massaged the bridge of his nose.

She wanted to crawl into a hole with the bugs — or better yet — into the sunshine.

"You have great instincts." He shifted his hips and adjusted his pants.

"I'm sorry," she whispered.

"No." He cupped her face and pressed a long, tender kiss to her mouth, slow and warm and so very possessive. "No apologies. I am the one who is sorry."

"You're not mad?" Her heart triple beat and she slid his shirt off his shoulders, wishing for a head lamp or any light source so she could appreciate those cut abs. She wanted him like no other.

He moaned and caught her wrists in his hands.

"You don't want me?" The question rhetorical since she knew the answer. Stomach sinking, she tried to gather the tatters of her dignity. No pouting. Definitely no crying. If a tear formed, she'd punch herself in the eye.

"Woman." He slid her off him so they lay facing each other, and he gripped her hair. "You are driving me wild."

Her thighs pressed together, a strange fire burned even the darkest, most secret part of her. "Viktor." She didn't know what she was asking for, her heartbeat an erratic beat against her ribs.

Viktor was careful of his strength. The cramped confines limited what they could do. It also trapped Trixie with a monster whose restraint tended to dissolve easily. He craved her like drowning man craved air. "Your deflowering will not happen inside the trunk of a car." Those were the most difficult words he had ever managed to say.

Her breasts pressed against his chest as she breathed heavily.

A growl escaped his throat. He fought the urge to tear off her clothes. "It is not the right thing to do."

"Oh." She sounded so defeated that he pressed her to the floor of the trunk before he restrained his wild needs again. So close. So soft. How were they going to survive each other until nightfall?

Trixie shifted instinctively under him, cradling him right where he wanted to be.

The hot, sun-heated lid of the trunk burned his back. Pain grounded his passion. "This does not mean I will not play." So he kissed her again. Her mouth was open and he was so tempted to sweep his tongue inside, savor what he craved with every hard inch. He fisted his hand in her hair tighter. She might not believe it, but he was trying to be good.

Trixie needed release. He would damn well give her one. Those urgent little movements of her body were charming him out of his good intentions. She arched up, rubbing her chest against his.

"Baby, I am not a good person. Do not test me."

"I know exactly how bad you are." Her hands swept along his sides as she scratched her nails over his skin.

"Harder." He hissed and had his mouth on Trixie's before he could think about the consequences. He would keep his promise and not take her virginity in this pit of darkness, but he *would* have her eventually. That promise he would keep. The violent need to claim her to the core was a gnawing ache in his gut. He wanted the world to know she was his — make certain no one would dare lay a finger on her. Running his tongue along the seam of her lips, he urged them to part. When she did, he swept in without hesitation, taking, tasting, claiming.

Her kiss was hesitant, and shy and so arousing, he had to lock his arms to keep from tearing her shirt asunder and cup her sweet, plump breasts in his palms while taking her wholly in a more demanding and sexual fashion. Instead, he let her sip at him, let her explore with the tip of her delicate tongue. He shuddered, his pants so tight the zipper would leave a permanent mark on his cock.

She did it again. Trixie was proving to be a quick study.

His lips curved into a feral smile before he sucked on her bottom lip then bit down.

She jerked, changing position slightly, tilting her hips so the heat between her thighs was right where he wanted it. She gasped and clung to his shoulders. "V—Viktor."

Her stutter was adorable. That mouth so lush and wet he could not resist imagining what he wanted her to do with it. She rolled her hips instinctively against him.

"Give in," he whispered. "I will make you feel good.

Trixie's throat dried up. Hands on her hips. Warm. A little rough. She sucked in a breath when his fingers traced the edges of her jeans to the fastenings.

He kissed her neck, sucking on the beat of her pulse. At the same time, he undid the button and zipper. "Can I touch you?"

Gasping in a breath, she buried her face in his hair. He smelled of desire and heat that was pure aroused male. Would it be like this with any other man? No, she already knew this answer. It would never be like this nor would it ever be again. She nodded, not trusting her voice would work.

His still-covered cock pressed against her as he slid his fingers smoothly inside her panties, parting her with more intimacy. He pinched her clitoris, that nub of nerve endings, and rocked their hips together. "Do you like that?"

She pushed into him, her body taking control, but his delicious weight held her in place. "Oh, yes."

"More?"

"Yes, yes…"

Another kiss, another intimate touch, but her body was silken with need for him and she found herself arching into the finger he stroked inside her. The pleasure-pain was the most exquisite sensation. Tiny muscles she hadn't been aware of clenched. More and more.

"Move on me, baby," he murmured as his fangs ran a teasing line along her throat.

She couldn't stop if she'd tried. The fluid motion of her hips pushed him deeper inside. "I want you."

"You are too tight." He slid a second finger inside and pumped.

A stretching ecstasy. Her arousal soared higher and higher and higher.

His thumb brushed her clitoris.

"Oh." She arched into him as everything exploded. Viktor cursed in Russian as her muscles convulsed around him and her orgasm tore her apart. Nothing mattered. Only them, here, together. Like a feather, she eased back, glorying in the weight of him. With tender kisses and petting, he soothed her down from her sexual high. She stroked his back, fingers catching on his pants. "What about you?"

He caught her hand. "Later." And guided it above her head. "You need to rest. We have a busy night ahead of us." Pressing kisses to her lips, he rolled to cuddle her close to his side. "We have eternity to explore this." As her eyes fluttered close, she sensed his mouth curl into a smile. "And I want to take my time."

CHAPTER SEVENTEEN

What felt like seconds later, the sound of metal grinding and squealing in protest startled her awake.

Viktor's body still pressed along hers but his muscles strained as he pushed against the trunk door. It popped open like a tin can.

She threw her arms over her head in reflex, but who was she kidding, they weren't going to protect her from the sun and an agonizing death. The pull she had felt earlier, when Viktor taught her to sense the sunrise, had moved considerably since then. Instead of going up like a roman candle, she remained alive, curled in a little ball.

Viktor stroked her hair. "I did not expect it to make so much noise and wake you." He kissed along her neck, taking his sweet time, and she melted into his arms. They had crossed a line last night and there was no going back.

Distant starlight greeted her gaze as she allowed Viktor's hair to stream through her fingers. "It's night already. I slept so good." She stretched, her body arching into his.

He raised himself on an elbow, admiring the lines of her motion.

"I'm still tired though."

"You have not fed today." He closed his eyes as she tugged him by the hair, back to her lips for a small kiss.

"Neither have you and you seem fine." She glanced at the bent and broken trunk lid. "More than fine."

"That is nothing." He nipped her throat.

"Well, your nothing is quite impressive."

A husky laugh. "Thank you."

She had walked right into that one. It was wonderful, lying here, being teased by her…*boyfriend* didn't quite describe their relationship. Neither did *lover* since they hadn't completed the deed yet. Master? *Never.* She decided on *sire* for now. Until she could use one of the first two. "Eoin is going to kill us once he finds his car." She stroked her hands over Viktor, more than happy to pick up where they had stopped.

"Me, yes. You? He would not dare risk the wrath of Angie. He is an angry dragon. Not a stupid one."

She brushed her fingertips over his kissable lips. "Why would she care? We only just met."

"Ken is her best friend."

"Betty's Ken? Well, that makes us almost family." She giggled at Viktor's wiry smile.

He sat, dragging her along. "We must start our journey if we are to ever reach the city."

She groaned at the thought of the long walk.

A car passed their hiding spot.

So, maybe not a long walk? They could try to catch a ride. Two vampires in a dark forest seemed harmless enough that someone might stop.

She climbed out of the trunk, smoothing the wrinkles out of her clothes. There was a faster way to reach Riverbend from New Port. A lovely interstate, but had Viktor chosen a rural, two lane highway to avoid Eoin's search pattern. Just because it was rural didn't mean no one used it though. "How far do you think we have to go?"

"I can carry you." Viktor sounded sincere.

She bit the inside of her cheek. It would be cozy being in his arms. "No." A woman had to draw a line as to how helpless she was going to act. Trixie had been lugged around enough in the last twenty-four hours. That was not her. She lived by her own rules, created her own paths. She caught stray animals and helped them find homes. She loved pink and drawing in detail, and she was good with cars. She never let peer pressure change her values and she still believed in true love.

That was Patricia Russell. Except she was now a vampire. She couldn't forget who she was at the core.

She walked to the edge of the dark road with Viktor on her heels. "I don't need you carrying me." She didn't need to walk a bazillion miles either.

Headlights appeared in the distance. She held out her thumb to hopefully hitch a ride.

"They will not stop." He crossed his arms, leaning on a tree.

The car sped past.

She ground her teeth, wishing he'd been wrong this once. "Doesn't mean I won't try."

Viktor slung her over his shoulder, like a caveman, and ran. Not at human speed. They traveled so quickly the trees blurred. It was as if he barely touched the soil and glided over the ground. So awesome, and probably another super power she wouldn't have until she was an adult vampire.

After what seemed like an hour. Viktor slowed to a stop and caught his breath. He set her on her feet. She stretched the spasms in her lower back from being in such an awkward position for so long. Twinkling lights on the horizon drew her attention, sparkling in a dance under the stars.

He pressed against her back. "Riverbend."
"We're almost there."
"No, we have still a lot of ground to cover."

"It looks so close."

"Because the land is flat. And?" he whispered his question in her ear, sending a shiver down her spine.

"I can see even farther since I'm a vampire." If she rolled her eyes any harder, she'd go back in time. "It's beautiful."

"She *is* beautiful." A rough sound. Impatient hands that turned her to meet his kiss.

And, oh, what a kiss.

It held the same dark temptations as this morning, but it also held something else — a tenderness, soft pleasure, with a playful nip. Shuddering, she pulled away, her mind blank and it took her a moment to recall what they'd been discussing.

"So —" She cleared the husky roughness from her throat. "Will we reach it before daylight?" She didn't want to hide underground.

A set of headlights burned in the night and grew brighter. They were close to the road again! She waved her arms over her head in her best impression of a cheerleader.

A pickup truck slowed to a stop. "Are ya stranded?" shouted an elderly gentleman wearing jean overalls. The vehicle and driver appeared to be the same age.

"Yes," she answered simultaneously as Viktor said, "No."

"Well, which is it? You need a ride or not?" The driver peered at them through thick glasses.

"We need a ride." She grabbed Viktor's hand and tugged him to the back where she jumped into the empty bed. "Thanks," she called to the driver.

Viktor followed with a thunderous scowl. She half-expected him to drag her out kicking and screaming. He settled next to her, knees bent, arms resting on them.

She nudged him with her elbow. "Say *thank you*."

Viktor's frown deepened. "Thank you." It came out threatening.

The truck pulled onto the road, wind blowing in their hair, and them on their way to Riverbend.

"I could have run the remainder of the way. I was not tired."

"Save your energy."

Heat flared in his eyes. "What do you plan on doing with my extra energy?" He scooted closer, fingers slipping under the hem of her shirt to tease along her abdomen.

"I—I don't know." Blah, so she needed to practice her flirting. She'd spent so much time deterring men's attention that she didn't know how to act if she wanted it. She hadn't any muscle memory.

Trixie's awkwardness charmed Viktor.

His retinue of acquaintances consisted of lieutenants that helped run his territory and his few shifter friends, who were all dominants. Trixie brought out his protectiveness. Her new life was filled with predators, including him. She had to be kept safe. It would be such a loss if she lost her Trixie-ness.

"I have a few ideas on what we can do with my extra energy." When they found some alone time, he planned on showing her a few of them. There was no need to hurry in his seduction. Trixie was his.

The truck rumbled along the two-lane road at the same speed he could have run. The ride wouldn't save them time, but it did give him a chance to plan their next move. He didn't visit Riverbend often.

The vampire nest was small since the city was not as populated as New Port and it had a higher population of shifters, which vampires didn't feed upon. Their blood tasted awful and didn't sustain them.

The local lieutenant kept a tight rein on the nest so he didn't need to watch them closely. They also didn't get along. He wondered who could have fathered a dhampir, which were the offspring of a vampire and a human. Procreation with humans was still possible, just rare. His lieutenant might know where to find this child who tattooed black magic. The dhampir might be from another nest and hadn't reported to the local one. Too many possibilities.

Trixie snuggled against him, pressed along his side, head resting on his shoulder. Their hair tangled in a mix of black ink and pink cotton candy in the wind. Arm around her shoulders, he held her tight, luxuriating in the sense of companionship.

She filled a gaping hole in his soul he hadn't known existed. He'd been surrounded by people and never realized how alone he was until he'd met her.

She sighed. A happy noise filled with such simple satisfaction.

He stroked his fingers under her chin and raised it to plant a tender kiss on the tip of her nose. He knew he unnerved her. Truth be told, he was more nervous. There were so many things he could do wrong in their budding relationship and he was an expert at making mistakes

"Where are you folks heading?" The driver shouted out his window as he came to a stop light.

They had finally arrived at the outskirts of Riverbend.

"Downtown," Viktor replied. They would start their search in the bar district, which was a block from the main shopping area. Tattoo parlors dotted the neighborhoods between.

"I can drop you off on the corner of Twelfth Avenue and Charlevoix Street."

"That is sufficient, my good man." He knew Charlevoix Street. It ran through the whole city, dividing East from West.

Trixie pulled out the cell phone her sister had given her the night before. "Crap, it's dead and I don't have a charger. I've never been to Riverbend." She twisted around for a better look. "It looks like a city." She laughed. "I'm not sure what I was expecting. Do you have a smart phone?"

He stared.

"I'll take that as a no. We have no GPS, map, or Google. This search might prove to be futile."

He smiled on the inside at her word choice. His vocabulary—the one she had teased him about—was affecting her own.

"Is there at least a river in Riverbend?"

The truck pulled over by the curb. They thanked the driver, *again*, and jumped out.

"If we follow Charlevoix, it will cross the river that runs through the city." He winked in reply to her happy grin. "Yes, there is a river."

She pointed across the street. "There's a coffee shop and it's still open." She grabbed his hand and pulled him along to her destination.

"I do not have any funds." He had wanted to be in and out of the city before his presence was noted by any of the supernatural creatures.

"Don't sweat it. I have a little cash."

"Coffee has little nutritional value."

She rolled her eyes. "I want to charge my phone. They usually have charging stations." She hesitated. "We can drink coffee?"

"Anything liquid. Sometimes it tastes off." He shrugged, confused by her little dance of glee.

They claimed the closest table, where she used the coffee shop's universal charger to plug in her phone. "I'll search the area for tattoo parlors and make a list."

He ordered two coffees in to-go cups. "Your plan is to wander parlor to parlor asking questions?"

"That's what detectives do."

He nodded. "Or we could ask Betty."

Her eyes narrowed. "She's on her *honeymoon*."

"Do you think she would mind the interruption if it caught this dhampir?" The coffee arrived and he took a sip of the liquid lava. "Fuck." Vampires could still burn their tongues.

Trixie growled something under her breath as she typed furiously on her phone. "There are fifteen tattoo parlors in the city."

"And we have no transportation." He raised an eyebrow as she bared her tiny, kitten teeth. "That is a lot of walking."

She went back to typing.

"We could contact the local nest." He frowned. If he did, they would expect him to visit. Make his presence known. "Somebody should know the dhampir's name. They are very rare and I doubt she has gone undetected all this time."

Trixie remained focused on her phone.

"Are you listening to me?"

"Sort of. Something about the dhampir and I don't even know what that is."

He leaned forward. "What are you doing?"

"Texting Betty." She tossed him a scowl as he hid his smile behind the coffee cup.

CHAPTER EIGHTEEN

Betty? Trixie texted and cringed when she hit send. Betty was on some tropical island with her soul mate Ken. He'd said Betty could pick any destination as long as it was bikini weather.

She's asleep

Ken? She fought the urge to crawl under the table. She still couldn't look him in the eye even though he'd forgiven her for shooting him in the ass with a tranquilizer dart. Well, a few darts. Who knew she had such great aim?

Who else would have access to her phone? And be in her bed?

Really must be true love if she gave you the password to her phone. God, she hoped Betty had deleted *those* pictures. The ones where they were wearing party streamers and hats and not much else.

We're soulmates.

She could hear his mic drop from this side of the world. *Okay, never mind.*

What's wrong, Trix? He used his beta tone through text. Impressive.

She hesitated and glanced at Viktor. *Nothing.* Could a werewolf sniff a lie through text?

You're lying.

How do you do that?

Waiting…

I need to know the name of the tattoo artist who screwed up her life.

There. It was done. If anyone would help her with this, it was Ken. Betty was the center of his universe and her skin art had almost destroyed their future together.

After a moment, he finally responded. *Why?*

Viktor was staring out the coffee shop window.

She angled her phone slightly and took a picture. Quickly, she sent it to Ken. *HE wants to know.*

!!!Stay away from him!!!

Too late, Ken. She tongued her fangs. Boy, were they in for a surprise when they came home. *Do you know the answer?*

Jade Ellington. She worked at Reckless Tattoo. I already sent someone to chat with her but she couldn't be found anywhere in the city. Then he sent. *Do you know what he is?*

Yes.

There are rumors about him. His pets tend to disappear. Please tell me you're not his pet.

What's a pet?

Are you feeding him?

No! She was being honest. She didn't want to wreck his honeymoon. If they knew the truth, Betty would jump on the first plane home. Trixie shouldn't have sent that picture.

Don't worry. Eoin is with us. Thanks! Make puppies. I want to be an Aunt ASAP.

She waited for a response, or worse, a phone call, but nothing happened.

She met Viktor's piercing gaze and told him the information. "What is a vampire pet?" She needed to know where she stood with him. If she was one, she'd reconsider Ken's warning with more seriousness.

Viktor reached across the table and grabbed her phone, scrolling through her text conversation. She wasn't fast enough to stop him. He paused on his picture. "That is not my good side." He returned it to her. "We call the humans who feed us, of their own free will, pets. The wolf is right. Some of my pets have vanished. I killed them."

His chair squealed with the speed of his standing.

She stuffed her partially charged phone in her pocket and tossed a couple of dollars on the table to cover the coffee they'd barely drunk.

Outside, Viktor waited. "I know where that tattoo parlor is located. It is a short walk from here. But first you must feed."

The bottom of her stomach dropped out. "I'm a little hungry but I can wait." She wasn't in any hurry to drink blood. No matter how much she craved it. The thought still repulsed her. How long before that changed? She feared the last trace of her humanity would vanish when it no longer bothered her to feed.

"Waiting is the first step to losing control. You must stay ahead of the hunger. Keep it banked low, otherwise it burns through you." He sounded like a man speaking with firsthand experience.

"Is that what happened to you?"

"Happened?" He met her gaze, his eyes dead and cold. "You mean happens." He stalked down the empty sidewalk.

She followed on his heels. "If you know this is a problem, then you can prevent it from happening again."

"No." He crossed the street without looking and cars squealed to a stop.

She didn't let that stop her though. She waved an apology to the drivers as she ran across, following. "Are you crazy?"

He stopped, his glare a sharp-edged dagger. "Sometimes." Then he continued his march.

She ground her teeth, which proved to be difficult with fangs. "I don't believe that. I think you use that as a play to—to…" She came to a sudden halt, staring at Viktor's retreating broad back. "So Eoin will punish you."

Viktor's steps slowed. He turned and strode until he loomed over her. "I did not have the privilege of having a teacher when I was made a vampire. No one explained certain rules as I do for you. Do not take these teachings lightly. Do not ignore them unless you want to bear the burdens that I do."

"What burdens are those?" She could guess. A person didn't tattoo hundreds of names on their body because they were feeling friendly.

"I am a killer."

"Tell me something I don't know."

He blew out a frustrated breath. "If you fight the hunger, try not to feed, it grows out of control until you are a ravenous beast and ruled by bloodlust. You awake from it surrounded by whatever crimes you have committed. Live with the consequences." The last part he whispered so low she barely heard him.

She wanted to touch him, to comfort him. Offer him the solace that he obviously needed. Instead, her mouth opened. "Is that why you have so many names on your body?"

Viktor pushed his shirt sleeve up over his wrist. The button on his cuff flew at slingshot speed, pinging off the brick wall. "Including yours."

There on the inside of his wrist, all by itself sat her name.

"You gave me a second chance." This time, she did follow her instincts and covered her name with her hand. "You didn't kill me. The stairs did." She didn't belong among those names. Viktor was her hero.

He covered her hand with his. "I made your heart stop."

"Dude, you could do that with a wink."

His small crooked smile appeared shy. "Come, Trixie. You make me blush."

"I don't see it."

"Closer." Eyelids heavy, he drew kissing close. "Do you see it now?"

What was she looking for again? She focused on his full, soft lips remembering how skillful he was with them. Her hand still pressed to his solid chest, sizzled with their connection and she curled her fingers.

"You make it so easy." He ran the backs of his fingers over her cheek. "So easy to forget what we were supposed to be doing." His eyebrows furrowed. "No distraction, Tricky Trixie."

"You didn't go there."

He chuckled. "We will both feed then continue our search."

She glanced at the time on her phone. It was late but she felt energized. She'd been working the night shift with animal control for a while so it wasn't a big switch to live without the sun.

Her diet, though…

That sucked.

Viktor led her to a livelier area of the city. Bars lined the cobblestone street with tasteful neon signs lighting her and Viktor's way. A few places even had terraces for customers looking for some fresh air. Like most club districts, they played dance music. The distant beat thumped in her chest.

"Is this what being a vampire means? Hunting in clubs?" This would grow old fast.

He shrugged. "Would you like to hunt in the twenty-four hour grocery store? Not many places are open all night."

She pictured her choices at this hour. Moms finishing their late shifts and stopping for milk or college students grabbing beer. "Nah, this is good."

Viktor took them into the busiest place on the block.

"Do vampires own this one?" She pressed against his back as they navigated through a crowded hall.

"No," he whispered. "I'd like to avoid contact with the local nest if possible."

She gripped the back of his shirt, fear a tangible pulse in her veins. "I thought this was your territory."

"It is, but my lieutenant and I have a bad history. I do not want to complicate our visit with posturing. I would rather take you home as soon as possible."

He turned her blood to liquid honey. Take her *home*. His home?

Viktor paused by the entrance, scanning the crowd. "We are in luck. I see a New Port pet."

The club was sunken into the ground so they had a great view. Heads bopped in rhythm on the crowded dance floor. She found her own chin dipping in time to the thumping music and her shoulders swaying to the groove.

"See that empty corner to our left?" Viktor pointed. "Wait for me there."

"Where are you going?" She was in a strange city in an unknown club. How would she find him if they lost each other? He didn't even carry a cell phone.

"To see if the pet will feed us."

"Oh." What did one say to that? She navigated her way through the crowd. Someone touched her hair, another her ass. It was too crowded to see who. The music no longer had her attention and she searched the crowd for a familiar dark head. Finally, she crossed the human sea to the secluded spot Viktor had pointed out to her. She tongued her fangs, not sure how to use them. With the blood bags, she'd been so hungry she'd bitten on instinct. She wasn't as hunger-crazed now as she had been. That was good. With the bags, she didn't have to worry about hurting them. This was her first time biting anyone and she didn't want to hurt them.

Trixie wouldn't have called this corner *empty* but it was less crowded. She stood with the wall to her back, hands in her pocket, and waited. What people wouldn't see was the sweat trickling down her spine or the tremor in her hands. Now that she knew dinner was coming, she grew hungrier fast.

The pound of the music slowly slipped away, replaced by the beat of their hearts. She could smell them.

Humans

Their blood sang to her.

Food.

Warm and fresh and salty and —

Viktor appeared. A man in his mid-twenties next to him. He cupped her face. "I feel your hunger." He closed his eyes and shuddered. "We will both feed." He opened his eyes and the predator looked back at her. "Carlos works for the New Port nest as a *donor.*"

"I thought you said he was a pet."

Viktor's gaze narrowed.

"Pet," Carlos interjected, "is a derogatory term. We prefer donor." He smiled. "I don't care what you want to call me." He winked.

Viktor continued to speak. His mouth moved but she couldn't hear him. The beat of hearts called her. The urge to follow them strong. "Trixie?" He cupped her chin, pulling her attention back to him.

"I smell them," she whispered. *Them.* It was no longer *us.* Closing her eyes, she swallowed reflexively. A predator. A hunter who would prey upon humans for the rest of her unnatural life. Her mouth watered. They shouldn't smell like fried chicken though. That wasn't fair. It had been twenty-four hours since she'd fed though. Her control was growing better. She had managed to sit in a coffee shop surrounded by people and not think about draining of them dry.

Silver lining, she would take it.

"The hunger makes your senses more acute." Viktor drew her aside, forcing her to open her eyes or trip over his feet. He gestured for Carlos to follow and led them to the farthest corner of the club where even the dance lights didn't reach that well.

She held out her hand to Carlos. "I'm Trixie."

He shook her hand. "A pleasure to feed you." His eyes were caramel soft as they caressed her curves. Carlos glanced at Viktor, whose smile appeared feral. "We could do this at my hotel room." His gaze stoked over Viktor in the same manner as it had her. "I wouldn't mind."

Viktor's expression darkened. "Be careful with such invitations. You might not walk away one day."

Carlos dropped her hand. Her hearing suddenly focused on his heartbeat alone and left her dizzy. She wanted him to run. Not to escape, but so she could chase. His fear would smell delicious.

She caught a glimpse of Viktor's face and realized how dangerously close Carlos was to dying. "Maybe we should get take out like at my apartment?" She stepped between the men, forcing Viktor to break eye contact.

He shook his head. "No, you need to learn this."

This being how to bite people.

Carlos' pulse slowed as he pressed against her back, his hands on her hips.

She froze. "Take it easy, Carlos." What kind of deal did vamps have with their donors? Because she didn't like the way Carlos kept eyeing her. Yanked from his hold, she found herself engulfed in Viktor's arms.

"I do not share."

"No problem, boss." Carlos met her gaze. "I hear it's your first time though. Don't worry if you hurt me. I've fed fledglings before." He undid the top button of his shirt.

"No." Viktor frowned. "We will use the wrists."

Carlos shrugged. He rolled up his sleeve and offered Viktor the inside of his wrist.

Viktor bent over, his gaze catching hers. "Come closer and feel the pulse."

Feel? She could freaking see it. She set her fingertips over the spot.

"You want to feed from the arteries. They flow easier and it is oxygenated blood, which is what our bodies need. Press your fangs along that spot."

Hunger burned in her veins. It was a full body ache. She glanced at Carlos—all sun-kissed skin and caramel eyes. How had he gotten mixed-up with vampires? Would his name grace Viktor's skin one day? What if she killed him with her lack of knowledge?

"Maybe you should show me first so I don't harm Carlos." She'd spent a good part of her life rescuing animals. She didn't even kill spiders in her house. Being bitten seemed painful.

"Trixie." His glare snapped her out of her racing thoughts. "You can do this."

Sure, she could. She just didn't want to. "What's wrong if I choose to live off blood bags?"

"Bags are not always available," answered Carlos. "The Red Cross keeps a tight lock on theirs. New Port and Riverbend have catering services but they aren't reliable. Only so many bags per day, and if someone buys them all, then you're shit out of luck."

She blinked. "You know a lot about this."

"I donate. It's a livelihood." He offered her his wrist. "People are always available. Come on, baby. You know you want it." He sang in a teasing voice.

If Viktor frowned any deeper, it would turn into a full-blown snarl.

She laughed. How could she not? Setting her fangs on the spot, she could sense Carlos' pulse soar.

"Now," commanded Viktor.

She sank them in, quick and deep. Warm liquid flooded her mouth. Salty and thick, it coated her parched throat and eased the burn in her veins. She was surprised how little she required this time. But how did she stop without making Carlos bleed out? She made a questioning noise.

Viktor stepped in and took her place at Carlos' wrist. The man leaned against the wall, eyes closed, a look of ecstasy on his face.

Okay…

She licked the blood off her lips. He didn't taste like chicken. He tasted better.

Viktor waved for her attention. He'd finished drinking and was now pressing his tongue to the wound. Not for long, maybe five seconds before he straightened. "Our saliva has properties to heal."

"Nice." The bite mark closed and was already beginning to fade.

Carlos pressed his hand to his wrist. He seemed a touch paler.

"Will you be all right?" She touched his forehead but he seemed warm and steady.

His eyebrows rose. "I'm fine." He regarded Viktor. "She's sweet. Too sweet. You better take care of her or they'll eat her alive."

Chapter Nineteen

A muscle in Viktor's cheek ticked as he watched Carlos fade into the crowd. He had some brass balls to flirt with Trixie.

His unsolicited advice still rang in Viktor's ears. A human worried about a vampire's welfare. His gaze traveled to Trixie. The blue flashing lights turned her hair violet. Eyelids heavy, she leaned against the wall as if savoring Carlos' flavor.

A pang of jealousy pierced his icy heart. He had sensed her growing hunger from across the club. The bond between them was stronger. He had not experienced this with his sire. Most likely because his sire had died shortly after Viktor was made. Trixie's hunger had not driven his too hard this time. Not like at her apartment. With her distress, his instincts to protect had flared instead.

He needed to explore this more. Her blood needs should have sent his over the edge, yet even as he'd fed, he had only taken what was needed. He had been concerned with her the whole time.

Carlos wasn't wrong though. Viktor had witnessed the desire in his New Port lieutenant's eyes when he'd seen Trixie. She wore her innocence openly and carried so little baggage in comparison to them. She inspired things in men and not all of them good. Defending her from their people's bad tendencies would be difficult.

He should have left her with Eoin. The dragon was developing a kind heart with the aid of Angie, especially for stray vampires. Viktor had been selfish though. It had been so long since he had felt…anything.

Caging her between his arms, he leaned in for a taste of her lips. Sweet and shy response. He erased Carlos from her mouth. Only he would remain.

Her slender hands stroked his sides. Her touch tentative and unsure.

The veil of his long hair shielded their kiss from view. He ran his fangs over her swollen bottom lip and she shuddered. He loved how she responded to his touch. There were no lies in her reaction. For the first time in centuries, he was tempted to let another close to him. To give her his trust.

She was just too perfect.

He jerked away at the sudden thought.

Eyes closed, she followed him, lips pursed for more, and then she blinked her eyes open. "Okay." She smiled sheepishly and smoothed his shirt. Her cheeks flamed, matching her hair, and it took every ounce of his will power to not bite her. Slide his hand past her waistband and touch her—

"I've fed. Let's go." She pushed past him, heading toward the exit.

He hung his head and took a cleansing breath. Like an imbecile, he let her go. If he claimed her, he would only hurt her. Everything he loved, he destroyed. He wasn't much better than those he tried to protect her from. The monster she needed to stay away from the most was him.

She melded into the crowd but her hair was like a beacon. He wouldn't lose her. Not that easily.

He followed. Weak and infatuated. She was doomed.

It didn't take long to catch up. Where the crowds parted for him, Trixie was prone to getting stopped by men. He weaved his fingers with hers and stared down the man offering to buy her a drink. "She is taken."

The human swallowed visibly and left mid-sentence.

"You need to teach me how to do that." She squeezed his hand as he led her outside the club.

The night air was a cool balm on his skin. He would teach her many things. "Our destination is this way."

It was late but the nature of the tattoo business meant late hours. A perfect job for a vampire. He had heard of Reckless. Their poor reputation preceded them. They needled anyone who just wandered in, sober or not. Like a heartsick shifter girl.

Poor Betty. He would right the wrong done to her. He'd burn that book then take Trixie home.

His home?

Not the nest. Not with Paulo and his hungry stares. Viktor had wanted to protect her from himself. Now… he could not imagine letting her go.

Still holding hands, they strolled down the sidewalk. Some restaurants were open and a few patrons moved along the street.

"Was Carlos inviting us for a threesome?"

"Does that shock you?"

She was silent for a moment. "Yes. I mean, he was so open about it." She glanced quickly at his face. "Have you ever?"

He was not the sharing type. "No." If he took a lover, they belonged to him and only him.

She looked so relieved he wanted to hug her. "He didn't even know us and we're vampires." She sounded so adorably shocked. "Does he have a death wish?"

"Carlos knows me. I have used him as a donor before tonight. That is why I recognized him at the club." It was sheer luck he had been there.

She bit her bottom lip. "Did I break some vampire etiquette by refusing his advances?"

His smile faded. "No." He shrugged. "It is easier to feed if your human feels rewarded. Some want sex, others money or drugs—"

"I am *not* crossing any of those lines." Her nostrils flared. "Well, except money. I'd pay to be fed, but my bank account is usually hollow." She screwed up her face. "How much are we talking?"

"Don't worry about cost. As your sire, I'll cover your expenses."

"Forever?" She snorted. "I'd rather you teach me how to feed myself than hand over cash." She made a frustrated noise. "I don't want to hunt. I don't want to hurt anyone."

He chuckled. "Carlos didn't look like he was in any pain." The donor had enjoyed feeding them both. "You worry too much about the natural course of our kind."

"I do?" She tossed her hands in the air. "What if in a hundred years from now I'm too broke to buy blood? Then what? I'd have to seduce someone. That's not me. I don't want it to become me."

"You are worried about a hundred years from now?" He grabbed her fisted hands and kissed them open.

"I don't want you to take care of me. I want you to show me how to care for myself." She cupped his face. "I don't want to end up—"

"Like me." He sighed.

"I was going to say prostitute for blood, but hey, whatever floats your boat." She smiled. It was so infectious he grinned back.

"What if I want to take care of you?"

"There are many ways we can take care of each other."

"I plan on teaching you everything I know, which is quite a bit. It took me centuries to build this mass quantity of knowledge so do not expect it all over night." It would take years and years, but he did not mind. She was a ray of light in his otherwise dark life.

"How much further to the shop?" She glanced at the night sky. "Looks like rain." A strong wind blew as if it had heard her prediction. He loved the rain, especially thunderstorms, but he hurried his steps so Trixie would stay dry.

Two blocks over, the storefronts changed. Fewer restaurants and retail to more pawn shops and liquor stores. "Stay close. This is a rough part of the city."

She smirked. "Like where I grew up and live?"

"I just thought you were down on your luck and needed a cheap apartment."

"I've been down on my luck and needed a cheap apartment since birth." She frowned. "It's not easy to escape, you know. Nobody has ever given me and Ruby handouts. We both bust our asses to make ends meet." She chuckled softly. "Sorry, touchy subject."

"Obviously." He had been born a lord. A silver spoon in his mouth so when faced with poverty for the first time as a vampire degenerate, he had been useless. He had no survival skills, but the instincts of their kind. He smiled a little. Not like Trixie. She seemed at ease on these streets.

Her walk confident, her eyes watchful, and he noticed, her stance ready to fight.

She caught him staring at her fists. "I'm a nice person, Viktor. Not a stupid one. If someone attacks me, I'll kick ass. Not well, but I try."

He slid his arm around her. Pleased that she didn't shy away. "I would kill anyone who hurt you."

"Don't." Her gaze snapped to the open V of his shirt and the visible names peeking from under the material.

He shook his head and patted his chest. "These are people who suffered for my lack of self-control. My hunger demon's victims. If I murdered someone who dared touch you, I would be in full control of my mental capacity."

"That's sweet in a Jack-the-Ripper kind of way." She grimaced. "The things that come out of your mouth are disturbing."

"I was born in a different age. You cannot expect me to be—"

"Civilized?" She quirked her eyebrow.

"Civility is like beauty. It is in the eye of the beholder." He paused in front of their destination. "Let's have a chat with our dhampir." He had not met one before. They were the unicorns of their race.

"We should have a plan of action. What if she's been tattooing people with black magic on purpose? What if she's a witch and tries to curse us? Or maybe, she's plotting against the Riverbend pack. We should—"

He pressed his finger to her lips. "This is a reconnaissance mission only. We will talk to her, maybe make an appointment then ask to see samples of her work. From there, we will find shelter for the day and only then make a plan."

She sank back on her heels. "That's pretty anticlimactic."

"Did you want me to bust through the door, fangs ablazing?"

Trixie laughed. "I didn't think this far. I just wanted to find her."

"What would you do?"

"Ask politely for the book?"

He kissed her forehead. "In a different situation, that might work."

She shrugged. "What do I do? Stand there and look pretty?" Flat tone and expression.

"Not at all. Listen. Observe. We will compare notes afterwards." He opened the door for her and whispered for her ears only, "Follow my lead."

She stepped inside and halted just past the threshold.

Three barber chairs lined one wall and a table the other. Tattoo machines were set at each station. Silence greeted them. The place was empty.

The back door swung open and a tall man came out, wiping his hands on a white towel. Wide shouldered with a scowling expression, he marched across the shop. "We're closing early."

Trixie's face fell with genuine disappointment.

Viktor worked with what she had inspired and set his hand on her shoulder as if to offer comfort. "She was hoping to meet one of your artists, Jade Ellington. She had done work on her best friend. She wanted a matching piece."

The shop owner scratched his chin. "Jade? All my artists are men."

Viktor's gut dropped. It had been a long shot that the dhampir would still work here. It had been years since

Betty had had her tattoo inked. He had still hoped. "Maybe you know where she works now?"

"Well shit, you're the third person to come around here looking for her this month. She's been gone over a year. Her mom got sick and she had to leave suddenly and take care of her." He set his hands on his hips. "Is she in some kind of trouble? She's a good kid. I'd hate to see her hurt."

Viktor gave him a slow blink. Good kid?

"Thanks for your help." Trixie made to leave but he did not budge.

He had to find this book more than ever. If the dhampir was an innocent in all this, her safety was his responsibility. Not to mention he had to keep the peace between the hot-headed wolf pack alpha and the local nest. "Who else came looking for her?"

The shop owner drew closer, his eyes widening. "I know you."

He sensed Trixie stiffen as if ready to flee.

"You're Viktor Petrov." His mouth dropped open. "They featured your work on the New Port dragon in *Tattoo News*." His eyes sparkled with excitement. "I can't believe you're here. I'm a huge fan."

Trixie looked at him oddly. "You're a tattoo artist?"

"We all have to make a living. It was how I met Eoin."

"You never *once* mentioned this."

"We have been preoccupied," he said under his breath. He shook the shopkeeper's hand. "It is always good to meet another artist in the business."

"How do you do it? I mean, work on a dragon. Their hides must be tough as hell."

"Diamond tipped needles." He also used a silver infused ink, but he was not going to reveal all his secrets.

The shop owner nodded. "I didn't know they made those."

"Special order. Very expensive."

"Can I get a picture of us together? Nobody will believe you were in my shop." The shop owner handed Trixie his cell phone before Viktor could answer. "Just press here." He showed her then threw his arm over Viktor's shoulder.

That stupid article had been Eoin's agent's idea. Publicity. Since then he had been booked solid. Well, he *had* been. Who knew the state of his business since he'd been locked in Eoin's castle.

Trixie snapped a few pictures.

"Thanks." The owner retrieved his phone.

"The others?"

The shop owner went still. "Werewolves. I didn't ask what pack." He gestured to Trixie. "Why don't *you* ink her?"

"Because I'm not a dragon who needs diamond tipped needles." Her sarcasm sharp.

Viktor followed her outside. The rain was a steady down pour now. They huddled under the awning.

"The werewolves were from New Port. Ken sent them," she said.

Viktor nodded, recalling the text conversation he had read. "Makes sense, but the shop owner said we were the third group. Ken would not have sent people to the same location twice."

She crossed her arms. "When were you going to tell me you were famous?"

"Famous only in certain circles." He searched the street for a taxi, but the area seemed oddly deserted. It was late, but not enough for everyone to vanish. "Come on."

"Where are we going?"

"A hotel. We will spend the day there and then query other shops tomorrow evening."

They hurried from shelter to shelter, trying to stay dry.

"What if she moved away from Riverbend?"

That would be too convenient and make his life simple. The alpha would not get his revenge and the local vampires would not up rise in war. "I wish," he muttered. Glancing over his shoulder, he caught a shadow moving in the darkness.

"If she left Riverbend, she could be spreading her evil somewhere else," Trixie said.

He sighed. Trixie's good heart could be the death of him.

Another shadow moved in the corner of his eye. He kept their pace fast but casual, trying not to appear frightened. "Trixie," he whispered. "Run, when I give the signal."

CHAPTER TWENTY

Heart in her throat, she glanced over her shoulder and tried to spot any and all danger.

Viktor nudged her with his elbow. "Don't look suspicious. Control your scent of fear." He rested his arm over her shoulder, his hand loose and relaxed, as if they were out on a romantic stroll in a torrential rain storm.

"How the fuck do I control my scent?" Her whisper sounded like a hiss. If he had wanted her not to smell of fear, he shouldn't have warned her to run. That jacked a girl's heart rate.

Though he appeared relaxed, Viktor propelled them along the sidewalk at a faster and faster pace. "See the intersection ahead?"

She nodded, resisting the urge to wring her hands. "Sort of." The rain made it difficult, but she saw the better lit area and cobblestone.

"That's the street to the clubs. Once we reach it, I want you to sprint to Carlos. Tell him you are in danger and need help hiding. He will get you home."

With narrowed eyes, she glared at her sire. "What's going on? I don't see anyone following us."

"Werewolves." He nodded to the deep shadows of an empty alleyway. "On the hunt."

"What about you?" Trixie could sense hostile gazes digging in her back. She wouldn't abandon Viktor to face the pack alone.

"We have to split up. They only want me. You should be safe once I'm far away."

"I've met the Riverbend alpha at Betty's wedding. He should remember me." How many pink haired girls had he met at his ex-girlfriend's wedding? Especially ones who spilled champagne on his shoes?

Viktor grunted. "Who do you think is leading the hunt? Riverbend is not like New Port. The vampires and werewolves do not have an easy truce. It is more like I had to force feed it to them. The alpha is a hothead."

"And the nest leader?" Because every conflict had two sides.

"She is a sadistic bitch."

"Nice, when's their wedding?"

He stopped suddenly. "I cannot believe you can still joke." His gaze darted ahead as he crouched, ready to fight.

She wiped her soaking hair from her face and blinked the rain from her vision.

Shadows detached themselves from the dark, blocking their way to the intersection. Standing easily a foot taller than she with night-glow eyes, the werewolves stalked them in beast form. Shifters didn't change shape to look like their animal cousins. They were more of a blend of human and animal. Bigger, bipedal, and with the same mind as before. It wasn't against the law for shifters to run around in this form, but it was frowned upon.

Humans technically were weaker than supernatural creatures, but they outnumbered them ten-to-one. Pissing off humans never turned out well, and she was no longer on the winning team. These werewolves could kick her ass and there was nothing stopping them because vampires didn't exist to the rest of the world. Shit with a cherry on top.

"Cut off." Viktor circled slowly, back facing her. "They are surrounding us."

"What's plan B?" High pitched and thready. She knew how to throw a punch and to take one. She hadn't any problem with biting, kicking, or pulling hair, but it wasn't like she was part of some girl's fight club. These wolves moved like Viktor. Like predators. Maybe one day she would walk with such deadly grace, but today was not that day. Instead, she was on the menu.

A growl behind her. She spun around. The shifters stuck to the dark, shunning the faint street lights, but with her new vampire vision, she could make out their movements. Hunting as a pack within city limits in an area not marked as a hunting ground *was* illegal.

And here she was, thinking like a human again. Because no one gave a crap about a vampire.

She retreated, reaching behind her to get Viktor's attention. "There are more on this side." Her hand felt only air.

"Run!" Viktor commanded from high above her head. She glanced up, almost drowning in the rain, and glimpsed him hopping from one rooftop to another, away from the clubs and the intersection.

He'd left her?

"Run, dammit," he shouted again.

She glanced at the werewolves that been gathering and saw only darkness. Then in the distance she spotted a tail. The pack was chasing him.

He was leading them away from her.

She took a step in their direction as if she had the ability to fight off a pack of werewolves all on her own.

A werewolf strode out under the streetlight, arms crossed over his furry chest as if daring her to try to pass him. Another wolf crossed the street behind him, smaller and dainty, yet no less feral looking. She eyed Trixie from head to toe and licked her muzzle. "Fresh meat," she said to her pack mate.

Wait, what? She retreated, tripping off the sidewalk into the deserted street, ankle deep rain run-off. Scanning the street for an escape route, she came back empty handed. "This is all a big misunderstanding." She held her hands in front of her in a symbol of peace. "I met your alpha not long ago. We're friends." She bent the truth. He wasn't going to win the Mr. Personality award any time soon. She'd been secretly happy that Betty's relationship hadn't worked out. She was much better off with Ken.

Neither werewolf reacted.

"Stop toying with her," the wolf shifter behind her shouted. The one blocking her path to the bar district. "Get her already."

Trixie held her breath. Her vision focused on the werewolves to the point where she could count each individual hair. The rain slid off her skin unnoticed and the sound of heartbeats filled her ears. Her pulse galloped and her muscles tensed, ready to spring.

Self-preservation kicked in. Years of street living in rough neighborhoods had honed those instincts. She spun on her heel and rushed toward the intersection guarded by the asshole shouting for them to *get her*.

People. She needed to be surrounded by witnesses. The shifters wouldn't dare hurt her in public. She was a vampire, but to the humans, she looked like one of them. If they saw werewolves picking on a girl, the National Guard would be called.

The shifter blocking her way stood rooted to the ground, muzzle unhinged.

She was *moving*. The rain drops hung motionless in the air as she smashed through them. The shifter's mouth closed in slow motion.

"She's a vampire," he shouted, the sound dragged out and unnaturally deep.

She tucked her chin to her chest and rolled into a tight ball, right through the werewolf's long legs. It worked. The rain poured on her head again. She had more momentum than she'd thought and instead of rolling to her feet to continue running, like she normally would, she stopped on her ass and bounced over the wet pavement like a skipped stone. The impact left her teeth rattling in her head.

"She's supposed to be human." Female voice shouted. She could hear their clawed footfalls, closing the distance.

Leaving her DNA on the asphalt, Trixie scrambled to her feet. Head spinning and ass smarting, she ran onto the populated cobblestone street lined with night life. The werewolves had thought she was human and that was what saved her. Why would they think she was human when she was with Viktor?

She ran at human speed, not looking back and straight for the club where she had met Carlos. What was the donor going to do for her? He couldn't fight off a pack of shifters — she pressed between the parked cars to cross the street — but Carlos might know some of the local nest. They could help her save Viktor. Yes, that was the plan.

A familiar face watched her from the humans. He stepped into her path, his eyes flashing amber. His tight T-shirt soaked and molding to his muscled chest.

Trixie stopped on a dime in the middle of the road. Crap, in her hurry, she'd forgotten they could look human too.

A car honked long and hard.

Before she could blink, she was yanked into his thick, veined arms and out of the way of danger.

She waggled her fingers in a little wave. His face mere inches from hers. "Hi, Chris."

The wolves were good. Moving like a military unit, they herded Viktor yet managed to stick to the shadows and out of the humans' sight. It was an unspoken rule to hide their battles from the humans. His real concern was their goal.

He snorted. When had he last been prey? The beat of his heart was a palpable thing. His blood sang in his veins and he wanted nothing more than to leap into the fray of battle and confront the pack. Have a good honest fight.

Not tonight. Not in this city. The truce was too fragile. One little crack would shatter all civility. It was a bad omen that pack felt confident to hunt him. The hostilities must be worse than he had been informed. Aggression came naturally, but as Master of the City, he led by example. Until he knew the facts of what had happened between pack and nest, he would not resort to violence. If war broke out in Riverbend, the vampire and shifter ruling bodies would want it extinguished fast. That meant sending him in to kill them all.

He had to focus before he tripped off the rooftops. The rain made the footing traitorous. Instead of fighting, he let the pack continue to guide his steps. The only blessing was that Trixie had escaped. He had seen her ingenious roll and awkward landing. Then she'd run to the bar section of the city. She would escape them there. He had faith in her.

He smiled. She was not used to her new strength and speed, but she'd managed it well. The look on that wolf's face as she'd rolled between his legs would be added to his cherished memories.

A clothesline full of soaking sheets crossed his path. He turned direction to keep the pack's attention from Trixie.

Werewolves awaited him on the adjunct roof.

He stopped his jump, pinwheeling his arms for balance. He spun around. Shifters closed in from behind.

He tore the sheets aside and came face-to-face with the pack's second in command. "Jeffery." He pulled up short before trampling him. "Thank you for the workout. It was exhilarating." They had never met but he made sure to know the faces and names of any major players in his cities.

"It's Ryan." The big shifter folded his ears back.

"What happened to Jeffery?" So, he did not have the best memory.

"Dead. He didn't recover from his wounds after our challenge fight."

He made note of Ryan. Not sure why he bothered. Riverbend's wolf pack changed betas almost on a yearly basis. That didn't speak well for pack stability or the alpha's leadership skills. Hell, he was a vampire and he understood this. What was the alpha thinking?

"I'm happy to oblige in hunting you down, Master of the City, but my alpha would like a word with you."

Viktor eyed the suddenly polite werewolf. "You should've asked before hunting me across the city."

"You ran before we could."

He opened his mouth to respond and paused. Ryan spoke the truth. Had Viktor overreacted when faced with Riverbend's pack while alone with Trixie? He thought not. "You could have approached me in a less threatening manner." If they had been in human form, he would not have sent Trixie off alone.

Ryan smirked. "Yes, I could have." He gestured to the other wolf shifters. "Bind him."

"That is not—" Shoved from behind, he lost his balance.

It took every shifter on the roof to hold him down and bind his wrist behind his back with silver chains. The metal was of poor quality and did not even burn his flesh. Snapping it would be easy, but he did not want to escape yet. How else would he find out what the alpha wanted?

Trixie had had enough time to find Carlos. Viktor had sensed the human had a protective streak for new vampires. Carlos would make sure she returned to New Port. At the next chance, he would call the nest there to meet her feeding needs. Maybe he should ask Angie if Trixie could return to the castle. Viktor would not tolerate her living with Paulo.

Ryan took him by one arm while another soldier took the other. They guided him off the rooftop.

"How long of a run do we have? The sun will be rising soon."

"We arranged a car." The beta stood a head shorter than him. In single combat, a vampire would always beat a shifter, but werewolves tended to fight in coordinated groups. Something his kind lacked.

The staircase leading to the first door was empty, the building silent as the occupants slept. Outside, a car pulled up and parked in front of the exit.

One of the pack opened the back door. Inside sat Chris, the pack alpha, in human form. Soaking wet. He leaned back so Viktor could see the other passenger.

Viktor's heart dropped.

"Hi." Shoulders slumped and rain soaked, Trixie waved, a sheepish look on her face. "He caught me outside the club."

Viktor broke loose of his werewolf guards. Before he could reach her, Chris pressed his clawed fingers around her throat. Viktor halted so fast the guards missed their mark as they tried to restrain him again. "Did he hurt you?" he asked his precious fledgling.

She shook her head and mouthed the words *I'm sorry*. He wanted to gather her in his arms and sooth the dejected expression from her face. Make her laugh, make her smile. She'd thought she'd failed him, but the opposite was the truth. He had failed her. He had placed her in an impossible situation.

His eyes narrowed as he glared at the alpha. Viktor had placed her in an impossible situation. Chris was smarter than Viktor gave him credit for. The alpha could not do him any real damage or keep him prisoner, but Trixie... She was still so young and fragile. The alpha could easily kill her.

Viktor entered the car.

CHAPTER TWENTY-ONE

Trixie had let Viktor down. She could see it in his eyes even though he smiled reassuringly as he sat across from her in the stretch limousine. She had never ridden in one before. The back part had two benches facing each other. Though their lives were in danger, she couldn't ignore the fact that she was riding in a freaking white limousine with the pack alpha and the city's most dangerous vampire. Two of the hottest men on the planet.

Ruby would never believe her.

The vehicle rode smoothly while both males glared daggers at each other. Werewolves had piled inside the limo on either side of Viktor, still in their shifter form. It left her feeling like a sardine.

"Viktor, I presume." Chris, a.k.a. Betty's ex-boyfriend, rested his arm over the back of their shared bench.

"You are correct." Viktor's gaze washed over her as if making note of every scrape and bump on her exposed skin. What he didn't know was that all of them had been self-inflicted in her so-called fancy escape.

"I'm Chris Jenkins, the—"

"I know who you are." The vampire struggled against his chains, but the alpha growled and rested his hand back on her neck in a veiled threat.

"Easy boys." She gestured slowly for Viktor to relax. "I'm fine." She aimed that directly at him. "The scrapes are from my dumbass roll." Not to mention the bruises on her ass.

"She's a fledgling, Christopher. Only a couple of days old and very delicate. You best be very careful." One didn't need to see Viktor's fangs or vampire strength to understand his own threat.

"I go by Chris." The alpha's hand remained on her neck but it was gentle, as he stroked his thumb along her carotid. "So, only a few days old. I *knew* you were human when we met. Were you turned against your will?"

Viktor snarled but stayed on his side of the limo.

"Viktor saved my life. If he hadn't turned me, I'd be dead."

The oxygen seemed thin and she couldn't catch her breath. There was way too much testosterone in the air. She cracked the window open.

Chris raised an eyebrow in question to her action.

"Claustrophobic."

His eyes narrowed. "I'm faster than you and not in the best of moods. Don't make the mistake of trying to jump out."

According to Betty, he was never in a good humor.

"Dude, seriously, did you miss the delicate comment made by Viktor?" They were driving at least fifty miles an hour. "I don't care to leave pieces of me on the road."

The shifters on either side of Viktor stiffened and glanced at each other with ears back. They apparently didn't like her tone. However, treat her like a numbskull and she'd return the favor.

Chris gave her a tolerant smile. "I see why Betty likes you."

Yeah, because they could both be bitches when they wanted.

The alpha turned his attention back to Viktor. "I understand you are the real master of the city."

Her vampire quietly assessed the alpha. She squirmed as the silence grew longer. Finally, Viktor nodded. "I monitor the city's vampire nest. Not the day to day events, but they answer to me."

Chris nodded. "Good. Where do you make your home then?"

"Why?" Viktor asked.

At the same time, she responded, "New Port."

Viktor frowned in her direction.

She rolled her eyes. "You were featured in a magazine. I'm sure Chris knows how to Google. It's not exactly a secret."

She scaled back, tired of the games. While they drove through the city, they could have been trying to find the dhampir.

"You didn't attend the mating ceremony of the alpha's only son. I thought relations between vampires and shifters in New Port were better than here."

"I was otherwise occupied."

Like chained in a dragon's dungeon. She had to bite her bottom lip to keep her mouth shut.

"The New Port nest's leader went in my place."

She blinked. Paulo had been at the wedding? There'd been so many people. So many supernatural types, she had been overwhelmed. Paulo hadn't even hit her radar. Viktor would have and she wished he could have seen her in the only gown she owned. She had rocked that dress.

Ken had footed the bill for the wedding. Something about shifter rules and him being more dominant than Betty. Whatever. It worked for her, otherwise Trixie would have shown up as maid of honor in a paper bag. She was that broke.

The limo slowed to a stop and the shifters dragged Viktor out. Chris offered her a gentlemanly hand and helped her exit the car.

She paused outside the vehicle. They stood in front of a brick building that resembled her craptastic apartment. Rusty metal fire escapes lined the alley walls, ladders connecting them. The windows were all intact but the paint peeled. Huge chunks of missing paint chips exposed the aging gray wood underneath. She glanced at the fancy expensive limo as she crossed the uneven and cracked sidewalk to the entrance.

Chris caught her. "I don't own the car. The driver owns a limo rental company and he is pack. He lets us borrow one when needed."

"Oh." What else could she say? The alpha in New Port was rolling in dough. She'd assumed all shifters were rich. Honestly, the only poor werewolf she'd met was Betty and she'd come from Riverbend. Who was Trixie to judge Chris? She lived paycheck to paycheck on a tightrope budget. If she and Ruby were lucky, they could buy a nice steak to share once a month.

Keeping her mouth shut, Trixie followed the alpha as he climbed the stairs to the top floor. If she'd been human, she would have been gasping for air by now.

Only three of the shifters had joined them. The way Viktor glared at the werewolves made her realize he was thinking of beating the shit out of them and escaping.

Chris unlocked the door and gestured for everyone to enter.

She hesitated. "Chris, what is the point of capturing us?"

When he answered, it was aimed at Viktor. "I think we have a common goal. Maybe we can help each other out."

"Then why the chains?" This time Viktor did show his fangs.

The alpha chuckled. "I heard rumors that you liked them."

Trixie spun to face Chris. "You can't be that stupid. Do you have a death wish?" Like a paper barrier, she stood between two super predators. "Play nice." She used her sit-and-lay-down voice that she'd learned as an animal control specialist.

Viktor met her gaze and she nodded to the unasked demand in his eyes. Sure, Chris wasn't going to win werewolf of the year, but he could have hurt Viktor. Well, maybe not, but he could have killed her easily. Someone needed to start trusting the other if they were ever going to get anywhere.

Chris tossed a key to Ryan, who unchained Viktor.

Hey, the voice had worked. Who knew?

Her sire scanned the small and sparsely decorated apartment. She bet he knew every escape access point once done. "I will listen." He crossed his arms, legs spread apart, his presence taking up most of the living room.

Chris went to the connecting open kitchen and pulled meat and bread from the fridge. Absentmindedly, he started the process of making sandwiches on the counter facing the living room. "Go change," he spoke to the other werewolves. "I'll be fine."

The werewolves went into what must be the only bedroom and closed the door.

Viktor raised his eyebrows. "You sound so sure."

"I have her." He winked at Trixie. "I'm young, but I'm not a fool. You said it yourself—she's delicate for a vampire." His hands moved with a hypnotic grace as he made five sandwiches at the same time. Cheese, meat, mayo—

"Can we stop threatening to kill me?" She stood across the counter from Chris. It was L-shaped with two stools on one side. "You're very practiced at this." She pointed at his sandwich making skills.

The other wolf shifters exited the bedroom. All of them in human form and lean with muscled tension. They wore matching sweatpants and T-shirts. She had hung out with enough shifters to know that stashes of clothes were kept for packmates to borrow.

Chris handed out the food as they passed the kitchen. "I have to be. Hungry shifters are dangerous shifters." He folded his arms and grinned "I also own the sandwich shop on the river shore."

Viktor pressed behind her, his hard chest aligning with her spine. "How nice." He circled his arms around her in a possessive hug. "Which of my goals were you referring to?"

Viktor did *not* like the flirting. The wolf was treading on thin ice as it was, yet he thought he could try and steal Trixie's affection. Unlike most of vampire kind, Viktor had no problem draining a shifter dry. Blood was blood and he could always use mouthwash to get rid of the taste.

Trixie leaned into him. It felt natural wrapping his arms around her, as if they had been like this forever.

"Don't play dumb." Chris snapped at him, his gaze darting to Viktor's hold on Trixie. "We've been monitoring your movements since the coffee shop. Why did you go to that particular tattoo parlor?"

He smirked, very aware that though the other shifters in the room were eating, they also listened intently. "I am a tattoo artist myself. I like to check out the competition."

Werewolves could smell lies. He was experienced enough to know how much truth was needed to mask them. The undercurrent of tension in Riverbend always tasted old and spoiled. It was his place to police the nest in the city, but not to mend old feuds.

He could hear Christopher grinding his teeth. "Bullshit," the alpha spat out. "You don't have competition at the shop. If the owner wasn't a bookie and using his place as a front, it would have closed years ago."

"Then why would I go there?" Viktor rested his chin on Trixie's head. She was the perfect height. He could hold her like this all night, smelling her sweet shampoo. Strawberries? Yes, definitely strawberries.

Christopher's eyes narrowed as he circled around counter.

Viktor slid Trixie behind him in an easy move. She was graceful in the transition and stayed close, resting her hands on his hips and peering round his arm.

"Betty." The alpha stated the name like a curse.

Viktor blew out a frustrated breath and glared at his companions. "I know Betty's story. I was the one who discovered the magic in the tattoo." Sometimes he hated it when he was right. The alpha was looking for revenge. "I also know the dragon called you." And inadvertently possibly started a war.

He pulled Trixie with him toward the loveseat, forcing the shifters occupying the space to move. He and Trixie sat.

Him with his legs crossed and arms resting on the top of the couch. Trixie straight-backed, knees pressed together. The piece of furniture was small and forced them close together.

"I'm here to prevent things from escalating between your pack and the local vampire nest," said Viktor. "One of ours wronged one of yours. I want to—"

"Wronged one of mine? Wronged me!" Christopher slapped his chest. "That dhampir monstrosity wrecked everything."

The growl in his voice triggered the other shifters. They set their food aside, eyes focused on the floor, and none of them moved.

Interesting. He assessed the young alpha carefully. "How so?"

Trixie's elbow embedded between his ribs. He had to stifle a laugh or the alpha might explode in bits of fur.

Christopher's eyes glowed the pale icy blue of Nordic wolves. "She stole my mate. If it wasn't for her, Betty would still be mine."

"No, she wouldn't." Trixie shook her head, indignation in the line of her spine. "You need to get over—"

Viktor slid his hand over her mouth from behind. It was one thing for Viktor to taunt the alpha—the wolf could not hurt him—but Trixie was still almost human weak. "Let's not rile the werewolf any more than we have to."

She nodded. He could sense her lips pressed together as if fighting to keep her words. Then he let her go.

The alpha paced. "We won't ever know the truth, will we?" He bared his teeth. "But I can taste my revenge. The parlor is where Betty was cursed with that fucking tattoo. Once my scouts spotted you entering there, I knew there was a connection."

Trixie leaned forward. "You were the other shifter that interrogated the owner. I didn't think Ken would have sent two separate parties to question him."

Christopher rolled his shoulders. Viktor could see the joints shifting below his skin as he struggled for control. "Ken never asked permission to cross into my territory."

"Yes, yes." Viktor waved his hand, brushing aside the issue. "That is another problem for another day. The artist we seek is gone and the owner does not have any information as to where. We are both shit out of luck."

Trixie sighed.

Christopher hesitated in his stalking pace.

Viktor leaned forward, elbows on his knees. "*You* know where Jade is." The real question was why the dhampir was still alive when the alpha was so obviously pissed.

Christophe nodded. "When news of Betty shifting reached the city, word spread like wildfire. Betty's father told me about the tattoo." As part of the Riverbend pack, Betty's father would have to report to his alpha whether he wanted to or not. "I looked for the witch that day but she'd already gone into hiding."

"Not a witch," he corrected. "A dhampir. She is half-human, half-vampire."

"I know what a dhampir is." Christopher grabbed a sandwich on the counter and destroyed it in three bites. He gestured to his pack mates to finish eating. They visibly relaxed and retrieved their food.

Trixie's eyes were wide. "I think his jaw unhinged."

"Probably."

The alpha darted a glare their way. "Shut up. I stress eat."

His fledgling bit her bottom lip, her cheeks flushed with poorly hidden amusement. Her adorable little fang peeked out and Viktor could not pull his attention away from it. "But you found her."

"Her mother is a member of the local nest. I'm sure she's hiding in there."

"How does that work?" Asked Trixie. "I mean, how can a vampire get pregnant?"

"We're still fertile post-change. It's just extremely rare that we conceive. Obviously, those odds are better with a human. The dhampir must have been raised by her mother's nest. That means that they will protect her."

Christopher nodded. "We can't get anywhere near the place." He grinned. "But you can."

CHAPTER TWENTY-TWO

Trixie pumped her fist. "Yes, this should be easy."

The look Viktor gave her said otherwise.

She groaned. It had *sounded* so easy. "I forgot about your issues with the nest's leader. You're *their* master. Shouldn't she be afraid of you?" Trixie made sure to be clear that he wasn't her master.

Viktor leaned his chin in his hand. An amused expression on his overly handsome face. "When is anything easy when dealing with politics? And for your information..." He gently clasped her chin in his fingers and drew her close enough that their breaths kissed. "I am not afraid of her. I just don't like being in the same room with her." He released her.

She let go of the breath she'd been holding. "Can't you just go in demanding for the dhampir?" Now that she said it, she wasn't sure that was a great idea.

His smile confirmed her thought.

"I watch too much television, don't I?"

Chris laughed. "I guess I do too. That's what I was hoping he could do." He sat across from them. At his laughter, the other shifters seemed to finally breathe. She had noticed how nervous they'd been when Chris was angry. "What is stopping you?"

"How would you react if someone strode into your pack, demanding one of your children?" Viktor shook his head. "I will not do it. Our children are so rare. I will not turn her over to you."

Chris punched the arm of the chair. It broke off with a loud snap. He stared at the broken piece. "Fuck, I just bought this." He massaged the bridge of his nose. "I'm not going to kill her. I just want to…" He growled.

"Throttle her?" Trixie offered, because that was what she wanted to do.

Viktor tossed her a concerned glare.

She shrugged. Nothing like a lover scorned to bring on murderous intention. They'd all been there. In the end though, the murderous thoughts were just poor wishes they'd never actually act upon. Chris had it bad. Betty had left Riverbend years ago; she was mated to another wolf shifter, and *still* Chris pined for her.

This wasn't healthy. "You might kill the dhampir."

"I just need to understand why she did it. That tattoo wrecked everything. The lack of motive is driving me mad. I never wronged the vampires before then. Neither did Betty. Why attack her?"

"We actually did not come for the dhampir." Viktor clasped his hands, looking very sane, and very much a seasoned leader. He had changed so much since she'd met him. Maybe having a purpose helped? Living for so long must get boring. Enough so that someone could lose their mind and end up in a dragon's dungeon.

Was that her future? Not if she had it her way. She knew how to keep busy. There were so many things she wanted to see and learn. She'd drag Viktor along with her and keep him sane.

"We came for the book she owns. The one Betty chose her tattoo design from. I suspect that's the source of the black magic and it must be destroyed."

"Have you checked anyone else in your pack for similar tattoos?" she asked.

"As soon as I heard about the incident, everyone was checked. No one used that artist but Betty. The place is more of a human hangout than a shifter one."

That made sense. Betty had gotten tattooed just before the pack had declared her human. She might have been trying to connect to her mother's people by hanging out with them.

It didn't really matter why Betty had gone. What mattered was preventing any harm happening to others.

Chris rubbed his chin. "So, there's a book of black magic involved. Not surprising when it comes to vampires."

"Hey, they're not all bad." Out of the corner of her eye she caught Viktor absentmindedly opening the collar of his shirt and exposing a name. She frowned at the alpha. "Well, I don't plan on going bad." For fuck's sake, couldn't she get a break?

"Trixie and I will visit the nest tomorrow night and try to locate the dhampir. Then they will see if she still has the book."

Chris' frown deepened, concern aging his young face. "I think they still have it. The book's existence explains some weird incidents lately."

"Like what?" Fear tiptoed along her spine. Tomorrow night's visit to the vampire nest had the fixings of a disaster.

The alpha rubbed his chin. "There have been two reported spontaneous combustions in the last weeks. At least, that's what the humans are calling it."

"You think they were vampires?" she asked.

Viktor grew still as stone. "Yes."

She couldn't imagine the pain. She didn't want to. "Why would they walk out into the sunlight?" Suicide?

"That's not the weird part." Chris' eyebrows rose. "It was midday and they went up in flames far from any shelter." He counted off on his fingers. "First one went up in the middle of Belfurred Park, and the second was at the farmers market. It's not like they jumped out of a window or exited a building and then went up in flames."

"They died a distance from their shelter. That's impossible." Viktor's dark eyes swallowed the light. They did not reflect anything from the room as he sat in silent contemplation.

"You do tattoo magic?" Chris asked.

Viktor quirked an eyebrow. "I have not a drop of magic in my blood." He winked. "Only charm."

One of the shifters made a gagging noise.

"I mean, how would a tattoo stop a shifter from changing shape?" Chris' face was pinched with concern. "It's just ink and flesh."

Magic was rare and weird, but she loved watching the documentaries on witches. "It's not just ink and flesh if the dhampir was born with magic. Add the symbol from the black magic book and *voilà*, a spell. Betty had never changed shape so all the magic had to do was continue that trait. If you had gotten that tattoo, it probably wouldn't have worked because you could already change shape. I'm not an expert, but that doesn't sound like a hard spell to do."

Chris rose to his feet, clapping his hands together. "Then it's decided. Viktor goes to the nest tomorrow night and retrieves the magic book."

"I have already explained that this plan wouldn't work." Viktor rose more slowly.

"That's when I asked you to go in after the dhampir. I understand your people being protective of their children, but they shouldn't refuse you the book. Or are you afraid?"

Her sire stood toe to toe to Riverbend's alpha, meeting his stare. "What do you want with this book?"

Trixie wanted to yank them both by the ears. They had the same objective and they'd be stronger together than apart. Couldn't they corroborate without the macho posturing?

"I'm going to burn it and make sure your kind doesn't mess with mine again." The alpha crossed his arms, his pack mates gathering behind him.

"See." Trixie got to her feet. "He wants to destroy it too. Can we be friends now?"

Viktor tongued his fang as if a piece of food were caught. How? They were on a liquid diet.

She elbowed him again.

"Fine." He spoke. "I will keep you apprised of what I discover." He snaked his arm around her waist and made to leave the room, but the werewolves blocked their path.

"You'll be my guests until the book is in my hands." Chris suddenly seemed much bigger. He took up more space without actually shifting. She'd met the New Port wolf alpha at Betty's mating ceremony. He had the same aura. Somehow Chris had hidden it until now.

But there was a flaw in Chris' thinking. When they went to the nest, there was no reason for them to come back. She smiled. "Okay, where are we sleeping? Has to be light proof."

Viktor didn't look happy. She would explain it to him once they were alone, then he'd understand that they had nothing to worry about.

"We have accommodations in the basement," said Chris.

"You have a change of clothes?" She gestured to her wet T-shirt and jeans smeared with dirt from the car trunk and her rough and tumble over the pavement. "I don't want to make a bad first impression when we go to the nest tomorrow night." Who knew—maybe she would visit this nest again?

Chris squished his eyebrows together. "You're not going. You're my collateral in case Viktor skips town with the book."

"What?" She glanced at Viktor for confirmation.

"He thinks you are his hostage." Viktor grabbed the closest wolf shifter by the throat. He moved so fast she hadn't had time to blink.

Unfortunately, Chris moved just as quickly. Claws pricked her throat. This game was getting old.

She slapped at it and tried to wiggle free and only managed to cut her skin on the claws sharp edges. Yeah, no luck there.

"It won't take much effort to tear her head off." Chris kissed her cheek.

Viktor's ink black eyes flared with dark heat that seared her retinas. He set his captive down.

"You made it very clear that she belongs to you." Chris stroked her hair. "I would hate to hurt someone that Betty cares about, but for my pack, I would make any sacrifice."

Trixie wanted to slap the stupid out of herself. All that flirting had been on *purpose*. He had been testing Viktor's reaction. Chris was smarter than he looked, and if his claws hadn't been pressed to her jugular, she would be impressed.

"You might be strong enough to beat all of us, but not before I kill her."

"You'd kill me?" She kicked him with her heel.

"Nothing personal. Pack safety always comes first. Cute, pink haired vampires second."

She couldn't fault his priorities. "We want the same thing as you. There's no double-cross to be had."

"Then your being my guest shouldn't be an issue."

Viktor growled. "No harm will come to her?" It was more of a command then a question.

"As long as you fulfill your part of the deal."

"And if I'm killed?" Viktor set the shifter he'd been holding aside and slowly drew closer.

"Killed?" She and Chris parroted each other.

Viktor pursed his lips. "I have already explained that I am not on good terms with the nest's leader." He rubbed his chin. "If I recall, I left her tied to a tree outside the city for breaking a cardinal human law. Or was it for stealing one of my lovers?" He scratched his head. "I cannot recall which was last."

"Yeah, we get it. You're not friends." She crossed her arms and gave Chris the side eye. "Are you planning on holding me like this all night?"

He retracted his claws. "You're their leader. Lead." Chris seemed genuinely perplexed.

"We do not govern our nests like pack. If I stride in making demands and threats, it would only incite rebellion," responded Viktor.

She had to side with her maker. As a person raised in a democracy, she would buck against any dictator-ish demands.

The alpha looked like he had a splintered bone stuck in his gums. "Escort my guests to their rooms."

"We will share one." Viktor possessively wrapped his arm around her shoulders. "Trixie will need to feed again when she wakes. Can you manage to acquire some blood without a massacre?"

His regal tone obviously rubbed Chris the wrong way.

"We can." The alpha took her hand and kissed her knuckles, lingering a few seconds too long. "I will be sure Trixie's every desire is met in your absence."

She could sense Viktor's predator tension climbing. For all his intelligence and finesse, he was still a killer. She tapped Chris on the nose hard. "Behave."

He looked stunned.

If he was going to act like a dog, then she'd treat him like one.

A shifter guard opened the door and ushered them out before things escalated. Smart wolf. Chris also could use a few lessons. She eyed Viktor. So could he. "You shouldn't let him goad you."

"He should not be touching you." Viktor tossed a death glare at the smirking alpha, who leaned against the apartment doorframe, watching them descend the stairs.

She poked Viktor. "Stop it. You're only encouraging him." Part of her was flattered. She'd never had anyone except Ruby and Betty stand up for her. Viktor felt responsible since he was her sire, but this seemed like more than that. She didn't want to place words on those feelings yet. It would give her false hope.

The werewolf boys took them to the basement where they had a nicely decorated room waiting for them. Desk, chair, books, television... She stared at the single twin bed.

"He's the one insisting you share." One of the guards nodded at Viktor. "Change your mind?" He directed the question at her.

"No," Viktor responded before she could.

The guard closed and locked the door.

She spun a slow circle. No windows. "Does everyone have a dungeon except me?"

"By dungeon standards, this is not bad." Viktor turned on the television and flipped through the channels. "Clean and furnished with entertainment." He glanced at her. "I would guess that this is really a safe room used by the pack." He tested the door by pushing. "Steel reinforced." Then he scratched at the walls and licked his fingers. "Silver mixed into the concrete. Definitely a safe room."

Fighting to keep disgust from showing on her face, she stared at the scratched spot on the wall. "You can taste silver?"

"It tingles on your tongue. In larger quantities, it would burn." He held up his finger. "Want to taste?"

No matter how curious, she would not lick his dirty finger. "What is a safe room?" She thought she had heard Ken refer to one, but she still hadn't a clue what it meant.

"A place where shifters with control issues can stay." Viktor retrieved the remote and chose a fishing show. "I do not know much more than that. Shifters are a secretive race."

"Yeah, and vampires are so forthcoming." She stared at the fishermen reeling in a bass — trout — salmon? A big, fighty fish. "You like fishing?"

His gaze was fixed on the screen. "I like sunshine."

Blue sky, clear water, and sunlight sparkling on the ripples. She flopped onto the edge of the bed. She'd never see the sun again, feel the heat on her face, or tan at the park with Ruby.

Viktor slid behind her, lying on his side. "We can change the channel if it bothers you."

"No." It came out as a whisper. They had been so busy the last couple of nights that the reality of her vampirism hadn't had a chance to settle. "How long do we live on average?"

"If you survive the first decade, a few centuries." He sighed and rested his head on his hand. "If you survive that then you end up like me." He didn't appear happy.

The bed flattered him. Heck, he looked good in anything. She could hear Ruby's voice in her head *live in the moment* or Betty's *take a chance*.

The crease between Viktor's eyebrows deepened. "I never wanted the responsibility of governing nests. Making them play nice while I broke the rules. The hypocrisy of it isn't lost on me, Trixie." Darkness in his eyes pulled her into their depth. "I want to be a better person. Have been striving for it since I moved to New Port. It seems like an impossible task."

She crawled in next to him and kept his face in her hands, her heart breaking at his pain. His regret. "What's stopping you?"

CHAPTER TWENTY-THREE

He chuckled. "Where do I begin?" Trixie's hands warmed an empty place in his chest. "Have I shown you *all* of these?" Viktor undid the front of his shirt one button at a time and enjoyed her focused attention on his fingers. He pulled the edges open, displaying the many names on his flesh.

She traced her fingertips over one. "I didn't know you had so many." Her fingertips tickled as she traced her way along his rib cage. "Why'd you do it?"

His amusement sizzled. Most women would have been helping him pull off the remainder of his clothes at this point. "What do you mean?"

"All these names. You said they are your victims. Why tattoo them on your skin?" Her touch branded his skin deeper than the ink.

He held his breath, letting her caress move from name to name. "Regret." The words tumbled in his throat like stones. Viktor sat up, leaning his back to the wall, unable to think while her hands were on his flesh. "I need you to comprehend that I do not choose to do this. It's not on purpose." He pressed his lips together as Trixie's confusion showed on her face. "I did not choose to be a vampire."

Her eyebrows drew down. "Neither did I." He could almost sense her worry through her skin. She did not want to become like him. How could he blame her?

He pulled her onto his lap, caressing her cheek. He could not seem to be in the same room with her without needing to touch her. "I know and I will ensure that you have everything I never did."

"Viktor." Her voice shook. "What did you mean by that? If you want me to understand, to trust you, then you have to explain things better."

He glanced at the blue sky on the television. A vision flashed in his mind of the last time he had seen the sun with his own eyes. "Times were different when I was a young man." He spoke slowly, treading along very old memories he kept buried. The pain had aged like a fine wine, but it did not hurt any less. "At the age of twenty, I had been considered a man for many years. A seasoned warrior and leader of my people in what is now considered Russia. I was a Boyar…umm, a Lord is the best translation."

She sat up straighter. "How long ago are we talking?"

"Eight hundred years, give or take a few decades." He shrugged. "I did not keep records or pay much head to such things. I had bigger problems drawing my attention." Even now his soul cringed. He recalled standing on a hilltop, staring over the battlefield as a swarm of horsemen rode over his men. "It was a time of death."

"Disease?" she whispered.

"Nothing so simple. The Mongols were sweeping across the country. Many died in their wake, including myself." He smiled wearily, tired of thinking of the past. The burden heavy on his conscience. "I woke on the battlefield the night I died. Alone and changed. I did not understand what had been done to me. Like any man, I made my way home only to find my wife and children massacred."

She gasped, her hands fisting his shirt. "Viktor…"

He pressed his fingers to her lips. Not wanting to hear her sorrow. If she wanted to know what had driven him to madness, then she had to listen while he could still speak it. "I have had ages to mourn and made peace with that loss." He had also had ages to leave a trail of bodies. "What I want you to learn is something I discovered too late." He sat forward, pinning her stare with his. "I explained not to abstain from drinking blood. You will not win. The bloodlust is too strong and your instinct to survive will always overcome your desire not to kill."

Trixie swallowed visibly. "What if I can't find a willing donor? It seems so complicated. I'm not a hunter at heart."

He shook his head. "In this age, there are many options."

"Is that what happened? You tried not to drink anyone's blood."

"Unfortunately, yes. I did not know of vampires. My desire for blood seem so unnatural, my aversion to light and increased strength. I thought I had been made into a demon. Science had not been practiced widely yet and witchcraft was very strong in my land." He leaned back against the wall again and stared down at the names. "Every time I starved myself, my bloodlust grew worse and the less control I had on it. I killed many people and lived like an animal in the countryside."

"For how long?"

He scratched his chin. "I do not know. I discovered a vampire nest once I crossed into Europe. Italy, if I remember correctly. Their leader took pity on me. Chained me in their dungeon and fed me until my sanity returned." He closed his eyes. "Since then I have struggled."

She rested her head on his chest. "So, the moral of the story is don't fight what I've become." She took a long shuddering breath. "What about my sister? How long before she's safe around me? I've been around other humans without a slip."

"You have done very well and I was here to make sure you were always fed. Can you do the same by yourself? Are you willing to chance your sister's life if you do slip?"

She shook her head. "I still have a lot to learn."

"We keep you well fed. You do not visit your sister unless you've had blood within a few hours." He frowned, recalling her sister's stabbing glare. "We teach her as well. She must follow the rules or her death will weigh upon you forever."

"Oh God, I don't even want to think about that."

He opened his eyes.

Trixie had her hands pressed to her mouth. "I managed to feed from Carlos without hurting him though."

He grinned, pride swelling his chest. "Yes, you did."

She lowered her hands and smiled. "That's a step in the right direction."

He had not needed to restrain her or pull her away. Her kind heart contained a strength most vampires lacked. She would not become a killer, his beautiful Trixie. She would be a beacon, someone other vampires would try to emulate. Including himself.

"So, you can't go hungry." She met his gaze, her eyes clouded with confusion. "What's the problem, then, with all the modern options you imply we have? Why the continued murders?"

"I am weak." He set her aside Jumping to his feet, he paced the small room. The prison he could easily break out of, but where to go? The safest place for Trixie was under the protection of the wolf pack.

That admission burned like silver poured straight into his vein. Christopher was all snarl. He would not harm Trixie. The werewolf's soul wasn't that dark, and there would be too many repercussions to the action. She had powerful friends in New Port's pack. Not to mention, Viktor would kill every Riverbend werewolf in revenge.

"Hundred years ago, our race pledged not to kill. We want to live quietly. But the old ones, like myself, find control slipping through our fingers." He glanced at her, hoping to find understanding and did not.

She crossed her arms. "Murder is not a mistake."

"I know this," he shouted. "My threshold is thin. Every time I starved, it grew thinner. My need for blood stronger." He dropped his head into his hands. "The guilt is worse. I asked Eoin for help. He is the only one in the city strong enough to physically stop me." He flung himself in the chair, tempted to return to her bed, but Trixie sat so stiff and shocked. He had to wait. He did not wish to touch her until she could forgive what he could not. "It's a madness with no cure."

Viktor continued to stare at nothing, every muscle in his body tight until he appeared made of stone.

She wanted him to stop killing people for obvious reasons, but the top one was the guilt was destroying him. How long before it drove him permanently mad? The people she cared about were a short list and she protected them with every fiber in her soul. Viktor was now on that list. "What you're doing now isn't working."

He rose slowly to his feet, looming over her. "No."

"Alone. You've done this alone for centuries. Every addict needs a support group, Viktor. Consider me your sponsor. Let me help you."

He blinked and wouldn't look at her. "I have been alone since the day I woke on the battlefield." He cleared his throat. "I am not sure how to be anything else. Even when I lived among vampires, I had really lived alone. With them but apart. A wild thing no one wanted."

She kissed him on the jaw, on his cheek, her love fierce. He had been too stubborn to die, in those days, and she was too stubborn to let him go now. "I don't know how to be a vampire. We'll help each other."

He pulled her into a hug, her ribs creaking pleasantly from his strength. So, this was how it felt to be a couple.

"First, we need to break out of here." She glared at the locked door. There was no way Viktor was facing that nest without her and she wouldn't waste her breath trying to convince Chris otherwise.

Viktor returned to the small twin bed, his huge body taking three quarters of the space. "Number one rule of being vampire, never escape during the day."

"Well shit, I almost made toast of us."

"More like charcoal."

She shuddered. "Thanks for the visual."

He patted the mattress. "Come, show me how not to be alone in bed."

She snorted. "I thought vampires were supposed to be better at seduction than this." Yes, she moved closer.

"Too many movies."

She crawled in next to him. "Maybe you should watch more."

He rolled on top of her.

Caged between Viktor's strong arms and pinned to the mattress by his weight, Trixie gasped. All words lost as her throat locked.

He leaned in so close all she could see was the midnight of his eyes. "A kiss." He waited for her slight nod before his lips descended upon hers.

She had no words to describe this raw primal sensation that spread through her, melting her tense muscles. All because Viktor and his firm lips that tasted so slowly.

Too slowly.

She moaned into his mouth. Gripping his shoulders, she pulled herself up since he was too strong to budge.

He licked along the seam of her lips.

Oh, yes. Wanting more, she opened and dared to reach out with her tongue.

He made a low, deep noise which curled her toes.

When it felt as if he lifted his head, she arched her back toward him and demanded more.

He pressed a kiss to her throat, his fingers slipping under the hem of her shirt. "I want to taste your skin."

"Yes." Husky word.

Rising, he pulled her shirt over her head.

Automatically, her hands went to his chest, stroking the chiseled muscles that were Viktor.

"No touching." He pried her hands away. "I want to go slow. Touching me will make me…crazed." He undid her jeans and slid them off, leaving her exposed in only her bra and panties.

She had the power to make him crazed? It seemed impossible.

Looming, his gaze devoured her, lingering on her lace covered breasts. He traced the delicate pattern and she shivered.

It was instinct to curve her body up toward him.

His gaze snapped up to meet hers and then he was upon her, gripping her jaw so he could take her mouth in a feral kiss that was all tongue and fangs and heat. His free hand slid under her body and released her bra fastenings. Sliding the straps off her shoulders, he followed their descent with small nipping kisses. The lace vanished with her other clothes, tossed over Viktor's back. Big, strong hands cupped her breasts, kneading, molding, kissing…oh…sucking.

She moaned, thighs spreading to welcome his big, gorgeous body as it pressed her into the bed. Fingers plucked at her nipples as he continued to kiss lower along her abdomen.

That was when she realized she was in over her head.

He kissed her navel.

She couldn't catch her breath. Her head spun.

"Tell me if you like this." Skimming over the small triangle of black lace, he ran his fangs over her inner thighs.

A shuddering breath. "Yes."

He slid her panties off, following their path with more nips and kisses, then with a sinful smile, he pulled her legs over his shoulders.

Her heart stuttered. "What are you doing?"

"Tasting you." He gave her such an intimate kiss her mind blanked then sparked with such a fever of want. She'd never understood, hadn't known. Sure, she'd read about it in books and heard her friends discussing it. The act had sounded embarrassing. Right now, she wasn't embarrassed. She was on fire and needy and so pleasured it hurt.

She felt the surge of raw sexual delight until her thoughts fractured into a long, shuddering satisfaction.

Viktor rolled back along her body, licking and tasting his way to her throat. His heavy weight a delicious blanket.

Her hand traveled under his shirt once more. His skin hot and firm.

"Bad vampire." He nipped her skin and rolled her on top of him. "The sun is rising."

"What about you?"

He licked her bottom lip. "We have plenty of time for that another day. Now, we both need to sleep. Tonight will prove to be interesting."

Chapter Twenty-Four

The bang on the door rattled Trixie's teeth, jarring her awake to sit up straight in bed, blanket pooling around her hips. She pressed her hands to her ears. "I'm awake, I'm awake." She blinked at the unfamiliar surroundings and recalled yesterday's werewolf adventures.

The knocking stopped.

Viktor sat in front of the television but his attention was focused on her. Or should she say, her naked breasts. "Not an evening person?" Amusement pulled at his lips as if he'd discovered a special secret.

"No." She pulled on her discarded shirt and it fell to her knees. Oh, not hers. Viktor's. He was bare chested.

He abandoned the television and opened the unlocked door.

In the hallway, holding bagged blood stood a large tattooed man. Burly, like an older bike gang member. His glare could have melted plastic. "Not again. *Trixie*." He growled her name and she squeaked like a dog toy he'd just bit.

Betty's *dad*.

Viktor tossed her a concerned glance over his shoulder. Grown women shouldn't make those kinds of noises. She knew this, but she felt like she'd been caught…with no pants on, which was the truth.

She shut the door closed in his face before he could say anything else. Pulling off Viktor's shirt, she tossed it at him. "Get dressed." She fell to her knees, looking for her clothes under the bed.

Chuck shoved the door open, but Viktor blocked it with one hand. She heard an *oomph* as Chuck collided with the unmoving object that was her sire.

She mouthed a silent *thank you* as she dressed at hurricane speed, shirt backwards and jeans inside out, but all the important bits were covered.

Viktor dropped his shirt on the floor, before letting Chuck in. "I assume you know each other? I am Viktor Petrov." He held up his hand.

Chuck stared at it as if Viktor's touch was contagious. His glare darted to her. "So, the rumors are true. I thought the alpha was mistaken when he called me. You really allowed *him* to turn you into a vampire.

"Hey, Chuck." She gave a halfhearted wave, feeling eight years old all over again. Betty's parents had decided that since she and Ruby didn't have any, they would fill in that role.

It was a shifter thing neither she nor Ruby understood, but Betty's parents were awesome, so bonus. They got the occasional check-in phone call and obligatory dinner invite when they were in town visiting.

Trixie had never been on the receiving end of *the* dad glare. It was awful.

"I thought you had a better head on your shoulders." Chuck's ears were red as he held up the blood he carried. "You're going to have to live off this for the rest of your life. You'll have to hunt humans. What do you know about hunting?"

Her mouth opened and closed repeatedly. It was like her vocal cords had short-circuited. She had never seen him so upset. Heat coated her limbs as her skin flushed.

Betty's dad turned on Viktor. "And you." He jabbed his finger into Viktor's chest. "I'm going to personally skin you alive and use you as a throw rug if I find out you hurt her."

Viktor's eyes went dead. His skin felt cold to Trixie's touch. "What did you accuse me of?" He bared his saber tooth fangs.

She had to give Chuck credit. He didn't give Viktor an inch. "I want to speak with her alone."

"Why? I'm sworn to protect her and I don't know you from shit. What assurance do I have *you* will not hurt her?"

"That's enough." She held her hands, inserting herself between the pissed off supernatural creatures. She was tired of being fought over. All her life she'd had to take care of herself. It was wonderful both these men cared about her, but she was a big girl wearing vampire pants now. She thought she could handle an upset werewolf daddy. "Chuck is Betty's father. And sort of my adopted one."

"Sort of? We'll discuss *that* another day." Chuck set his hand on her shoulder and pulled her behind him. "And Trixie's well-being is also my concern."

She pleaded with Viktor, over the werewolf's shoulder, to calm down. "I trust Chuck with my life. He'd never hurt me. Look, he brought breakfast." She pointed to the bag blood.

"Let Trixie feed first." Viktor crossed his arms, those pecks flexing in the most inviting way.

Chuck passed her a bag over her shoulder. "Go for it, kid." He didn't move.

She sighed and wondered how Betty had survived being a teenager with such a protective father. "Why did Chris call *you*?" Eyeing the bag, she tried to figure out how to drink it without freaking Chuck out. She was hungry and her stomach cramped.

Viktor retrieved a glass from the bathroom. He gestured for her breakfast. With a sharp fingernail, he punctured the plastic and helped her pour the contents inside.

Betty's father frowned with thin lips. "You're Betty's best friend. You're family! Of course, he called me. We're pack."

Technically, she wasn't pack, but he didn't use the term literally. He meant he cared.

"No, she's not pack." Viktor discarded the empty blood bag and pushed the full glass back in her hands. "She belongs to me."

She could all but see Chuck's fur stand up on his spine. He growled. Viktor couldn't have said anything worse to an overprotective old werewolf. She'd been reading a lot on shifters ever since Betty's mating.

"You need to be quiet now." She pointed at Viktor. "I don't want to have to pick pieces of you out of Chuck's teeth."

Both men snorted and ignored their mutual reaction.

Trixie wiped her mouth and handed Viktor her empty glass.

Chuck eyed Viktor. "Interesting tats. Didn't know vampires' skin could be tattooed."

"Viktor's a tattoo artist. He seems to be well known. He was featured in tattoo news magazine for the work he did on New Port dragon." She bit the inside of her cheek before she continued.

Viktor poked at his skin where the densest patch of names existed. "It's a process to tattoo my kind. Not many would tolerate it."

Chuck leaned forward, inspecting the writing. "What do all those names mean?"

She elbowed Chuck in the side. "I thought you wanted to talk to *me*?" Betty's dad didn't need to know how many people Viktor had killed. That would give them another thing to fight over. She pushed between them. "Let's go. The night won't last forever and Viktor has somewhere to go."

Chuck exchanged nods with the guards in the hallway. He led her to another safe room at the end of the hall. She glanced over her shoulder at the two shifters quietly talking with her sire. "They're nervous about him."

"They have a reason to be." He held the door open for her.

She sat on a bed identical to the one they slept on. "How many safe rooms does your pack need?"

"Can't have too many. It's rough on the teenagers, especially the dominant males. Rumors are Chris spent almost a year down here." Chuck pulled the chair around to face her and set down. "When did this happen?" He gestured with his hand up and down her body.

She assumed he meant her vampirism. "A couple days ago."

"Does Betty know?"

"No, what kind of friend do you think I am?" Betty should be howling at the moon or hunting buffalo or whatever wolf shifters did to be romantic.

"One who is in over her head." Chuck went down on his knees in front of her and grasped her hands in his big rough palms. "Did Viktor force this on you? I can help you get away from him. Arrange a ride back to New Port. The pack will make sure you never see Viktor again."

She sat speechless for a second. He was being more than overprotective. He was frightened.

For her.

Nobody seemed to understand her sire like she did. He hadn't done anything but take care of her since she'd woken up a vampire. "I'd be dead if Viktor hadn't turned me into a vampire." Sure, her choices had been limited, become a vampire or die. But it had been *her* choice. She explained to Chuck about the fall down the stairs and Viktor's offer. "He didn't have to do it. From what I understand, I'm the first vampire he's ever made. Give him a little slack. For me."

"The dragon was involved." Chuck shook his head. "I should have retrieved those kennels the night he adopted those cats."

"Hush. Shoulda, coulda, woulda won't change the present. It was fate." Or karma. "Viktor has been kind to me." Boy, had he ever been last night. "Anyways, I doubt your alpha would allow me to leave."

If Chuck wanted a bad guy to blame, she'd point him to his overbearing alpha.

"Why wouldn't he let you go home with me?" He rose to his feet and returned with a chair.

The door swung open. No knock. Chris strode in with a very angry looking Viktor in tow. The alpha held a lovely, long black gown in his arms. "Change of plans." His gaze landed on Chuck. "Why are you still here?"

She jumped to her feet, followed by Betty's dad. "Didn't your mother ever teach you any manners?"

"I never had a mother." He stared at Chuck until Betty's dad left the room.

"You're not a very nice man." Trixie folded her arms.

He tilted his head in a very wolf manner. "I'm not a man. I'm an alpha. He's mid-level pack. It's for his own safety." He handed her the dress. "Change. We're all going to the nest tonight."

She examined the gown she was given. "Won't I be a little overdressed for a hostile takeover?" The black number was silky and soft. It flowed like water over her hands and she'd never worn anything so beautiful.

Viktor had changed while she had been talking to Chuck. He wore a black on black suit with no tie. He held up what looked like a card. "An invitation. Seems as if Sybil knows I am in the city and a guest of the pack. She is upset that I did not stop at the nest first. She is holding a party in my honor this evening as retribution."

"Retribution?" she whispered. "In my experience, parties are supposed to be fun."

"Not vampire ones." Chris frowned.

Her heart plummeted. "I'm no genius, and I'm out of my league here, but this smells like a trap."

"Of course, it is." That's when she noticed the alpha didn't look like a sandwich shop owner. He wore a navy power suit that set off his eyes. It made him look more dangerous. "That's why I'm coming. To protect my investment." He stared pointedly at her.

And why Viktor look like he could chew nails.

"Why are you taking me? I can't be of much help." She wasn't a fool. There was bad blood between all three leaders. Putting them in the same room seemed like playing with dynamite while juggling matches. Last time she checked, bombs killed baby vamps and she liked living.

Viktor handed her the invitation.

Her name was listed under his. "This can't be good."

CHAPTER TWENTY-FIVE

They borrowed the limousine again. Trixie leaned forward in her seat and inspected the contents of the minibar. Teeny, tiny bottles of liquor, soda, crackers… "Oh, hard candy." She inspected the bag, looking for her favorite flavor. "Can I eat hard candy?" That couldn't be considered solid food.

Silence.

She glanced at her quiet companions. Chris sat legs apart, arms crossed with a stern frown aimed in her direction.

Viktor grinned from ear to ear. He sat next to her with his arms extended over the back of her bench, jacket button undone, his long legs taking most of the space. "Yes."

She plucked the strawberry shaped one and popped it in her mouth. The sweetness was muted but not unpleasant. She made note to buy a bag if she ever returned home.

Chris eyed the candy bag. "That doesn't belong to us."

She sighed and set it back inside the bar, but continued to investigate, no matter how hard the alpha glared. "They won't miss *one* candy. I won't take anything else."

"You could have whatever you want." Viktor leaned closer to Chris. "Fucking bill me."

"I really don't want anything else." She needed a clear head walking into Riverbend's vampire nest. No alcohol for her. Neither her sire nor the wolf alpha liked Sybil, the nest leader. Trixie expected she and Sybil wouldn't be exchanging best friend bracelets at the end of the party. "I've never had a chance to explore a limo and have never seen the insides of a minibar. I'm just curious." She pulled out a box of condoms. "Oh."

Viktor threw back his head and laughed while Chris snatched the box out of her hand and returned it inside the minibar.

"What kind of limo service is this?" She quirked her eyebrow and bit back her own grin.

Chris straightened his tie and glared out the window. The alpha didn't answer.

Viktor winked then leaned toward the werewolf. "Do you have a business card? Maybe I will rent this vehicle for Trixie and myself to tour the city later tonight."

Her blush matched Chris's. "Viktor." She kicked him in the ankle with her sharp heels.

Chris pointed at her sire but stared at her with narrowed eyes. "Why him? What could you possibly see in him?"

The limo pulled to a stop.

Viktor leaned forward, elbows on knees. His dark eyes a pool of mischief. "I am waiting for the answer as well." They both stared at her expectantly.

The driver opened the door.

She kissed the tip of Viktor's nose. "A girl has to have secrets."

This time Chris roared with laughter as he climbed out. He extended his hand to hers and helped her exit the vehicle.

She appreciated it. The heels were higher than anything she owned. She felt like she was walking on stilts. The slightest breeze and she'd fall over.

Viktor joined them. He stood a head taller than her even with her new shoes. Her sire half-naked and in chains had weakened her knees. In a suit, he was devastating. He withdrew her hand from Chris's grasp and set it on his arm.

She then remembered what a jealous lover she had. She didn't want to hurt him and set a shy kiss on his cheek.

The quiet of their surroundings piqued her curiosity. "Not a nightclub." She took a step forward as her gaze landed on a sprawled mansion. "Nice." White, colonial, with a huge flower garden.

"The Riverbend nest inherited this home before I took over the territory. I no longer approve acquiring wealth by turning the rich."

Offering eternal youth in exchange for wealth seemed quite a deal. But that was the poor girl in her talking. "Look at all the space." She had thought Betty's new home massive. It was a normal bungalow in comparison to this gorgeous piece of brick and mortar.

"It's a very pretty place." Viktor stood stiffly next to her, face devoid of emotion.

"The nightclub is finer though." She leaned her head on his shoulder. "I mean, it must take all week to sweep the floors of this place."

He kissed the top of her head. "They have housekeepers."

Damn, he wasn't going to make this easy. They strolled to the front door via a garden path. "And the flowers can only be enjoyed in the day…" She paused to smell a pink rose, inhaling the sweet fragrance.

He plucked it and wove it into her hair. "I will buy you a prettier home."

She slowly blinked as he climbed the stairs to knock on the front entrance.

Chris took his place. "Did he just offer to buy you a mansion?"

She nodded.

"Is that why—"

She snapped her teeth at him. "No."

"I don't understand women." He gave that distinctive wolf expression.

"Obviously." She joined Viktor as the double doors swung open and golden light poured out onto the front lawn.

"Master." A man well into his forties bowed, sweeping the floor with his hand. "We've been expecting you and Ms. Russell."

"Of course, you have." Viktor maneuvered past their greeter, taking her along. She would have remained rooted at the front entrance, staring at the golden marble walls and floors. A chandelier hung overhead, sparkling. Little reflected lights swam over her silk dress. She traced their path and realized she and Viktor had stopped moving.

Chris' way was blocked by the vampire.

"He is with me, Henri. The alpha of Riverbend pack deserves better courtesy than that."

"Courtesy? His pack did unspeakable things to me a few months ago." Henri managed to appear dignified as he gave Chris inches to squeeze by. "Unforgivable animals."

"But you lived." Viktor's eyes narrowed as he hissed at the alpha, "What did they do?"

"There was tar and feathers involved. That's all I know," whispered Chris.

Viktor slowly closed his eyes. A quiet phrase in Russian slipped past his lips.

Chris met her wide-eyed stare and shrugged. Not an ounce of guilt or regret in his eyes.

"This way, please." Henri sniffed as he passed the alpha and guided them out of the foyer.

And into an honest to God ballroom. Her hand fluttered to her chest as Viktor drew her through the threshold. Candlelight everywhere. Enough to light the room but keep it intimate. Music played from deeper in the house, not the trance stuff from the nightclub. Classical and soft, the kind needed for couples.

As they crossed the room people turned to stare. Many bowed or curtsied. She cleared her throat and loosened her hold on Viktor's arm. She shouldn't be at his side. She would just slip back with Chris while Viktor dealt with the nest.

Her sire pressed his hand over hers, forcing it to stay. Forcing *her* to stay. He turned a soft smile her way. His gaze not on the vampires gathered to greet him, but focused on her. "Promise me the first dance."

A flutter of nerves in her stomach. "I've never danced to this kind of music." The moves seem so calculated and trained. "I'll make a mess of it."

"Nonsense, I'll teach you." He lifted her fingers to his lips. The claim very public.

Suddenly every gaze in the room seemed to train onto her. Hushed whispers followed their wake.

Her flutter of nerves evolved into a slight tremble. She didn't know where to put her hands and her ungraceful steps grew heavy.

Guests parted to allow a woman in a golden gown made of gauzy, flowing material through. It moved like air around her body and appeared transparent without revealing details. She held out her hand, forcing Viktor to clasp it. "Master Viktor, I'm so pleased you have joined us."

"Sybil." His answer short and quick. He released her fingers without any further contact. "How could I refuse your invitation?"

A flash of sharp teeth. "This must be Patricia Russell." Sybil aimed her attention directly at Trixie.

"Pleased to meet you." She wasn't sure if she should curtsy or not, and decided to hold out her hand. She knew her full name? Very few people did. Someone had done their research.

"I understand you are a dogcatcher in New Port." Sybil wove her fingers together. The condescending tone sharp and lethal.

Trixie dropped her ignored hand. "I don't deal in just dogs. I rescue any animal in need."

"And put down the rabid ones," she muttered under her breath.

Viktor's gaze softened as he turned away from Sybil, amusement clear in his dark eyes, and Trixie realized he had heard her soft words.

Their host sighed at the sight of the alpha. "Christopher. I don't recall your name on the invitation."

Chris had somehow managed to snatch a flute of champagne from somewhere and was gulping it back. He wiped his mouth. "Sybil, nice place. Where's the food?"

Trixie bit her bottom lip to avoid grinning and gave Chris a mental high-five.

"This is a vampire only event. Only liquids." Sybil gave him a tart smile. "Next time, I will call your sandwich shop to cater."

He raised an empty flute. "I'd appreciate the business."

Viktor scanned the crowd, looking for familiar faces and found none. The guests watching this farce unfold were young. All of them less than a decade into vampirism. He had avoided visiting the nest too long. They watched with fear and curiosity. With Sybil as their role model, it did not bode well for any of their futures. That did not explain why he could not spot any of the older, more loyal vampires that called this place home. It was their support of Viktor that kept Sybil in check.

Chris brushed shoulders with Trixie. "Come on, I'll get you a drink and we can leave the grown-ups to talk."

Viktor hovered close to Trixie, not wanting her alone with the nest. But the wolf was correct. He needed to speak with Sybil alone. In Trixie's presence, the bitch would only have barbed words. He trusted the alpha to protect Trixie in his stead. They shared a common interest in her safety, if for different reasons.

"Sybil." He offered to take her hand. "A dance and then?" He had wanted to save this dance for Trixie. Teach her the steps to a simple waltz, but this was a time of danger, not of leisure.

Sybil set her manicured, long fingers in his grasp.

He escorted her to the sectioned off part of the dance floor. Over his shoulder, he glimpsed Trixie watching while Chris whispered in her ear. He would throttle the wolf later. Even from this distance, he could see the hint of hurt in her eyes. Trixie nodded to something that Chris said and weaved her fingers with the wolf's. He would skin the wolf too.

Sybil dug her nails into his skin. "She's very young."

He settled into a dancing stance, holding Sybil at a distance. With ease, they flowed into the pattern of the other couples. They were both of an age when such skills had been expected at one point in their lives.

"I made her only a few days ago." Only, and she was already an integral part of his existence. A night without Trixie sounded empty and meaningless now.

"What do you want, Sybil?" Better to start on the offense, especially since she had something he desired.

"Whatever do you mean?" She twirled a long strand of his hair around her finger, tighter and tighter.

"You did not invite me here for nothing. I have visited the city often without being *summoned* to the nest."

"My nest." She tugged hard.

He bared his fangs. His grasp on her waist tightened. "*My* nest. Do not make me remind you."

"Maybe I want you to." She released his hair and laughed. "I miss our play."

He did not. At the time, he had used Sybil for self-punishment. That was before he'd met Eoin. "My tastes have changed." He wanted more. He had witnessed the relationship between Eoin and Angie develop. The…happiness his friend now enjoyed. If the self-proclaimed harbinger of smoke and fire could find love, why could not Viktor?

"I see." Her eyes narrowed. "I asked you here to show you something I have discovered."

A whisper of memory licked at his thoughts. Ashes. Christopher had mentioned the recent death of vampires. "A discovery?" They continued to dance reflexively, but he moved them farther from the center, toward a quieter section of the ballroom. "Tell me."

"Did you know my nest birthed a dhampir forty or so years ago?"

"Rumors of her existence have reached my ears." He did not mention how recently.

"Smart little girl." Sybil scowled. "Always had a mind of her own."

He kept his face impassive yet laughed inside. That meant the dhampir did not let Sybil control her. He was not sure if this was a good thing or not, considering the dhampir's past transgression. "Why have I not been introduced to her prior to tonight?" He had visited the nest in those forty years and never seen a child.

Sybil's lips twisted. "Her mother hid her until she was an adult."

"Is this why you asked me here? To meet her?" That would be too convenient, but he could only hope.

"No, no, silly." She traced a sharp fingernail along his jaw. "So handsome. I almost forgot how pretty you were. You really should visit more often."

"Sybil…" He broke off the dance as she pressed her body against his. It would be simpler if he played her games. She would be more pliant. It would not take long and these dark hallways had many private nooks.

His stomach rolled at even the hint of the thought. His heart and body belonged to a certain animal control officer. He could not bear even the thought of betraying Trixie. Her affection was so pure and generous. He could not recall the last time anyone had cared for him.

He had not realized how empty he had been inside until Trixie had filled that hole.

"I will confess, Viktor, that I am hurt that you would visit these animals before your own people." Sybil twisted away, the edges of her dress twirled with calculated practice. She had to own a heart for it to be hurt. Insulted was more her style. Sybil flung open the French doors that led out to the night garden and sat on a stone bench just outside the exit.

Viktor remained where he had stopped, waiting for the next level of verbal attack. He hated these games.

One thing was for sure—Sybil had spoken the truth when she'd said the nest was hers. He still had not recognized anyone during their spin across the dance floor.

CHAPTER TWENTY-SIX

Watching Viktor lead Sybil to the dance floor left Trixie bleeding inside. Had he forgotten he'd asked her for the first dance?

Chris leaned to whisper in her ear. "This place stinks of death and betrayal. How long do you think he can keep her busy?"

Viktor glanced over his shoulder, his heated stare pinning Trixie's. Over that distance and in only those few seconds, understanding gonged in her head. She entwined her fingers with the alpha's. "Let's find the dhampir."

Viktor was distracting Sybil. That had to be it, because why look at her with such longing and go with that bitch? Nobody would pay attention to a dogcatcher and a werewolf. Sybil had made sure of that. They were below her or her nest's standards.

Chris' lips spread into a vicious grin. His eyes flashed amber. "Let the hunt begin."

She strolled as best she could in the heels Chris had provided. "Next time you buy some shoes, try to be more practical."

He eyed the slit that ran down the side of her gown, which gave her some room to move. "I think they're sexy."

"Don't make me smack you in public."

"Then you'd be forced to marry me, because only my mate would be allowed to live after such a transgression." He turned his wolfish gaze on her.

"Did Betty smack you?"

He growled. "Repeatedly."

"And you still have no common sense." She scanned the crowd. "You know what Jade looks like?" Jade Ellington, dhampir tattoo artist, sounded like someone who would stand out in a crowd.

"No, but I would know her scent." His sharp smile turned sheepish. "The tattoo parlor still had some of her stuff in storage. Apparently, she left town so quickly she never returned for it. I bought the box. Her scent is still on her needle gun."

"Even after all these years?"

"Packing it in the box helped. The smell was faint, but…" He shrugged. "I am an alpha."

And he had the ego to go with his acute sense of smell. They combed through the guests quickly. "Are you getting anything?" Who knew how long Viktor and Sybil's dance would last. She and Chris had to work fast.

The werewolf shook his head.

She eyed the sweeping staircase and rejected the idea of climbing to the second floor. Everyone would spot them since it was central to the room. "Come on. Let's look for a back way." She jerked her head toward where one of the servants exited. Sybil didn't strike her as someone who would let the help use the same public hallways.

They crossed a dining room to the kitchen then to a narrow hallway that followed the back wall of the mansion. It ended at a wooden stairwell. "Ha! And I knew watching TV would come in handy one day."

"Why do you think Jade is upstairs?" Chris asked.

"I don't. I think the bedrooms are. With your nose, we'll locate her room and hopefully the book." She doubted that Jade would keep it in the nest library for anyone to use.

Chris scowled, taking the lead and making sure she stayed behind him. "I want her, not the damn book."

"Stick to the plan. We destroy the book." Her feet were cramping so bad she could barely think straight. She kicked off her heels and followed close behind Chris, trying to move as silently as the alpha. The stairs groaned under her weight and she frowned at how quietly Chris managed when he was twice her size.

The second-floor hall looked like the servant quarters. They treaded passed quickly until Chris stopped so fast she walked straight into his solid back.

She rubbed her nose. "What is it?"

"I smell her." He bent to one knee, sniffing the bare, unpolished wood floor.

"Here?" She glanced at the yellowed plastered walls and ancient cracked doors. Something didn't feel right. Why was Jade in the servant quarters?

Chris moved them back to a doorway they had just passed. "Her smell is strongest here." He tried the knob. "Locked." That wasn't surprising, considering what Jade had in her possession. Chris used force until metallic parts of the knob and lock cracked. The door swung inward.

Together they peered inside the room.

Light glared from a bare bulb that hung from the ceiling. A young woman dressed in a threadbare T-shirt and torn jeans sat on the metal cot, reading a worn paperback novel. She rose to her bare feet, skeletal thin with bruises lining her arms and face. "Who are you?"

Chris jumped to his feet so fast he almost slammed into Trixie's head. Win for vampire reflexes kicking in. "Jade Ellington." The alpha tossed Trixie a smug look over his shoulder. "I'm Chris Jenkins, alpha of Riverbend Wolf Pack."

"I'm Trixie from New Port." She waved her hand over Chris' broad shoulders. "Why are you locked inside this room?"

This wasn't going according to plan. They had a starved-looking dhampir, no magic book, and Jade didn't look like a criminal mastermind.

Jade clutched the novel to her chest and took a step closer to Chris. "Are you here to rescue me?" Hope in her voice, a cry of desperation.

She and Chris exchanged confused looks. The alpha crossed the room in one long stride. He gripped Jade's chin in his hand and examined her frail face. "Who's been using you as a punching bag?" His fury was surprising, considering he had wanted revenge on the dhampir himself.

She jerked her chin loose. "Sybil lets them beat me when I fail. She calls it *incentive*." She looked from Chris to Trixie and back again. "You're not here to help."

"Yes, we are." Trixie grabbed her hand. "Come on. We don't have much time." No matter what Jade had done to Betty, she did not deserve torture. There was something else going on that they didn't understand, and the only way they could get answers was by helping Jade.

Chris didn't hesitate and took the lead. He was a bossy wolf but a protective one. He scanned the hall. "It's clear."

"Wait." Jade fell to her knees and searched under her bed. She pulled out a thick, black leather-bound book. "I can't leave without this."

It had to be the book they wanted. Trixie didn't know how to confirm it though.

Chris glanced back. "Is that the book you used at the tattoo parlor? The magic one?" Apparently, he knew.

Jade's eyes went wide. "How did you know that?"

"Long story." Trixie pushed the alpha to move.

"My mother is this way." Jane went the opposite direction. "We have to rescue her too."

Chris threw his hands in the air. "What the fuck is going on?"

Trixie chewed on her bottom lip and followed Jade. There was no other choice but to keep pushing forward. She wasn't leaving anyone behind.

Sybil sat on a stone bench, facing the gardens. "I have always wanted to see my flowers in the morning light."

"They have cameras for that. You can watch them in safety." He crossed his arms as he leaned against the doorframe. Noting Trixie and Chris had vanished from the party. He could only hope the alpha kept her safe and that they took this opportunity to search for the dhampir's magic book.

"It's not the same. I want to enjoy the warmth on my skin."

"You would get very warm if you tried it." Sybil was trying to hint at something, but he was in no mood to play games.

"Viktor." She patted the bench next to her. "Join me."

"I am fine where I am. What did you want to show me, Sybil?"

"Power." She leaned forward. "Real power. Something that could turn the tide for our kind forever."

"The news, the people the humans claim spontaneously combusted, that was you're doing." His arms tightened across his body and he gave her a fake smile. "What have you been up to?" Since they had entered the nest, he had been uneasy. He had come knowing it was a trap, but Sybil was acting too civil.

"I have discovered a way to walk in sunlight."

He blinked, not sure he had heard correctly.

Her smile turned shy but she did not have a shy bone in her body. "Well almost. Those *spontaneous combustions* were failed attempts, but we are *so* close."

"How is that possible?" He slowly approached her, his feet heavy with wonder. Sunlight was every vampire's regret at some point in their lives.

"The dhampir I spoke of…"

He didn't hear her other words as the puzzle pieces fell into place. Sybil was using black magic to alter the vampires of the nest. She was using the dhampir to do her dirty work.

"… extensive testing, we're close to developing a foolproof spell. Viktor, are you listening to me?"

He stared out over the gardens. "How extensive were your tests?" There were too many young vampires in the mansion and none that he recognized.

"I don't know what that has to do with anything."

Deepening his tone. "How many of your nest have you killed with these tests?"

She pressed her lips together and turned her back on him. "Their sacrifice was for the good of vampire kind."

"Did they volunteer?" Even if she said *yes*, he could not bring himself to believe her.

She refused to answer.

"I did not think so." He stood, looming over Sybil. "I am relieving you of your rule of this nest. You are obviously too unstable to be left unsupervised." He flexed his fingers, resisting the urge to fist his hands.

The scent of blood was in the air. Close. He shook his head. There were humans in the other room allowing some of the vampires to feed. When had he last fed? Chuck had brought them blood at the pack house. Had he not drank?

Sybil gave him a knowing smile. "I don't think taking my rule away will be quite so easy."

"Fine," he snapped. "I will just kill you and be done with the whole fiasco." He tired of Riverbend and all its politicking. It was why he'd chosen to never settle here. Too much strife fed into bloodlust and that was the last thing he needed.

She tutted, wagging her finger at him. "Not so fast."

ᴄHAPTER ᴛWENTY-ꜱEVEN

ᴛrixie followed Jade. The dhampir seemed to know where she was going. Sure footed, she led them farther from her bedroom and down a narrow hall to what appeared like a closet until inside they found a hidden spiral staircase that led to the basement.

"Not another dungeon," Trixie mumbled to no one in particular.

Chris maneuvered past her and Jade. He stared at the dark hole below. "Why is your mother being kept down there? I thought you were both members of this nest. *Family*."

Jade tried to move past the alpha with no success. "We were until Sybil discovered what this book can do." She pushed Chris to descend the stairs and he surprisingly complied. "And vampires don't do family. I wish I'd never found the fucking thing."

The stairs ended in a dark room similar to Eoin's dungeon. "Déjà vu," whispered Trixie. If she recalled properly, that hadn't ended so well.

"Which cell is your mom in?" Chris moved a few inches ahead sniffing the air.

"I'm not sure."

The alpha gave a surprised growl.

"The only thing I know is she's down here. It's not like they gave me visiting rights. They always brought her to me." Jade leaned against Trixie as if exhausted.

"You *knew* you were doing black magic? Harming people?" Trixie pointed at the leather-bound tome in her arm.

"Not at the time," Jade hissed back. "It's only when things started to happen and I grew sick that they realized the book was magical and had bonded to me. I didn't even know I had magic in my blood. When I refused to do as Sybil ordered, she imprisoned my mother and forced me to work on spells."

That explained why Jade had vanished suddenly from her job.

"Wait, what kind of spells?" That didn't sound good, even to an amateur like her. Evil leader plus black magic spells equaled disaster in movies.

The pop of the gun went off, the sound familiar. It wasn't gun powder fueled, but air triggered. A tranquilizer rifle, like the one in her animal control truck. She glanced at Chris.

He pulled a dart out of his shoulder. "What the —"
Another shot.

He jerked and slapped his ass. His knees buckled. "Run," he managed with a slurred voice.

Trixie hurried to his side and caught his falling heavy body. She groaned under his weight, even with her vampire strength. No way could she carry him alone. She twisted to ask Jade for help, but she was already running up the stairs like a frightened gazelle.

Two vampires appeared behind Chris. One grabbed Trixie by the arm. The other dragged Chris into an empty cell then locked the barred door behind him.

"You know who I am?" She tugged free of her captor's hold.

He smirked. "The dogcatcher who arrived with Viktor."

"Yes." She nodded, her bubble popped. "That's *Master* Viktor to you."

"Did you catch the other girl?" Her captor shouted up the stairwell.

"Got her." Someone shouted from above.

Crap, they'd caught Jade as well. Weren't they the best rescuers ever? Wait until she told Viktor about all this. Prisoners and black magic and all this time they thought Jade had been the mastermind of all evil.

Her guard guided Trixie away from the dungeon back up the secret stairwell into a small room next to Jade's. A tattoo table was the centerpiece with manacles at each corner. "I thought we were going to see Sybil?" And hopefully Viktor.

"We already have our orders." The guard turned toward her. "Take off the gown."

Her every breath jagged, she clutched her neckline. "Excuse me?" Eyes darting around the room, she tried to find an escape, a distraction, anything.

"Take off the gown or I'll tear it off." He gave her a soft smile. "It's not what you think. Now undress and lie on the table."

Another guard walked in. This one even bigger. "Need help?"

"No, she's going to cooperate. Right sweetheart?" He nodded for her to start.

Heart in throat, she blinked back tears. She would not give them the satisfaction of seeing her fear. She knew predators like these guys. Seen them on the streets in her neighborhood. They lived off terror. The zipper on the dress was difficult to reach. She'd do what they asked and wait patiently to strike.

"Is Viktor occupied?" Her original guard asked the bigger one.

"Sybil is doing her sales pitch."

"Think he'll buy it?"

"If it works? Sure." The guard glanced in Trixie's direction as she lay on the table in her bra and underwear. "If this one flames out like the others, then we're all dead."

Flames out? Had he said *flames out*? What deal were they talking about? She knew Viktor. He wouldn't accept anything from Sybil. *Shit.*

"On your stomach, sweet thing. Bring in the girl."

She did as told and her original captor locked the manacles around her limbs. "What are those for?" she asked.

"So, you don't try anything stupid and force me to hurt you."

The door opened and Jade was pushed inside. Her gaze was so wide the whites showed all around her irises. "No, not her." She retreated.

"Jade, we've been through this before. Every time you say no your mama gets a bone broken." The guard crossed his arms. "Do I go break her legs again?"

Jade shuffled across the room, book in hand. "I'm sorry," she whispered to Trixie.

"Now, if you do the tattoo right this time, Pinky will get to live." He sounded so chipper Trixie wanted to spit.

He'd said *tattoo*. She glanced over her shoulder. Jade was preparing inks and her needle gun. Trixie broke out in a cold sweat. Jade was going to ink her with black magic. "What is the spell going to do to me?"

Jade met her pleading stare. "Makes you resistant to sunlight." She grimaced. "If it works."

Lowering her voice to a whisper. "It hasn't worked yet?"

Jade shook her head.

Trixie turned her face away, her attention back on the guards. "Is this where I make a deal? Because I'm ready." Viktor had said he had heard vampires agonizing screams as they burned under the sun. She didn't want to burn. Sybil had to find another toy to fight over and Trixie needed to buy herself some time to figure out an escape.

The guard shook his head. "Time for deals is passed. If your sire rejects Sybil's offer, then you're the backup plan."

She squirmed and tugged her restraints. As backup plans went, this one sucked. The nest was placing all the bets on her survival. They had to be desperate to think they could coerce Viktor. If she flamed out, he would kill every single one of them — her heart broke — and he probably wouldn't stop there.

"Don't do this, Jade. If Viktor loses his shit, he'll kill most of Riverbend before they take him down." Hell, he needed a dragon to stop him. The city only had a wolf alpha and he was out cold in Sybil's dungeon.

Jade stroked Trixie's hair before sliding the long strands over her shoulder. "They will keep hurting my mother until I do this." She pressed her hand in the middle of Trixie's back. "Hold still. One line out of place and the spell will not work. Trust me, Trixie."

Viktor searched the party quickly for either alpha or future lover. How long had Sybil kept him outside talking? Bargaining?

"Enough." He cut his hand across the air. "The magic is unstable, Sybil. No one knows what ill effects it will have on us with time."

She sighed. "Then we take our time studying it. Any way you want. All I ask is for your patience and support."

He paced the patio. It would be a lie if he said he was not tempted. To walk in the sun. To be human-like with vampire immortality. The fountain of youth complete. But everything had a price in time. What would theirs be? "If vampires could be day walkers, would not all humans want to turn? Then who would feed us?"

"Humankind can be turned into cattle." Her matter of fact comment.

He shuddered. Why could Sybil not see this for what it was? The possible end of the world. Their kind had evolved such weaknesses because they had such strength in other areas. There had to be a balance and Sybil was trying to break it. "I did not travel to Riverbend to negotiate. Hand over the book."

"So, you can take the power for yourself? I think not. Do you take me for a fool?" At those words, soldiers slid out of the darkness surrounding them.

No, he would never think of her as foolish. Sybil had risen in the ranks because her wits were sharp and her heart ruthless. He used to admire such traits. But her bed was cold and her affection colder. He found his soul draining empty around Sybil and she fed his darkness. In those days, he'd had so little control over his bloodlust.

Unlike a certain pink haired dogcatcher who had rescued him like all the other strays. Her love was a beacon he craved. He scanned the soldiers. Young, strong when they had been human, and from their stances, they had some training. Military would be his guess. Modern, newly made, and had no idea what he was capable of.

"Speaking of the sun…" She yawned. "Will you be spending the day?" Mocking him. She twisted her head to the side and spoke to the closest vampire. "Is it done?"

He nodded.

Viktor had been so intent on their *conversation* he had lost track of time. Morning was upon them, and he had not seen Trixie or Christopher in all that while. "What is done?" He clenched and unclenched his fists. "Where are they? Where are my companions?"

Two of the soldiers stepped forward as if ready for his attack.

"Don't worry about the girl and the wolf. The nest has kept both occupied. A few of the females even find the alpha attractive, you know. He might make a good pet in time."

Viktor snarled. "Trixie?" If any harm befell her, he would not forgive anyone, including himself. He should have left her in the safety of the pack. That he considered the company of werewolves securer than his own people convinced him this nest needed purging.

She smiled. "No worries there. I know firsthand how possessive you are. Trixie is quite safe. She's spending time with the dhampir."

He jerked his attention away from the soldiers drawing closer. "What have you done?" The dhampir created the black magic spells. The anti-sunlight tattoos that had all failed. He glanced at the fading night in the East. "No…" He turned on Sybil. "Where is she?"

"Somewhere secure." Sybil smoothed her dress as she got to her feet. "Kill him."

Before she finished her command, he had her by the throat. Blood pounded in his ears. "*You* will die if you harm her."

The soldiers moved as one, taking hold of his arms and trying to pry his fingers free of Sybil's frail neck. Their efforts did nothing. Would *do* nothing. They were seedlings to his deeply rooted vampirism.

"Too late." Sybil pointed, her voice hoarse from his hold. A streak of sunlight speared the sky.

Reflexively, he retreated deep into the shadow, dragging Sybil and the soldiers along.

Sybil struggled to get free of his hold. So much had gone wrong in Riverbend due to his apathy. How many of the older vampires had Sybil murdered for her need of power? The nest's well-being was his responsibility and it had gone rotten. All these young fools scrabbling at his limbs thought Sybil a leader when she was truthfully a spider.

They could not remain on the patio any longer without burning. Sunlight burst through the night like a tidal wave and they were directly in its path. He would not sacrifice all these young lives. Not for a spider. Sybil's role was to protect the nest, make it thrive, give the vampires of Riverbend safe haven. A home.

Instead, she'd corrupted the nest and killed good people in the process. He held her glare and waited a second longer for the sun to reach her precious garden.

Her eyes went wide as comprehension dawned.

Viktor was not a ruthless leader, but he had the capacity to be. Once he saw her understanding, he tossed Sybil far into the gardens, such a distance she would not reach shelter in time, and let the sunlight wash over her.

His speed so fast, he had enough time to shove the young soldiers into the mansion. They tripped and stumbled with the momentum of his power. Some blinked in confusion.

Viktor closed the French doors behind him. His skin smoked as he stared at the suddenly emptying ballroom.

Trixie.

Sybil's cries of agony tore through the morning quiet but he did not pay them any attention. He focused on the fools in front of him. "Sybil is dead. She led you astray from my laws. You have two choices—self-confinement in your rooms or death. Any vampire I see will die." The party had been an orchestrated roux to keep him occupied. Trixie's name was on the invitation. The trap had been for her, not him. "Now, where is my fledgling?" He trembled with his roared question.

Those who had flexed their muscles and thought themselves powerful cowered. They shook their heads and no one gave him the answer he needed.

There was no time. Sybil had done something to Trixie and the sun was on the rise. He stormed across the ballroom, slamming through doors, tearing them from the hinges as he did not bother opening them in his haste.

The sun had risen.

Sybil would not have dared to place Trixie outside. It was a lie he had to believe; otherwise his grip on his darkness would slip. His fall complete.

CHAPTER TWENTY-EIGHT

Curled in a shaded corner of an enclosed garden, Trixie watched the sunlight spear through the open roof of her enclosure. Her broken fingernails bled from clawing at the locked door. The guards had dumped her in Sybil's private walled-in garden, complete with a fucking fairy fountain in the center.

The walls were too smooth to climb, not a tree to use in sight, and some sadistic bastard had placed metallic bars over the opening to the sky. Fear squeezed frozen fingers around her lungs. From the scratches in the wall and the one slightly bent bar, she would guess she wasn't the first vampire who had been imprisoned here. She stared at the scars on the wall above her head and blinked back tears. A camera watched her from across the garden. She would *not* cry. She would *not* scream. She *would* hide from the sun and give Viktor a chance to find her.

Stupid fledgling vampire strength. If the others couldn't break out of here, then she had little chance.

Sunlight crept closer.

Knees to chest, she pressed farther into the corner, running out of space. Her heart drummed so hard it hurt. Maybe the tattoo Jade had given her would work? The dhampir had said to trust her.

Tentatively, Trixie reached forward with her hand. Time was running out. She bit her bottom lip, blood coated her tongue. She would *not* cry. She would *not* scream. She would not give that bitch, Sybil, the satisfaction.

The sunlight caressed her fingertips and smoke rose from her skin.

In his blind tirade through the mansion, Viktor hit a door that rebounded him. He staggered back, shaking his head. There weren't many things that could repel his strength. He pressed his fingertips to the surface and shoved. Nothing. It wasn't a coincidence. Why else have a door reinforced against the vampires unless you wanted to keep them imprisoned.

He spun a slow circle and noticed many monitors on the desk. A security post.

"Trixie!" He heard Chris' shout from the depths of the house, but Viktor could not respond.

His voice was frozen. He touched one of the screens with his fingertips. "No." The word a graveled plea. Trixie huddled against a wall, hiding in the fading shade. Sunlight was almost upon her.

"Christopher," he shouted. Viktor could not save her. He would be a torch before he could even reach her. But the wolf could. "Christopher." His bellow echoed in the building.

The alpha appeared in full beast form. Eight feet tall, a creature of death, coated in muscle, fur and claws.

Viktor pointed at the door. "Through there." Viktor tore his jacket off. "Cover her with this before carrying her back in."

Together they attacked the thick metal door until it groaned and bent and shattered outward.

At the last minute, Chris shoved Viktor back inside before he tumbled out into full daylight. The alpha had saved him. He fell back into the room on his ass, his gaze on the television.

Blood trickled from the corner of Trixie's mouth. She stared defiantly at the camera. He twisted toward the exit. He should see Christopher on the television. He turned back and checked the screen again, but could not see the alpha. "No, no, no." He rose to his knees, watching the sun touch the edges of her gown.

The alpha charged back inside. "I can't find her. It's just a garage. Parked cars and shit." His chest heaved, searching for air, gaze riveted to the screen. "Viktor."

"I know." He could not turn away. His existence would end today. Everything beautiful and good in the world was about to burn before his eyes.

Christopher stormed across the room. He tore the monitor off the wall with an animal roar and tossed it against the floor.

Metal shards and broken glass bounced off Viktor. He sank to the floor on his back among the sharp debris and stared at the ceiling. "You should not have done that." Chris was trying to be merciful but now she would die alone.

The alpha fell to his knees next to him. "I can't watch her burn."

It did not matter. Nothing did. Not anymore. Viktor had wanted to show her the world, explore the night, and see it all again through Trixie's eyes. He rolled to his feet, blood trickling along his back. Instead, he would destroy this nest one at a bloody time. An inhuman growl rolled off his tongue. Storming from the room, he headed toward the wing that housed the nest's bedrooms.

"Viktor." Christopher followed on his heels. "Don't do this, man. She wouldn't want it." The werewolf jumped onto his back, dragging him down.

Bloodlust burned in his veins. It made him strong. He would drink this city dry and kill them all. This time not even a dragon could stop him.

A young woman, skeletal and frail, scurried into the room from the basement stairs.

Strong clawed arms wrapped around Viktor as Christopher struggled to hold him back. "Jade, get out of here. I can't hold him much longer."

Jade cupped her hands around her mouth and shouted over Viktor's ear piercing snarls. "She's not dead. I tried to tell you, Chris, but you ran out of your cell so fast."

"What?" the alpha shouted back.

The stranger crossed the room, grabbed Viktor by the ears, and shouted straight in his face. "Trixie's not dead."

He backhanded her against the wall.

The alpha shook him. "She's okay, Viktor." He punched him. "She's alive." He glanced at the girl. "Are you all right?"

Viktor staggered back, hope a flickering flame of light in the darkness that threatened to drown him. "Trixie lives? How?"

Chris punched him in the face again.

"Stop it," he snarled. "I heard you." He shoved the alpha off.

Christopher pointed to the girl. "This is Jade. She's the dhampir who does those fucking tattoos." He blocked Viktor's path. "*Don't* hit her again."

"Trixie is in the solarium. Follow me." With Christopher's aid, she rose to her feet and hurried from the room with both of them on her heels.

"What's the solarium?" asked the wolf.

"An inner garden and Sybil's testing grounds."

"I saw Trixie on the television. The sun—" Viktor's throat locked, the words stuck. "The sun was about to touch her."

"I know." The dhampir paused in front of a wall. She pushed back one of the wooden rosettes in the moldings and inserted a key into a hidden lock. "I found these down in the dungeon. I've seen the soldiers use them on this door." It wouldn't turn. She tried another. "One of these must work."

Viktor punched through the wall. "Then we go the hard way."

"Stop." She shouted as plaster and dust showered her face. "I gave her the proper tattoo. And you might break the fucking mechanism that opens this door." The fourth key clicked and a section of the wall slid outward. "Careful." She pushed him away and then opened the door completely.

Sunlight spilled into the mansion and Viktor fell back, hope punching through his diaphragm to grip his heart.

In a golden halo, his Trixie stepped out of the sunlight. Her radiant skin sunburned and smoking, but she was alive.

Crushing her to his chest, he breathed her in. "My heart," he whispered. "My Trixie."

She cupped his face between her hands. "Beautiful man, you're squeezing me too hard. I'm a little on the crispy side."

He loosened his hold. "I thought…" She should be dead. Looking at the burns on her skin, he saw she would have been in a few more minutes.

"So did I." She laughed and threw her arms in the air. "I didn't go up like a Roman candle."

He drew one of her arms closer, brushing his fingertips over her already healing skin that no longer smoked. "The tattoo worked."

"Sort of. I don't think I could have stayed out there all day. I won't lie, it hurt, but I'm alive."

He spun on the dhampir. Fury burned in his veins. "You." Any misgiving he had about handing Jade over to the alpha for punishment was gone. Actually, on second thought, Christopher would have to wait his turn until Viktor was done with her.

Trixie blocked his path to the dhampir. "Wait, she was coerced into this by Sybil."

Trixie and Christopher explained Jade's unfortunate situation.

The alpha extended his hand to the dhampir. "Come on, Jade. Let's go free your mom."

Jade pressed herself to the alpha's back as he led her away.

Trixie unzipped her gown and exposed her lower back. An intricate symbol was tattooed on her skin forming a lacy circle.

He traced it. "Sybil told me this was her ultimate goal. For vampires to walk in the sun."

"The spell isn't perfect. I'm not sunbathing anytime soon. It was more like I was slow roasting."

Viktor grimaced. "It is better than going up in flames in seconds." He touched her face, memorizing every detail. He could scarcely breathe. His mind could not even brush the thought of losing Trixie.

She pressed her lips to his. The intimate act started slow and tender then her hand caressed the nape of his neck, gripping hard. The kiss grew deeper and more desperate.

He fisted her hair, pulling her head back, opening her to him. She surrendered so willingly.

Someone coughed. "Get a room." The alpha returned, carrying the dark magic spell book. He was still in beast form. "There has to be an empty one that you can use in this place."

"There are plenty," said a woman Jade was helping walk. Viktor assumed it was her vampire mother since they looked so much alike. That Sybil would abuse one of their rare children was reason enough to have destroyed her.

The vampire lifted her face and pushed back her tangled hair.

"Lauren." Viktor pulled a chair over to his old friend and helped her sit. "I never realized you had a child." He had known Lauren since he had taken over the city. She was one of the original nest members.

Lauren beamed at Jade. "I kept my sweet girl a secret to protect her from Sybil. Where is the sadist? I have a stake with her name on it."

"Mother." Jane ran her hand over her face. "I think we've witnessed enough death."

Viktor glanced over his shoulder at Trixie, reassuring himself that she hadn't been a mirage. His lover had almost been another victim. His frown deepened as he returned his attention to the other woman. "Sybil is dead." He left out the details. "I did not recognize many of the vampires in the nest. Most of them seem new."

Lauren nodded. "Tell him everything, Jade."

"*Mother*…"

"He is the Master of the city. How can he help if he doesn't know the truth?"

The dhampir looked away. "Sybil thought the older vampires would be more resilient since they are — *were* so powerful."

Lauren snorted. "She killed them on purpose. Made my girl use the others as test subjects so she could be rid of any rivalry. The only reason I'm still alive was to control Jade."

"Rebellion?" He shook his head. Viktor had known of Sybil's animosity toward him, but that was personal. He had not known she had infected the nest with it.

"Not a rebellion. Sybil hadn't the power yet." Jade set her hand on her mother's shoulder. "Many of the older vampires, the ones most loyal to you, questioned Sybil about using me and that awful book."

"Then we agree about something at last." Chris held up the book. "This is bad news and needs to burn."

"No," shouted both Jade and Lauren.

The alpha bared his long, sharp canines. Viktor did not think he heard the word *no* often. "I don't understand. It's evil. You said you hated it."

Jade pressed her hand to the black cover. "The more I used the book, the stronger our bond grew. Now my life is tied to it. If you destroy the book, you will kill me as well." She glared up at the alpha. "Don't look at me like that. It wasn't my choice."

Christopher bowed his head, almost touching the top of Jade's with his nose. "Then the book stays with me. Nobody uses it. Including you."

She gasped. "But…"

"No buts." He shook his shaggy head. "I can't allow black magic in Riverbend unsupervised. It stays locked and secure with the pack so it doesn't hurt anyone again."

Jade let her fisted hands fall to her side.

"It's for the best." Viktor had half-expected the alpha to burn it anyway, but he trusted Christopher to keep his word. He had so far. Viktor glanced at Lauren. "Have any of the other original members of the nest survived?"

She slowly shook her head. "As far as I know, I'm the last."

He nodded. "These young vampires need strong leadership. Someone to keep them safe and in line. The nest is yours if you would accept it." He could not do it. His control was slipping already. The dragon was right—he wasn't ready to be among people.

Lauren grasped Jade's hand as her daughter came to stand behind her. "Together, we will make this nest a haven for our kind again."

Trixie yawned. "Sorry." She blushed. "It's way past my bedtime."

"My fledgling tires. I will take your leave until tonight. Rest well." He bowed.

"You will need to feed?" Jade asked.

Trixie came to stand next to him. "I don't think you fed since Carlos, Viktor. You really should."

That would explain his increased violent reactions. His incompetence to keep track was his weakest trait. Things had been happening so quickly since his arrival in Riverbend and he had grown dangerously distracted. "Do you have anything available?"

"Normally, yes, but with the ball, I doubt there is much left." Jade held out her arm. "You can use me. I'm half human. I can sustain you, at least until we can have something delivered."

It was a generous offer, a tempting one, but the girl was too weak. He would not steal her strength if he could help it. "No, I can wait a little longer."

He was the oldest and strongest vampire in the tri-city area. Of course, he could wait until he returned home.

Chapter Twenty-Nine

Waking with Trixie in his arms was a gift. Viktor watched her sleep, learning every curve and line of her face.

She smiled before opening her eyes. It was shy and rewarding. "Good evening, Mr. Vampire." She stretched then wrapped her arms around his neck. Her kiss, sweet and soft, the way she had of doing sometimes as if he was the vulnerable one. When it came to Trixie, her tender heart could cage him more effectively than any dungeon or chains.

"Good day, Ms. Vampire."

She rubbed her eyes and looked at the time. "It's early. Why are you awake?"

Hunger crept along his veins. A familiar enemy. He should have taken Jade's offer this morning to feed. Hunger would not let him rest, nor would it until he fed. "I want to be ready to leave as soon as the sun sets and arrive in New Port with time to spare." He had more resources in his home city and acquiring blood would be easier.

"No hiding in trunks." She nuzzled his jaw.

His fangs ached as they suddenly grew longer. He flinched. Time was not his ally. If he made himself wait until reaching New Port, he risked the bloodlust taking over. He never wanted Trixie to witness his loss of control. "First, I will feed before the journey."

She rose on her elbow and examined his face closely. "I'd say sooner rather than later." She threw off the blankets. She wore a short cotton nightgown the color of the sky, borrowed from the dhampir. "I'll find Jade." She strode from the room, determination in her every step.

Trixie had fallen asleep as soon as she had crawled into bed this morning. The temptation of her body pressed so close against his had driven him insane all day. But in his state of hunger, he could not be trusted to be gentle.

They had a few hours of daylight left. He rolled onto his back, arms behind his head. Her scent still lingered on his skin where she had rested her head on his chest. He inhaled deeply and had not minded being her pillow. If not for the growing burn in his limbs, he would be content. But this thing that he had allowed to evolve, this blinding hunger that consumed all things, would not diminish. No amount of joy or goodness could control it. One simple slip like yesterday could lead to disaster.

Trixie returned with Jade in tow.

He sat on the edge of the bed, still wearing his suit pants since he did not trust himself to wear less in bed with Trixie. Not yet. "That was quick."

"Jade was awake." Trixie stood by the door, her arms crossed so tightly she might as well be trying to hide. She cast her gaze away from his. "Do you want me to leave the room?"

He patted spot next to him. "Come sit."

Jade looked from Trixie to him. "Is something wrong?" A small frown.

"Trixie is of the opinion I will want to have sex with you while I feed."

His fledgling gasped. "Viktor." She covered her face with her hands. "I can't believe you told her that."

Jade only raised a curious eyebrow. She had, after all, been raised by vampires. She understood their ways and that feeding could be both sexual or just about sustenance.

"She watches too many movies," he whispered.

Trixie sat next to him and elbowed him in the ribs. "Stop it. I can't help being jealous. Jade is beautiful and I'm possessive." She gave him a sharp nod as if daring him to contradict her.

He was not stupid though. "How are things within the nest, Jade?"

The dhampir rubbed her chin. "I was going over Sybil's financial records and had Chris do some basic inventory."

Viktor raised an eyebrow. "The alpha is helping?" The wolf had surprised him again. Maybe there was hope for the Riverbend's pack.

Jade nodded. "I can't leave all this work for my mother. She'll be a fine leader, but she should concentrate on consolidating her power. Not checking if the electric bill has been paid, which it hasn't. Not in three months."

Viktor fought a grin, knowing he had left the nest in good hands.

"Anyway, Chris offered to help." Jade gave him a worried look. "I hope that's fine." She approached the bed, offering her wrist.

"Yes." He drew her thin arm to his mouth. Her pulse pounded in his ears. A tribal beat calling to an older instinct deep within his DNA.

"He's nice for a werewolf." Jade turned her attention to Trixie. "Have you known him long?"

"No, we met through a mutual friend." Trixie sounded amused. "You actually like him?"

"I don't—I mean… We just met."

Viktor set his fangs on her thin skin and sank them deep.

Jade jumped and made a pained sound. "Your teeth are longer than those of the nest."

Trixie was at her side. "He's very old."

Viktor tossed her an annoyed glance.

She grinned. "He's ancient, you know." Then she helped Jade to sit next to him. "As for Chris, he and his pack hunted us down in the city." She winked at Jade's wide-eyed stare. "Fun times lay head for you."

"I imagine."

The dhampir's blood tasted off. Human tainted with vampire. It eased his physical needs but still he wanted more. He tried to relax his jaw, release his hold, but his body would not respond to his commands.

"Ow, you're hurting me." Jade tugged but his hold was too strong.

"Viktor." Trixie came around, her face close to his. She pulled at his arm. "Viktor." She said louder as if he'd grown deaf.

"Let go." Jade pushed in his head, pulled at his hair. "Make him let go." Panic in her voice.

Someone crawled onto his back and tried pulling him away.

"Chris." A woman's voice shouted as another one screamed. He could not recall their names, their faces a blur.

The blood poured slower in his mouth, but there was still more to drink. He bit deeper, wanting it all.

The scream sharpened.

A face came into focus, inches from his. Pretty, pretty, pretty. Big blue pleading eyes. Her mouth moved. Succulent lips, kissing lips. He remembered how they felt. He let go of his prey, suddenly hungry for something different.

The prey fell back. A strong shove pushed him off the other side of the bed, away from the pretty. He rolled backward, landing on his feet. Fangs bared, he faced…

He faced Trixie's terror-filled eyes. She huddled behind Christopher with Jade. The dhampir pressed her hand to the wound on her wrist.

He shook his head clear.

"You with us again, Viktor?" Trixie asked.

"You have some serious control issues," Chris shouted. He was back in human form and dressed in borrowed clothes. He tore the bed sheets into strips. "You hurt her." He pointed at Jade then knelt to dress her wound.

Viktor sank to his knees, pressing his forehead to the mattress. Jade Ellington's name had almost been added to his body.

Trixie knelt next to him. She wove her fingers into his.

"No." He pulled away. He did not want her stained with his mistakes. "Thank you for stopping me."

"I didn't do anything special." She rewove her fingers with his, gripping tighter when he tried to pull away. "Don't you dare close me out."

He lifted his head. Chris and Jade were nowhere to be seen. He twisted around and leaned his back against the bed.

Trixie straddled his lap, hugging him close. "We'll figure this out. We'll make a feeding schedule and set alarms on our phones."

Running his hands over the silky skin of her arms, he sank into her comfort. Helpless to resist, he was an addict and Trixie his drug. "Schedules do not work." The solution would not be so simple. He had battled this for ages. "Blood needs vary, depending on activity and stress. Sometimes I can go days without feeding, others I can't get enough." He rested his head on her shoulder. "I wish it were so easy."

"Don't." She squeezed tighter. "Don't give up. We know dragons and werewolves and vampires. Even a mythical dhampir." She grew quiet. "Somebody might have a better idea than chaining you up in a dungeon." She sat up straighter. "Maybe you need a different kind of restraint."

He tilted his head. "What do you mean?"

She brushed the long strands of his hair from his face. "We need to talk with Jade."

"If she will see me." He sighed. "I have to apologize and make amends." He hated that he had injured the frail girl. She had already suffered enough abuse from his kind.

Together they dressed and searched for Jade. They found her sitting at a small table in the kitchen, out of reach of the evening sunlight.

"Hey." Trixie crept ahead of Viktor. "Is it okay if we join you?" She wouldn't take no for an answer but was willing to find Chris if it made Jade feel safer.

Jade stared at her with bruised eyes. A huge bandage on her wrist and a triple-decker sandwich sat on the plate untouched in front of her.

Chris came out of the pantry, carrying a jar of mayonnaise. "Found it." His glare fell on Viktor. "Out."

Trixie raised her hand. "We came to make peace."

Alpha and master glared at each other across the kitchen.

Jade took a delicate bite of the sandwich, ignoring the men. "This is good, Chris."

The alpha set the mayonnaise jar next to her. "This will make it great." He didn't take his eyes off Viktor.

Her sire came forward. "I wanted to apologize. What I did was inexcusable." He turned around and left. Spine rigid and shoulders stiff.

Trixie ground her teeth. Her vampire would accept blame and guilt, but never forgiveness. He was his own judge, jury, and executioner. She hung her head. He was hurting and she couldn't make it better.

Then fingers curled around hers. "The hunger drives him hard." Jade stared across the table at Trixie, her big eyes seeing more than she let on.

Trixie nodded.

Chris folded his arms and looked away. "He'll kill again, Trixie. Can you live with that?"

"It's not on purpose…" But her heart ached. "I'll find a way to stop this." Before it was too late. "I had hoped Jade might have an idea or two…"

"I might have something." Jade tapped her fingernail on the spell book. "I had a lot of time to study this book while locked in my room."

"It's black magic." Chris shook his head. "Trixie, this is a bad idea."

"Wait." Jade hushed the alpha. "Let me finish. People say black magic as if it's all evil. Well, most of it is, but in some instances, it can negate other evil."

Trixie blinked. "You understand what she's talking about?" She aimed her question at the werewolf.

Chris shook his head.

Jade pointed at her. "You're a vampire. Your existence is touched by darkness. Some, like you, are almost made of light, which is why the sunlight protection spell worked on you. If I did the exact same tattoo on Viktor, he'd go up like a bonfire." She flipped through her spell book. "This symbol is a dampening spell. By inking this on a darker creature, it will subdue some of his darker cravings."

She meant Viktor when she said darker creature. Trixie released the breath she'd been holding. "Okay, let's say I can convince Viktor to try this. What do you need for the spell?" At this point, she was ready to try anything. Viktor had only been away from Eoin's monitoring for a couple of days and already he had lost control. How many more lives would the dragon allow Viktor to take before he destroyed him? It was not a scenario she would permit. Not without a fight. Jade had already proved her magic worked with both her and Betty.

"This is true black magic at its core." Jade couldn't meet her stare. "And I don't have one of the key ingredients."

Trixie leaned forward, unable to read any of the writing in the book. "What is it?"

"The blood of a virgin."

Chris tossed his head back, roaring out a loud laugh. "Good luck finding *that* in Riverbend." He grew quiet suddenly and eyed Jade. "You don't mean a kid, right?" A growl rolled in his chest.

"Do I seem like a person who would harm a child?" A sharp tone. "It has to be an adult." She sighed and traced the pattern on the page of the book. "I once hoped I could cure my mother's vampirism with the spell, but it doesn't work that way."

Trixie rested her arm on the table. "How much blood are you talking about and does it matter that I'm a vampire?"

Chris' jaw unhinged. "No way."

Jade raised a questioning eyebrow. "This won't work unless you are *truly* a virgin."

"I am." She tapped her foot. "I mean, you are or you're not. There is no gray area."

"You never…" Chris inserted his index finger within a circle that he made with his other hand.

"No." Trixie hissed.

"You were sharing a bed," Jade replied.

"Yeah, at my place too," Chris added.

"And Viktor has been *very* patient." Too patient in her opinion, but in the end his patience might be his salvation.

Jade and Chris exchanged looks, then the dhampir took another bite of her sandwich. "I'll get my equipment and you explain to Viktor what we're about to try."

Trixie left Jade and Chris to prepare. The bedroom she shared with Viktor was empty. She combed the mansion looking for him. The other vampires kept to their rooms, avoiding their big bad master who had killed their bitchy leader. In the meantime, the sun had set and she expanded her search outside. In the gardens, she finally spotted Viktor watching the moonrise. "There you are."

"I needed to think." The sadness in his voice was devastating. "Once you are safe in New Port, I will leave the territory."

"What?"

"I think it's time I retire. Go somewhere quiet and isolated—"

She cupped his face. "That won't stop anything, Viktor. The hunger was still drive you to kill." She pressed a gentle kiss to his mouth. "Jade has a spell that will help." She explained Jade's theory and the spell.

"You want me to try this?" He didn't sound convinced.

"Yes, unless you have a good reason not to." Viktor's nights were numbered if he didn't get a handle on his bloodlust. If Eoin didn't kill him, then she was sure Viktor would find someone else powerful enough to do the deed.

He closed his eyes and hugged her tight. "To stay at your side, I would try anything."

They searched the mansion for Jade.

"She didn't say where they would be waiting." Trixie hadn't given the dhampir a chance before racing off to find Viktor. "She would need her equipment." Her stomach turned. "I know where they are." She led Viktor deeper into the nest.

Her heart out of sync, Trixie halted at the entrance of the room where Jade had been forced to tattoo her back. She hadn't thought she'd ever return here.

The dhampir dropped her chin to her chest. "Hope you don't mind, but all of my gear is in here."

Viktor strode to the table where Trixie had been tied. He fingered the manacles. One by one, he crushed them in his fist.

Trixie watched wide-eyed at the display of his strength. "Okay."

Lips thin and body tense, he then pulled off his shirt and sat on the edge of the table. "Do it."

Jade gestured for Trixie's hand and pricked her finger. She squeezed one drop into the ink.

"That's it?"

"Yes, what were you expecting? For me to sacrifice you on the altar?" Jade then proceeded to work.

Annie Nicholas

CHAPTER THIRTY

Viktor borrowed a motorcycle from the nest and returned to New Port. He and Trixie had plenty of time before sunrise so they took the interstate this time.

As they reached the border of the city, he took the exit off the highway and slowed to a stop by an empty field of wild flowers.

Trixie leaned forwarded, looking over his shoulder. "Is something wrong with the bike? Don't tell me we ran out of gas. I don't want to spend the day underground." Her grip on his shoulders tightened.

He pointed at the sky. "I have some explaining to do." The words left a sour taste in his mouth. Viktor was not good at apologizing, but he had stolen the dragon's vehicle and abandoned it in the forest.

Eoin came to a soft landing. "So." His tone sharp as he narrowed his glare upon them. "Where should I begin?"

"We had important business to attend to in Riverbend," Trixie interjected before Viktor could open his mouth.

The dragon lowered his head so he could look Viktor in the eye. "Did you get her?"

"Let us say that the black magic is stopped and the book in good hands." He would tell Eoin the details of this adventure on another night over a glass of wine when the weight of the world did not seem to press on him, or Trixie's heat warming his back.

"More importantly, did you behave?"

"Did I kill anyone? I disposed of my lieutenant, who conspired to usurp my rule." Viktor leaned on the handle bars. He would not be returning to the castle. Not now, not ever.

"I approve of this action." Eoin nodded.

Viktor removed his jacket and raised the edged of his short sleeve, exposing his newest tattoo. "I did get some work done by the dhampir."

The dragon sniffed and sneezed. "Black magic? Is this wise?"

"It's supposed to keep his bloodlust under control." Trixie caressed the ink. "I think it will work. Jade has had years to study that book."

"Jade?" Eoin shook his head. "This sounds like something I need to hear at length and not in some cold field."

"I am taking Trixie home."

The dragon nodded. "Come visit when you have time. I would like to hear this story and throw out those chains." He launched himself into the sky, wings beating a storm of wind.

Viktor pulled on his jacket.

"You're taking me home," she asked quietly.

"Yes."

Trixie clutched him tight the whole journey. Her lush body pressed to his back like a sweet temptation. As he parked in front of his home, his blood burned. Not to feed, but for his woman.

Viktor helped her off and her legs wobbled unaccustomed to straddling something for so long. He supported her under the elbows until she found her land legs. Her gaze wandered behind him to the old brick building. "Is this your tattoo parlor?"

He winced. "I prefer tattoo studio." He hung his arm over her shoulder and faced his home. Two huge picture windows, painted black, cover the front of the shop, his name scrawled in gold across both.

"I imagine you're only open at night."

"Of course. Let me give you a tour." He tugged her inside before she could reply, his heart a hummingbird in his chest. He wanted her to stay. To want to stay of her own free will, not because she had nowhere else to go.

She wandered along the wall where he had framed pictures of his best work, her fingers tracing the images. He did not have much furnishings since he only worked on one customer at a time. She glanced over his equipment and inks.

He leaned against the wall, following her graceful movements among his things, within his sanctuary. He had not invited another vampire inside since opening the shop.

Pausing by a mirror, she opened her mouth and examined her fangs.

"Is something wrong with your teeth?" He stood behind her.

"Just wondering. Will the New Port nest accept me? Are they prissy like Riverbend or can they tolerate a dogcatcher in their ranks?"

His brow furrowed. "You want to live with them?"

"I'm not ready to return to Ruby and I refuse to live with the dragons."

"This is your home." He kissed her cotton candy hair. His beacon in the night, his hope and future.

She glanced at him. "No vampire nest. No Paulo."

Viktor growled. "Not unless you want him dead." He traced the outline of her ear. "I had hoped you would remain here with me. Use your drawing skills to create unique tattoo designs."

She laughed and wrapped her arms loosely around his neck. "This feels right. A new home for my new life."

"A safe home, where I can protect you."

"And I can protect you." She kissed the tip of his nose.

"I know this is not a luxurious mansion. We could always look for a nicer home if you want."

"You're never going to forgive me for that, are you?" She twisted and wrapped her arms around his neck. "This place is perfect. I have had enough of mansions and fancy gardens. I've decided fancy balls are *not* for me." She pulled him down with her grip on his hair.

Taking her mouth with a slow fury, he made it clear she was the sole focus of his life.

She surrendered with a moan, opening herself to everything and anything he wanted. Fingernails teased over the tense muscles of his throat.

He scooped her into his arms and carried her to the elevator.

She pulled away and blinked at the pristine metallic walls. "Where does this go?"

"You do not think I sleep in the studio with those big windows." He chuckled at her blush.

"Maybe."

The doors opened and she slipped from his arms.

Stunned, Trixie blocked the exit from the elevator until Viktor guided her steps forward. The whole second floor was one huge apartment—gleaming wood floors, large living room with fireplace, and a bed against the far wall.

"No kitchen," she murmured.

"No food to cook. I do have a small fridge for drinks and blood." He brushed the hair away from her neck, his breath hot and heavy on her skin. His fingertips caressed her hips, his hands rising to slip under the hem of her shirt to splay across her lower abdomen.

She spun around, pressed her mouth to his, putting one hand on the nape of his neck, holding him close, never going to let go. He was hers. Her vampire. Her lover.

Not breaking the connection, Viktor lifted her up in his arms and carried her across the apartment. The comforter was soft against her back when he laid her down, his body a heavy, muscled weight.

She spread her thighs to accommodate him, her core aching for him.

He kissed his way along her throat as her fingers clenched on the muscled heat of his back. The cotton of his T-shirt crumpled under her grip.

"I want all of you," she whispered. She reached down and pulled her shirt over her head to throw it to the floor. It left her dressed in a bra of delicate lace, her breasts straining to be set free.

Viktor gazed upon her chest and snapped the clasp so the lingerie fell off her shoulders. He ran his rough palms over her nipples.

She moaned, arching her back into his touch.

Looking up, his long hair falling across her body, he closed his hand on her breast and settled his weight more heavily on her.

Then he kissed her and petted and stroked her torso with possessive hands that made it clear Viktor Petrov had claimed her as his. She'd never wanted anything more in her life.

Material ripped as he tore his T-shirt and tossed the rags to the floor and the naked heat of his flesh was pressed to her breasts.

She traced the complex spell tattoo on his shoulder, her blood permanently embedded in his pale skin. "Do you really think it will work?" All her hopes for the future laid in this artwork.

Closing his hand around her throat, he lowered himself until their breaths kissed. "Yours does. Betty's did. So will mine." She met him kiss for kiss. Her need for him a mad thing, she made a distressed noise when he lifted his body off hers.

A hot look before he undid the fastenings of her pants with desperate hands. It took mere seconds to pull off her jeans and panties and another to take off his own. "I am going to taste every inch of you." He knelt between her legs and nipped at her sensitive inner thighs.

"Viktor." Her mind exploded, her body howling, a soundless moan, his mouth hot and demanding on her flesh, his rough hands on her thighs as he held them apart. "I want—I want…"

He rose up over her body, bracing himself on his right arm, using his fingers on the other hand to brush back her hair. "Tell me." His voice an erotic caress against her ear.

"I want you inside me."

His thick eyelashes fluttered closed and his abdomen clenched as his erection pressed against her abdomen, impossibly hard. "There will be some discomfort." He settled his hips between her thighs, his weight deliciously heavy. "Tell me if I am going too fast."

She'd be lying if she said she wasn't nervous. She wanted to be with him. This magnificent, beautiful, caring

280

vampire. Trixie wrapped her legs around Viktor. "Love me."

His responding kiss was a naked demand. "Spread your legs wider," he ordered once he released her mouth. Their gazes locked as he began to push inside her.

A painful stretch had her hissing at the need that still wanted all of him.

He stopped. His jaw brutal line. "Are you hurting?"

Tight and full to the point it was almost painful and exactly where she wanted him to be. "I'm…perfect."

He shuddered and pushed farther in, withdrawing slowly then returning until he was buried to the hilt inside her. "Trixie." Stormy eyes with so much emotion, he moved in an easy rhythm. His body rigid, the tendons of his neck standing out starkly.

"Faster." A breathless demand.

His fingers dug into her hips. "You sure?"

"Yes." Clawing her nails into his muscled back, she attempted to help by arching her hips.

Viktor pulled out only to slam back in hard. He pounded deeper, over and over again, a primitive, rough, spectacular taking.

Coming so hard Trixie splintered. She clutched his sweat-slicked skin. Their hearts drumming to their own love song. It was a possessive, passionate claiming as she orgasmed.

Viktor came with a violent cry, his breathing harsh and his body rigid. He fisted her hair in his hands, molten stare pinning her gaze. "You are mine."

ℰPILOGUE

She parked the animal control truck in front of the new building for Almost Home Rescue. Though she would moonlight as an artist for Viktor, she still wanted to try to keep her job as one of the city's animal control specialists, as long as she could be home before dawn. Her tattoo made her sunlight resistant, not sunlight proof.

Betty and Ken had returned from their honeymoon last week. Her werewolf best friend had been less than pleased to find Trixie with a new set of fangs.

Trixie's phone dinged with a text.

Ruby: *I don't feel like going into work tonight. Can you introduce me to any hot, billionaire vampires?*

Trixie: *Sorry, they're all poor douche bags in New Port. I got the only good one.*

Ruby: *Betty forgive you yet.*

Trixie: *No, she's still angry. For now.*

Ruby: *When are you coming for a visit? I miss you.*

Trixie: *I'll stop by on my break tomorrow night. Viktor will chaperone.*

Ruby: *Great, I'll stock up on blood. TTFN.*

A whimper drew Trixie's attention. She reached back and scratched a floppy ear. "Betty is going to flip her lid over you, baby." She led her latest animal retrieval to the service door of the rescue and rang the bell. It was late, but she knew Betty was still here unpacking. Her best friend opened the door.

"Look who I found wandering the park all alone." Trixie stepped back so Betty could see the Great Dane puppy

Trixie had on a leash. She had spent the last hour chasing the pup and it had evaded her, even with her vampire speed.

Betty sank to her knees and greeted her distant cousin with ear scratching and kisses. "She has a collar and a tag. You could have just taken her straight home."

"I am taking her home. This is just a pit-stop for kisses. Am I forgiven now?"

"Trix," Betty growled, sounding very werewolfy. "There's nothing to forgive. I just can't believe you didn't call me when you became vampire. And I'm a little hurt." Betty rose and hugged Trixie tight, and punched her arm. "Then you dragged Chris into this and my *dad.* Am I the last one to find out?"

Trixie shrugged. "My boss doesn't know."

"Oh, how reassuring." Betty eyed her. "Everything okay at work?"

"Sure. Kennels retrieved and boss-man is thrilled I want permanent night shifts." She winked. No one at her job had noticed anything different about her. Viktor always made sure she fed before each shift. "I haven't bitten anyone."

Betty frowned. "And Viktor?" Betty had expressed mixed feelings about him. He'd helped save Betty, but he'd also scared the crap out of her when she met him mid-blood-thirst-craze.

"No signs of bloodlust. Eoin hasn't thrown his chains away." They still owed the dragon for the car they stole. Viktor kept mailing the dragon miniature toy vehicles and she kept expecting to find the tattoo studio torched.

"You know I'm not a big fan of magic." Betty rubbed the spot where her tattoo had been. "Especially when done by Jade."

It technically wasn't Jade's fault, but Trixie would pick her battles. She just wanted her best friend back. "Time will tell." She eyed Betty's flat stomach. "Any signs of pregnancy yet?"

Betty snarled. "Stop that. I'm not ready. You're as bad as Ken, my parents, and Ryota." She sighed. "You know this puppy is super adorable. Let's introduce her to Ken." Betty gestured for Trixie to follow. "I have a pot of coffee on." She paused as she crossed the threshold. "You can still drink coffee, right?"

"I'd stake myself if I couldn't."

Betty laughed. "I'd stake you too, if you couldn't. Some things are sacred." She went inside.

Trixie glimpsed a familiar shadow in the dark.

Viktor stepped into the light and dropped a seductive kiss on her lips.

"Are you spying on me?"

"Maybe I missed you."

"We need to find you some customers to keep you occupied." She took his hand. "I think Ken wants Betty's name inked on his body."

"No more werewolves." Viktor shook his head. "I had my fill in Riverbend."

She drew him inside the rescue. "Come on, it will be fun. You can even misspell her name if you want."

His mischievous grin filled her with hope for their future.

Did you enjoy your read? Want to try a similar series by Annie?

VANGUARD ELITE SERIES

You can start with <u>Bootcamp of Misfit Wolves</u>.

Ian's alpha tosses him out of his car at a training camp for worthless and weak wolf shifters run by a crazy vampire.

His only choice is to escape and go lone wolf.

Until he runs into Clare...

She actually volunteered for this gig.

Her wolf is all alpha but it's crammed into a petite package, and she definitely has no mercy when it comes to him.

The work is hard.

The training dangerous.

Surviving is optional.

Clare can't stand Ian's disregard for her authority and he hates her driven ambition.

Sparks fly and teeth are bared. Opposites attract they say.

If they don't kill each other first.

About the Author

Annie Nicholas writes paranormal romance with a twist. She has courted vampires, hunted with shifters, and slain a dragon's ego all with the might of her pen. Riding the wind of her imagination, she travels beyond the restraints of reality and shares them with anyone wanting to read her stories. Mother, daughter, and wife are some of the other hats she wears while hiking through the hills and dales of her adopted state of Vermont.

Annie writes for Samhain Publishing, Carina Press, and Lyrical Press.

www.annienicholas.com
Facebook
Twitter
Annie's Newsletter

Made in the USA
San Bernardino, CA
02 June 2019